These Hallowed Halls

Anne Louise Bannon

Healcroft House, Publishers

ISBN 978-1-948616-15-7
Library of Congress Control Number: 2020925300

Healcroft House, Publishers, Altadena, California, United States of America

Contents

Dedication VII

Acknowledgments IX

1. September 10, 1984 1

2. September 11-12, 1984 15

3. September 14-16, 1984 33

4. September 17, 1984 47

5. September 18 - 20, 1984 61

6. September 21 - 22, 1984 73

7. September 23, 1984 87

8. October 2 - 4, 1984 99

9. October 8, 1984 113

10. October 9 - 14, 1984 127

11. October 18 -19, 1984 141

12. October 20 -21, 1984 155

13. October 22, 1984 169

14. October 23 - 24, 1984   185

15. October 25, 1984   197

16. October 27 - 28, 1984   211

17. October 29, 1984   227

18. October 30, 1984   241

19. October 31, 1984   257

20. November 1 - 2, 1984   267

21. November 3 - 24, 1984   283

Thank You for Reading   293

Coming Soon   295

Other books by Anne Louise Bannon   297

Connect with Anne Louise Bannon   301

About Anne Louise Bannon   303

To my good friend and editor, Carol Louise Wilde, for whom a biology lecture really is a good time.

Acknowledgments

The problem with writing acknowledgments is that it seems like I'm always thanking the same people. Paula Bernstein, PhD, MD, is always on hand with my medical questions. My beloved husband, Michael Holland, listened to far more of this story than he read. My daughter, Corrie Klarner, also provided some good ideas, criticisms and some real praise (which your old mom needed, sweetie). Then, of course, there's Carol Louise Wilde, who helps in so many ways, but particularly gave me some fun stuff to work with in the biology department. Eunice Blakely had been created long before I knew Carol, but Carol's observations and thoughts did even more to bring her to life.

I've also got some new folks in my life who have been incredibly supportive. The Blackbird Writers have been an inspiration and a wealth of marketing talent that I can draw from. My author pod buddies, especially GP Gottlieb, have really helped me extend my social media reach.

And there's always you, the reader. Thanks for picking this up and sharing these adventures.

September 10, 1984

On my own.

There I was, however many thousand miles over Wisconsin, and I was on my own. Well, Sid would be there somewhere. But for the first time since I'd become a member of Operation Quickline, the two of us would not be working side by side. I wasn't even sure how much I was going to be seeing Sid.

I was nervous. We were going to be undercover, and that's always a scary thing. Yet, I was also excited. At last, a chance to prove myself. I mean, I knew Sid and I were good at this investigation and spy thing, but I didn't know how much of that was Sid or how much I was adding to our little team.

Let me explain. Within the structure of the FBI are several smaller organizations that mostly only the members know exist. Operation Quickline was one of these. Our core mission was to move information around, and that was usually what we did. However, every so often something would come up that was too hot for regular law enforcement, and we'd get called in to deal with it.

Which was why I was on an airplane flying into Green Bay airport. I looked out the window at the ground below. It was parceled off into bright green squares, which really looked strange to me. Back home in Los Angeles, everything that wasn't hemmed in by concrete was brown. After baking all summer, Southern California was in the middle of its traditional September heat wave. I was glad to be leaving the blast furnace.

On this last little leg from the flight in Chicago, the pilot had announced warm weather in Green Bay. I couldn't help laughing when he said the temperatures were in the low eighties. When I'd left Los Angeles that morning, it had already been ninety-five and getting hotter.

The seat belt sign flashed, and the pilot announced we would be landing shortly. Sighing, I put away my commentary on Shakespeare's sonnets. I'd been reading academic journals non-stop since late August when the assignment first came up. That was the one part I was terrified about. My cover was as an English professor at a tiny arts college in Appleton, Wisconsin. Now, I had taught English before, at a community college, but I'd been away from that job for over three years, and only had a master's degree. My cover had a full PhD and more years of teaching. I did not want to say something stupid or not know something I should have. [You wouldn't have been the first PhD to do so, on both counts - SEH] I had even begun some research for a journal article, or maybe even a book.

The plane landed with a bump. I slid on a pair of large-framed glasses. The lenses didn't help or hurt my vision any. They were just part of my cover. We'd been ordered to change our appearances. I used makeup to subtly change the contours of my face and had cut my hair and dyed it blond. As the plane docked at the gate, I drew a deep breath and waited until most of the other passengers had deplaned. Then I got my purse and backpack together and walked into my new role.

As I entered the terminal, an announcement was going.

"...Janet Mayfield to the desk at gate six. Paging Dr. Janet Mayfield to the desk at gate six. Thank you."

My alter ego. I swallowed. My real name is Lisa Wycherly. Fortunately, if I failed to live up to my new identity, there were very few people who would see it as anything but a lapse in integrity. Unfortunately, the people who would question it were the very people I needed to convince if I wanted to stay alive, let alone be successful. It was too late to run, not that I would have. I stepped up to the desk.

"I'm Dr. Mayfield," I said to the young man behind the counter.

"Oh, good." He looked around, then waved at somebody. "Sir? Here she is."

The man that approached was tall with a rounded belly. He seemed to be in his late thirties, with a round face and light-brown hair which was just beginning to recede. He wore a short-sleeved plaid shirt that was open at the neck and light-colored polyester dress slacks. He smiled pleasantly.

"Dr. Mayfield?" He held out his right hand. "I'm Dr. Ted Curtis, from Martin University. We heard you were coming in today, so I volunteered to come down and get you settled."

"That's very kind of you," I said, shaking his hand. "They told me that one of the other faculty would meet me, but not who."

"We only settled it last night." Ted chuckled. "Ever been to Wisconsin before?"

We started down the hallway to the baggage claim.

"No, I haven't," I said, and stopped. "Wow."

A wall proclaimed, "Welcome to Packerland" in big green letters on a gold surface.

"Yeah, that's Wisconsin for you," Ted said, shaking his head. "I was born and raised not far from here, but most of the faculty are from other places."

"Oh. What do you teach?"

"Sociology. I've got two intro classes this quarter and two experimental techniques for the upperclassmen."

"So, what are you doing hobnobbing with the English Department?" I asked.

Dr. Curtis laughed again. "They told you just how small Martin is, didn't they?"

"Well, yeah. I guess it didn't sink in," I said.

It was a tiny college and an arts school, with a music conservatory, a theater department, and fine arts. That's where most of the faculty were. The humanities department had half the staff of the conservatory, alone, and that was with humanities covering six subject areas. The math/science department wasn't any bigger. In fact, the humanities and math/sciences departments only existed to fulfill general education requirements for the underclassmen.

"Well, there isn't much hobnobbing to be done if we don't cross disciplines," Dr. Curtis said jovially. "We're a pretty tight-knit faculty and very eclectic. I hope you can talk about something besides Chaucer."

"I hope so, too. Chaucer isn't my specialty. I'm not much of a scientist, either."

"Don't worry. Most of your contact will be with the humanities people. You'll get to know us pretty well."

"That should be interesting," I said, looking around the baggage claim for the conveyor that would have my luggage. "Back at UCLA, I didn't even know the entire English faculty, let alone other departments."

A minute later, the luggage from my flight began appearing on the conveyor belt and Dr. Curtis left to pull his car around. I found my two suitcases and one box and lugged them out to the curb where Dr. Curtis' large, light blue Chevrolet had driven up.

"The dean set up housing for me," I told Dr. Curtis after he'd gotten out of the car and opened the trunk.

He took the box from me. "That's right. It was one of those weird bequests that the university got some fifty or so years ago. Basically, it's an old house with two apartments. We mostly use it to house new staff members until they can find their own places. But Fran Mercer, she's Communications, has been living there since she came, so she's been managing the place. She'll get you the keys and everything when we get there."

"Great. Now, all I'll need is a car."

"Well, the apartment is within walking distance of Lawrence Hall, where the humanities classes are, but you'll need a car." Dr. Curtis proceeded to give me a few tips on who to go to and who to avoid.

While he talked, I looked out at the window at the green countryside flying by. Then I saw something that made me chuckle.

"What's so funny?" Dr. Curtis asked.

I blushed. "This is going to sound pretty silly, but I keep seeing all these little red barns with silos. They remind me of a toy farm set I had as a child. I didn't think people had them anymore."

Dr. Curtis laughed. "Welcome to rural America. Those little red barns are the sign of one of this area's major industries, family farming."

"Really? I thought family farming had gone extinct. You have to understand, I was raised in California. There farming means the huge agribusinesses of the San Joaquin Valley."

"Family farms are alive and well here. That, dairies, and paper mills make up the bulk of the jobs around here. It's basically a blue-collar area. Good old Martin U. is something of an oasis."

I bit my lip and didn't say anything more. Sid had gotten decidedly snobby when he'd heard about the assignment. Appleton was a good-sized town, but as far as Sid was concerned, it was in the middle of nowhere. In fact, the term he used was obscene.

"What could possibly be going on out there?" he had asked. "The place sounds like something out of a TV show."

"I'm not sure that place was in Wisconsin," I'd said. "It could have been anywhere, which I believe was the point."

"There are no military installations, not even any secret missile silos."

"It's a university. Maybe it's some sort of research going on."

"It's an arts school. In the middle of nowhere."

As it turned out, there was some research going on. Someone was developing a nerve gas of some sort or doing the theoretical work on it. Someone else had stumbled onto part of the formula and had sold it to the Soviets. I still don't know what made the formula so special, but it was clear that the U.S. did not want the Soviets to get it.

The trouble was the formula was a high-level secret. In addition, the person doing the research had made it clear that he (or she) did not want anyone to know who he (or she) was. Local law enforcement was not trained for undercover espionage investigations. Regular FBI was not considered secure enough. So, Operation Quickline got the job.

Sid's cover was as a music student. Others were posing as students in the art and theatre departments. There was another faculty member in the computer science department, but he was from another agency (we apparently did not have the Need to Know which one). I was the only other faculty member on the team. Our mission was to find out who was stealing the formula and protect the researcher developing it, assuming we could figure out who that person was. Since I was faculty, my job also included collecting information from the other "students" and either sending it on or spreading it to the others, as needed.

I had thought that I would have been better posing as one of the students, being a lot closer to that age than Sid. But Martin U. had a whole program for "second-career" students, and I had actual experience teaching English composition.

We didn't know who the other Quickline agents really were. I had the names they would use, but had no idea what they looked like. The one thing we knew was that it was probably an amateur who had stumbled onto the formula then gotten himself under KBG control. It wasn't much to go on, but it helped that, as Dr. Curtis had said, I was expected to get to know the rest of the faculty.

We pulled into Appleton around a quarter after four, and a few minutes later, Dr. Curtis drove past a white clapboard house with two stories and a peaked roof. It was longer than it was wide, barely two windows across on the top floor, with a small alcove on the right side of the bottom floor for the front door.

"We call it The Box," Dr. Curtis said, pulling into the driveway. "Most of those old places were torn down in the 1950s and replaced with the tan brick boxes. This one survived because of the bequest. I have to warn you, there are those on the faculty who think the bequest may have actually been a sick joke."

"But you said Dr., um, Mercer?"

"Fran Mercer." Dr. Curtis braked and turned the engine off. "We're all on a first-name basis here. She's Fran. I'm Ted. None of this doctor crap."

"Okay. I'm Janet." I smiled weakly.

Ted nodded. "Yeah. Fran has stayed here, and we all think it's a little strange. Most faculty find someplace else to stay within the first month or two."

"Oh."

"It's still cheaper than a motel." Ted opened the car door and hefted his bulk out.

I followed suit. Ted went straight for the door in the alcove and rang the bell.

The door was answered right away by a petite woman in her early thirties. She had short, light-brown hair and she blinked a lot, as if she were permanently sleepy.

"Hello, Ted," she said.

"Hi, Fran," he replied. "This is Dr. Janet Mayfield, our new English person. Janet, Dr. Fran Mercer."

"How do you do?" I asked, shaking her hand.

"Very well, thank you." Fran stepped back from the door. "Come on in. Why don't I just take you right on upstairs?"

"Sure," I said, walking into the dark hallway. There was barely enough room for me and Fran. The worn tile was made up of tiny white hexagons, with black ones interspersed throughout. Dark wood paneling covered the walls and made the hallway even darker. The same dark wood made up the banister to the long, narrow, and steep staircase along the side of the house that led to another dark wood door at the top. Dim yellow light from a couple wall sconces lit up the fraying, threadbare carpeting on the stairs.

"Ted, can you bring Janet's stuff up?" Fran asked, as she started up the stairs.

They creaked loudly, all the way up.

"Wow, that's pretty noisy," I said, following her.

"Best burglar alarm there is," Fran said. "There isn't a spot on those stairs that doesn't creak." She tossed a grin over her shoulder. "And people wonder why I like this place."

The apartment was furnished, but sparsely. The door opened into a large living room with light-colored, though very scuffed, wood floors. The blank walls were white lathe and plaster and the two windows from the side made the battered sofa look a little lonely in the middle of the room. Another long, dark hallway ran along the side of the house from the living room to the kitchen in the back, with a small bedroom and a tiny bathroom in between on the left. The bedroom had a bed and linens, a bureau, and no closet. The bathroom had a toilet, sink, tub with shower, but these took up most of the floor space.

The kitchen was small, too, with battered dark brown linoleum, and plywood cabinets that had been stained a dark brown. Inside were a set of pottery ware for four, a couple pots and pans, some glasses, and some cheap stainless flatware and some cooking utensils. At least, the refrigerator and stove were full-sized and reasonably new. A back door led to a narrow wooden staircase down the back of the house, where there was a graveled alley.

"You can park your car in the alley," Fran said. "When you get one."

"Yeah, that's on my list," I said, opening the refrigerator. "I guess I'd better get some groceries in first, though."

"Of course," Fran said, heading back into the hallway.

"Hey! Hey!" Ted called from the living room. "I've got everything up here. Where do you want it all?"

I looked around the living room and noticed that there was a small desk and bookshelf on the wall near the front windows.

"The box can go there," I said, pointing to the desk. "I'll take the suitcases."

I took them into the bedroom as Fran told Ted that I needed to get some groceries. We went out to dinner, first, at a steak house called the Whistling Cow some ways out of Appleton. The dining room was dark and not terribly full on a Monday evening. We had just gotten seated and were looking at the menus when I heard a hissing sound. Sure enough, a couple waitresses were bringing a family their dinners, including three steaks, still sizzling on their platters.

I bit my lip. I have a voracious appetite. Worse yet, I'm one of those lucky people who can eat like a horse and never gain weight. On the other hand, I was undercover and didn't want to seem memorable. So, I ordered a medi-um-sized rib-eye steak with a baked potato. Fortunately, the salad bar was not that appealing, so I didn't heap my plate all that high, although Ted did. Fran nibbled on some of the lettuce with a little dressing on it.

When the steak arrived, it was utterly amazing. Perfectly tender, with a pool of butter on the top. I couldn't help myself. I cleaned the plate. Ted was vastly amused. He'd had the same size steak but had only finished half of it.

"Where do you put it?" he asked.

I blushed and shrugged. "I don't know. I'm just really energetic, I guess."

Inside, my stomach was churning. My first day and already I'd screwed something up. Fran was busy dressing Ted down for teasing me about my appetite.

From the restaurant, Ted drove us to the local used car dealership. He made a point of inspecting any potential car for signs that the dealer had covered up a rust problem and that the engine was in order.

"You don't want a piece of junk," he told me. "And you have to be careful about the rust thing. Winters are pretty hard on cars around here."

I found a Celica that was in decent shape, and Ted approved of it. So, I signed the papers and then took Fran with me to get groceries and Ted drove off on his own.

"I am so glad he was here," I told Fran, as I pulled onto the highway. "I would never have known to check for the rust thing."

"Ted just likes showing off," Fran said, genially. "In fact, I'm sure he heard you were young and single, and that's why he came to pick you up. But Ted's harmless. The person you really have to watch out for is Ernie Lavalle.

He's Poli Sci. Brilliant theorist, but what a lech. And not the only one, I'm afraid."

After getting groceries, Fran insisted we go straight home. I invited her to share a soda with me, but she begged off.

"You need to get settled," she said. "Classes start next week. I don't know why they took so long to hire you. It's out and out rude in my mind."

I showed Fran out and listened to her progress down the stairs. She'd been right. Those stairs made an excellent burglar alarm. However, that would only help if I were in the apartment. I made sure all the blinds were down, then double-checked the locks on my suitcases and the seal on my box and breathed a sigh of relief that they were all intact. From my purse, I pulled what looked like a face powder compact out. Well, it was a powder compact. It's just that under the compressed face powder was a super powerful bug finder. I popped that layer open and flipped the switch. The display glowed and a needled wavered.

Someone was broadcasting some signal or other, but based on the needle movement, it wasn't too close. I went through the apartment. The needle didn't waver much until I got to the kitchen. Near the door, it showed that the signal was stronger. I opened the door and looked outside into the dark alley below. There was no one there, but the signal was stronger when I pointed the bug finder to the south and the large tan brick apartment bannt house next door.

I shut the door and locked it, then went back to the living room. I could faintly hear Fran below and did not doubt that she could hear me. That would be inconvenient, but hardly worrisome. I got some more equipment from the backpack. I put the ultra-thin wiring on every window and door in the place. It wouldn't keep anybody out, but if someone went in, I'd know it.

After that, it was time to unpack and make the space my own for the time being.

September 11–12, 1984

My plan was to spend most of the week hunkered down in my apartment preparing for my classes. But there were two events that I was going to have to come up for air to attend.

Tuesday morning, I woke up late and had to scramble to get dressed for my meeting with Dr. Joseph Cunningham, the Humanities Department Chair. I'd been assured it was mostly a formality, but I still put on the one nice skirt suit I'd brought. I drove to the campus and promptly regretted it.

Martin University was a small collection of brick buildings with white columns on the fronts, surrounding lush lawns and huge, old trees of different sorts. The music conservatory was the one exception. It was modern and huge, with a glass dome and steel walls. It sat on the far eastern end of the campus. The rest of the buildings were grouped around a large, white Greek Revival building that was Petrie Hall, or the administration building.

Parking there was a nightmare. The one road that wove around the campus slid in and out of wooded nooks that screened tiny lots, all filled with cars. The only lot that wasn't full was festooned with signs warning of the dire consequences if one even thought about parking there without the appropriate sticker in the window. I sighed. The quarter hadn't even begun.

I muttered a prayer to St. Anthony, and on my second go-round, a car pulled out of a slot in the visitor parking next to Petrie. I grabbed my purse and hurried inside to get all the paperwork signed and my parking pass paid for before my meeting with Cunningham.

I got to Cunningham's office on the first floor of Lawrence Hall right on time for our meeting. Cunningham's secretary, Eliza Spinetti, a waspish looking woman with dark hair and glasses on a chain, informed me that the Chair was not in yet, and told me to take a seat to wait for him. I waited twenty minutes, thanking God that we didn't have to deal with these kinds of petty politics in the spy business, mostly because we almost never worked with our colleagues.

Dr. Cunningham finally swept into the office. He was a portly man, with brown hair that had gone gray at the temples, dressed in a dark wool three-piece suit with a white carnation in his lapel, a blue and gold tie, and a matching color in his top pocket. I stood and smiled, trying not to think about how much more gracefully Sid would have and did pull that look off. [A carnation? No. Far too over the top. - SEH]

Cunningham addressed Ms. Spinetti first, then finally deigned to notice me.

"Janet," he said with a fake smile. "You've completed your paperwork?"

"I have. I was told you'll give me a tour of the facilities, then get me my keys, course lists, and grade sheets."

Cunningham cleared his throat. "Miss Spinetti will take care of you." He looked at the secretary. "Won't you, dear?"

"Yes, Dr. Cunningham." Ms. Spinetti fidgeted with her wedding ring.

He turned back to me. "Good to have you on board, Janet. But before I forget, we need to amend your course outline for the Shakespeare seminar. The course description specifically lists the plays Coriolanus, Julius Caesar, and Titus Andronicus as the topics of study. I would appreciate a copy of your new outline on my desk by Thursday morning."

I forced another smile, wondering how far I wanted to push my new boss. I seriously doubted the course description had mentioned those plays and the only textbook that had been ordered that I knew of was a Complete Works of Shakespeare. On the other hand, some battles were simply not worth fighting.

"I'll do what I can," I said. "Given that I was planning on teaching Hamlet, Richard the Third, and The Tempest—"

"Surely you're comfortable with the listed plays."

"Of course, I am. But I will have to re-familiarize myself with the nuances of each. Will Friday afternoon be good enough?"

He sniffed. "It will have to do."

He swept into his office and shut the door.

Ms. Spinetti sighed as she got up, then looked at me. "Sorry to be such a grump on your first day here, but working with him..."

"I can well imagine," I said.

She pulled a split ring containing five brass keys from the top of her desk and motioned me out into the hallway.

"Your office is upstairs on the second floor." She held up a key. "This is the key to the building, so that you can get in at night and be sure you lock up after you. It's been a real problem around here."

She led me upstairs, explaining how to get to the faculty dining room in the Commons Building, reminding me that grades were to be entered into the computer system weekly during the course of the quarter and that the computer would see to averaging them out at the end and assigning a class grade to each student.

"Classrooms are on the left," she said as we turned into the long corridor filled with wooden doors with frosted glass windows, some lit, others not. Small bulletin boards were posted next to the doors on the side of the building that overlooked the front.

Ms. Spinetti went on. "Offices are on the right. Here's the key to yours. There will be a fifty-dollar charge if you lose it."

I smiled. She didn't know that I already had pass keys to every building on campus. But then, she wasn't supposed to know.

She opened the door into an airy space with three casement windows along one side. It was huge, bigger than my bedroom at the apartment. The bookshelves were half-full of volumes left behind by my various predecessors. The ancient wood desk's edges had been rounded smooth by years of use and the desk was filled with office supplies and all sorts of ephemera. The plaster walls held prints of Shakespeare and Wordsworth. Thomas Hardy glared at me from the wall in front of the desk. In between shelves and prints, notices of campus events and deadlines from years before had been taped to the walls.

"We can get you a computer, but it will not be hooked up to the campus system. Cunningham wants to be sure you survive a couple quarters before coughing up to wire this office."

I looked around in awe. "Yeah, I've heard you guys have a turnover problem."

Ms. Spinetti snorted. "And the reason why is downstairs. Come on. I've gotta get you your course lists and grade sheets."

She locked the door again and started back down the hallway.

"This last key goes to your locker at the campus sports club. It's a full luxury facility, complete with basketball, squash, and racquetball courts, two inside tracks, swimming pool, weight room, saunas and steam rooms, stationary bikes, and treadmills." She couldn't have sounded more bored. "One of the donors had it built a couple years ago because he was worried the students weren't getting enough exercise. They decided to make membership a perk for faculty members. A complete waste of time and money, if you ask me. No one ever uses it, not even the people who should."

We'd gotten back to Cunningham's suite, and she glared at Cunningham's closed door.

"Oh, and it's Mrs. Spinetti."

I smiled at her. "Well, thank you for the tour, Mrs. Spinetti. It was very nice of you."

She handed me my course lists and grade sheets and the keys and went back to her desk without another word.

I went back to the administration building to find that my ID card was ready for me, so from there, I went to the library and stayed there until after dark. I left for about a half hour in the middle of the afternoon to visit the Faculty Dining Room in the Commons. Another perk for faculty was that they could eat at the dining room for free. It wasn't much of a perk. The portions were insanely small. Even portions at home, which were always small by Sid's decree, were bigger. I was going to buy something extra at the Commons, but they were only set up for student meal plans.

I was starving by the time I left the library and stopped at the nearest burger place to load up on a double cheeseburger, onion rings, and a shake. I brought it all home and went back to work.

The next morning, Fran was at my door by ten to help me move into my office before the Faculty Luncheon. I told her my nerves were about fitting in and not ruffling feathers. In truth, I was terrified that I'd be found out as a complete fraud among all the other scholars. Fran insisted I'd be fine and told me not to get any more dressed up than I would for class. She was wearing khakis and a mint-green polo shirt, so I opted for a similar outfit, although I wore my armored running shoes. They looked like ordinary running shoes, but the soles could be popped open to reveal a variety of small tools and weapons. Fran and I walked to the university, with me carrying a good-sized load of books in my backpack for my new office.

"That's Petrie Hall, the first building built when the college was founded in 1879," Fran explained as we walked to Lawrence. "Not only has it got the university admin offices, but it also houses the computer science department because that's where the main computers are. Did you get any time to go through Lawrence Hall?"

"Not much," I said. "Mrs. Spinetti showed me my office, then dismissed me."

"I thought Cunningham was supposed to give you the tour."

"He was twenty minutes late for our meeting, then dumped everything on Mrs. Spinetti."

Fran sighed. "I hope you don't get too discouraged by them. Martin U. is a lovely place, and most of the faculty are genuinely nice. But you're right, Cunningham is a little bent out of shape about how you got hired. The chancellor insisted that he take you."

"Really?" I swallowed. I wondered if Cunningham also knew why I was there.

"Cunningham is a dyed-in-the-wool chauvinist pig." Fran said, then blinked. "Oh, and he is to be addressed as Dr. Cunningham at all times. The chancellor, however, knows that we stand to lose a boat-load of grant funding if we don't hire according to Affirmative Action principles."

So that was how my hiring had been manipulated. I had wondered. After all, someone in the school administration had to know I was there under cover. But I trusted my bosses. They knew how to make these things happen, and what they did, I didn't have Need to Know.

I was gasping a little as I opened my office door. I couldn't help but smile as I saw it.

Fran blinked and glared. "They didn't even get you a computer?"

"Apparently, they want to see if I'm going to stick around before wiring this office." I put my bag down on the desk. "I think the first thing I'm going to do is get rid of that print of Thomas Hardy."

"I wouldn't," said Fran.

"Why?"

"The ghost of Sherman Pendergast."

"What?"

"He's the only humanities faculty that's been here longer than Bob Farnsworth. Or was."

My eyes opened wide. "I'm only an associate professor. How did I get the office of a full-tenured prof?"

"Because Pendergast died in this office." Fran laughed. "The story goes it took a week to find him. Since then, every new English prof gets the Pendergast office and woe to him if he gets rid of Thomas Hardy."

"I loathe the work of Thomas Hardy." The words slipped out before I could check myself, although I knew at least two of my English professors had felt the same way.

My stomach lurched. The previous summer, things had gotten, well, traumatic doesn't even begin to describe it. [That's right. We weren't calling it PTSD yet. - SEH] It sounds weird, but I have this thing about dead bodies. I can't handle them. I know, given the business I'm in, you'd think I'd be able to handle them. But I'd always had Sid around to help me when the stiffs had shown up. I couldn't count on that this time.

I took a deep breath. "Do you think Professor Pendergast would object if I simply shifted Mr. Hardy to another place in the office? Maybe someplace that still shows respect, but where I don't have to look at him glowering at me?"

Fran grinned. "Probably the most diplomatic solution yet."

We swapped around the various prints until my view from the desk included William Shakespeare and Mr. Hardy glowered at the room from a spot next to the door. I'm not normally superstitious. In fact, my religious beliefs don't, technically, allow me to be. So, I justified it by telling myself that I didn't want that kind of distraction and, given that I didn't need those kinds of distractions, it was probably just as well.

Unfortunately, the wall adjustments made Fran and me somewhat late for the luncheon. Fran insisted that it wasn't a problem, that we would hardly be the only ones late, and that most of the faculty would try to get out of there as soon as they could.

"I'd better warn you, portions are really small around here," Fran whispered. "We'll go get a real lunch after the speeches."

Fran was right. Most of the other faculty were still milling about the Faculty Dining Room chatting when we arrived, and we were hardly the last to. My arrival raised a couple eyebrows. After all, I was one of three new faculty members. The other two were in the music conservatory and art department, respectively, and I was fairly certain they'd been hired through normal channels.

Fran, bless her, made a point of sticking close to me and introducing me around to the sciences and math staff. Only one of the professors stood out, Dr. Steve Carmona. He was a tall man, with reddish hair, horn-rimmed glasses, and a decided tendency to stoop. But the real reason he'd stood out was that I'd seen him before back in Los Angeles, only without the stoop or the glasses.

"Are you new as well?" I asked him.

He laughed. "Nah. I've been here at least ten-something years." He shook my hand. "Good to have you aboard, though."

I moved on. A small man, somewhere in his middle forties, slid up next to me, and ran his hand through dark hair that had the flat dullness of a bad dye job.

"May I have the honor of sitting next to you at lunch today?" he asked with a leer.

The back of my neck tingled.

"She's already sitting with Fran and me," said a tall, imposing woman with gray hair and a twinkle in her eye.

She stood next to Fran, and the two laughed softly as the smaller man sniffed and moved off.

"And that was Ernie Lavalle, Poli Sci," Fran said. "He thinks he's the department Don Juan."

I smiled. "I take it he's not."

"That is painfully obvious," said the older woman.

"To everyone but him." I replied.

The older woman looked at me with a warm smile. "Your repartee is quite good. You'll do well here. I'm Eunice Blakely, History, and the department old maid."

Fran rolled her eyes. "You're not even fifty-two."

"But I am the oldest single person on the staff," Eunice said. "It's a distinction I'm coming to enjoy, especially since it keeps Ernie at bay."

A little bell rang, and the room filled with the sound of chairs scraping the wood floor as people went to their department tables. Fran and Eunice directed me to the humanities table. It was one of the smaller ones. Fran and Eunice introduced me to everyone, but I only caught the names of the other two history professors, possibly because they were sitting next to Eunice, on the other side from me, and Fran, who had taken a place across from me. Max Beard had landed next to Fran, but the medium-sized, balding man seemed to barely notice that she was there. Eunice, for her part, kept her focus on me rather than the man on her other side, Ryan Martin, mostly because Martin kept laughing loudly and too long at stuff that wasn't funny.

Dr. Cunningham came up and put his hands on Fran's shoulders.

"Ah, Janet." He took a deep breath, filling out his round form even fuller. "I should warn you about these two troublemakers." He fake-smiled at Eunice and squeezed Fran's shoulders. "They are not the best examples to follow if you want to make tenure here."

"Blow it out your ass, Joe," Eunice said. "It's been years since anybody has stuck around here long enough to for the tenure committee to notice."

"There's Fran," Max said suddenly. He glared at Cunningham, then went back to contemplating his food.

Cunningham smiled and removed his hands from Fran's shoulders. "All the same, Janet, it doesn't hurt to be discerning when it comes to choosing one's companions."

"That's why we warned her about you," Eunice's tone was blithe, but her eyes snapped at the older man, who huffed off. Eunice looked at Fran. "You did warn her, didn't you?"

"I couldn't," said Fran.

But then the president of the university got himself to his feet and called for order. He introduced the department heads, some with more reverence than the others, with Eunice commenting softly. As the president spoke on the honor of serving the arts, Eunice muttered the same speech right along with him. It was no small trick to keep a straight face, and I didn't dare look over at Fran. At the same time, I couldn't help but worry. For all Cunningham tried to pretend to be jovial, there was pure malice behind his teasing.

I asked Eunice about it later that afternoon as she, Fran and I ate our second lunch at Gianotti's, a nearby pizza parlor.

"Joe Cunningham is a wart," Eunice said. "A carbuncle."

"Eunice," Fran groaned. "Does anybody even know what a carbuncle is anymore?"

She shrugged. "The easy answer is Joe Cunningham."

"Yeah, but why the animosity?" I asked. "He was really nasty to you two today. And you asked Fran if she'd warned me about him."

Eunice glared at Fran. "And you said you couldn't."

"The chancellor asked me not to. He must be writing grants again.

"No doubt."

Fran nibbled at a piece of pizza. "I did tell Janet that he's a male chauvinist pig."

Eunice snorted. "He is a blight, a stain upon the hallowed halls of academia."

"I noticed," I said. "But why?"

"He has tried to ruin the career of every woman academic who has come to Martin. Poor Fran, here, would have gotten tenure anywhere else two years ago."

"I'm supposedly on the tenure track." Fran's blinking grew worse. "I feel like I'm not even in the station, thanks to him. And all because I turned him down when he wanted a little fun and games."

"Fortunately, I already had tenure when Joe became the department head." Eunice held up her glass of iced tea. "To Sherman Pendergast, another male chauvinist pig, but one who could recognize brilliance when he saw it."

"Maybe I should just go to U-Dub." Fran wiped her eyes with her napkin.

"And start all over again?" Eunice asked. "Joe Cunningham is hanging on by a thread and he knows it. One more harassment complaint and he's toast."

"Really?" I asked. "He wasn't exactly nice to me yesterday, but I wouldn't call it harassment."

"Trust me, he's only biding his time," said Eunice.

"No," snorted Fran. "He doesn't want to get in trouble with the chancellor after he sent what's-her-name screaming three days before classes started."

"Believe me." Eunice leaned in close. "The turnover in young academics around here is phenomenal. Most of them are just trying to polish up the resume and get some easy teaching credits before going seriously tenure-track at a more prestigious institution. But the lovely young ladies, like you, they rarely last more than a quarter."

"Why hasn't the university gotten sued?" I asked, my mouth open.

"Oh, but they have," said Eunice. "I have personal confirmation on that one, at least twice. They settled and hushed it up to keep the enrollment numbers up. That's why they can't get rid of him. If they own up to what he's been doing, all those nice rich girls are going to go someplace else with Daddy's nice, green money. And do you want to know the worst part of all this? Cunningham is a terrible historian. History was his game before he became administration. Sloppy end notes. He comes to conclusions that are trite and were discredited years before. He can't even be bothered to verify the primary documents!" Eunice jabbed the table with her forefinger.

"I think she gets it, Eunice." Fran rolled her eyes at me.

"I could understand if he were studying pre-Conqueror England," Eunice went on, nonetheless. "That documentation is scarce, and the grad students don't always know where to look. But he's an American Civil War man! There is absolutely no excuse not to check and verify your primary documents."

Fran looked apologetically at me. "She's even worse when she's drunk."

I couldn't help laughing. "Oh, dear."

"And do not be afraid of him." Eunice sat up straight. "I can and will protect you, just like I protect Fran. She will get tenure here if she wants it. And if you like it here, I will see to it that you do, too." Eunice paused. "Assuming, of course, that you publish on schedule, your scholarship is sound, and you keep up on the teaching. Those are, after all, the appropriate criteria for tenure."

I grinned. "I'll do my best, Eunice."

Eunice drove us home the long way, lecturing me in a genial way about the town's history and the people that had settled there.

"Are you a Nineteenth Century person?" I asked.

"Pshaw. No. Obviously, I teach it all, especially Northern European History."

"What most places call World History," Fran said.

Eunice snorted again. "Utterly typical of the Northern European male mindset. I mostly publish on the English Civil War era. In fact, I'm getting some traction on women's daily life during the Jacobean and Civil War periods. That's my real interest, but it's hell getting the journals to take that one on. And I've been dabbling in the late Medieval Lowlands. You know, the area that would become Belgium. We have a large Belgian population in Wisconsin, and late Medieval, early Renaissance was certainly the area's heyday." She looked at me. "And you?"

I was prepared for that question. "I did my dissertation on feminist tropes in Hamlet." I shuddered. "I'm sorry. I'm still too traumatized by the oral defense to even think about it."

It worked. Both Eunice and Fran laughed loudly and went on to share their own horror stories about having to defend their dissertations, then the ridiculous nonsense that they'd chosen to write about.

"How did we get away with such chicanery?" Eunice asked as we pulled into the driveway at Fran's and my place.

"I don't know about you," Fran said. "But when I think about what the boys got away with. Good lord, what B.S. And David Watts. He's still talking up his dissertation on… What benighted poet is he so excited about?"

"Gerard Manley Hopkins." Eunice's eyes rolled. "It's not bad stuff and certainly has a ring to it within the context of his Jesuit origins. But the way David goes on about the sexual metaphors says a hell of a lot more about David's relationship with the Catholic Church than Hopkins' relationship."

I shrugged. "Hopkins had a few issues, but then, I've yet to read a Victorian poet who didn't."

That got another good laugh. Eunice grinned at me.

"Yes, darling. You'll do very well here. Would you do me the enormous favor of avoiding Ernie Lavalle and Joe Cunningham like the plague and stick around? We could use another good broad, and I mean that in the kindest way."

"Of course, Eunice." I smiled at her, my heart filling in spite of myself. "I'll do my best."

Fran cocked her head. "What brought you out here, anyway? If I read your CV right, you were at UCLA."

"I was an adjunct at UCLA and not even able to make rent without a roommate," I said, again ready for that question. Adjuncts were generally part-time staff and at the bottom of the academic food chain. "The broken heart didn't help, either."

Fran winced and blinked. "I completely understand that one. Eunice, do you want to stretch this into dinner?"

"I would dearly love to. Alas, I'm teaching a new course on Elizabeth I and have barely gotten the syllabus together. And I don't doubt that Janet, here, is in similar trouble."

"I am," I said. "My Basic Comp outline is in good shape. But I've had to completely redo the outline for the Shakespeare seminar. According to Joe Cunningham, the course description includes Coriolanus, Julius Caesar, and Titus Andronicus, and he told me yesterday to stick to those plays."

Both women recoiled in horror.

"That would be one of Joe's tricks," Eunice sighed. "Well, good night, ladies. Flights of angels sing thee to thy sleep."

I sniggered as Fran and I got out of the car. "I don't know if you realize it, but you're using the singular familiar for the second pronoun."

Fran laughed.

"What?" asked Eunice.

"Thee and thou," I said. "They're basically the singular familiar form of you. How the two got blended I don't know, but back in Shakespeare's time, they were separate, like tu and vous in French, and tu and usted in Spanish."

Eunice laughed loudly and waved as she pulled out.

"Really?" Fran asked, still laughing.

"Yep. Little known fact," I said.

"Eunice is right. You'll do very well here."

Fran waved at me as she went into her apartment. I mounted the stairs. I tried to be as quiet as I could, but three steps up, I realized there was no hope of avoiding any noise. So, I just went upstairs.

September 14–16, 1984

F ran looked nervous when I came down the stairs on Friday afternoon. We were again dressed casually. I had my purse, which doubled as a briefcase. She had an actual briefcase.

"Is everything okay?" I asked as we walked out the door and Fran locked it.

She blinked several times. "I just don't want you to get discouraged."

We both shuddered a little as we walked to Lawrence Hall.

"It's a faculty meeting. It's meant to be discouraging," I said.

"Well, I'm told ours aren't any worse than anyone else's. We'd better make a point of not sitting anywhere near Eunice, though. She tends to misbehave, and it's impossible to keep a straight face."

I agreed. When we got to Lawrence, I made a point of going to Cunningham's office first. He was just coming out of his office when I arrived.

"Ah, Janet, I asked you to turn that course outline in yesterday morning and I haven't seen it yet." He puffed himself up. That day, he wore a yellow carnation, possibly in honor of the meeting.

"It's right here," I said, handing him the papers. "I said Friday afternoon, and it's Friday afternoon. Now, I don't want to be late for the meeting."

I turned and found Fran in the hallway. She silently laughed as she led me to the conference room.

The meeting was terrible. Cunningham reminded the faculty that grades were to be entered into the computer system weekly during the course of the quarter, which brought on a debate about why it was necessary to do it that way and why couldn't someone hire a work-study student to do it? This, in turn, brought complaints that not all the offices were connected to the computer system. Fran commented that my office didn't have any sort of computer at all. Cunningham explained that there wasn't enough money in the department budget to wire all the offices, which inspired another extended discussion about getting a grant from the endowment, punctuated by complaints about whether people really needed computers in the first place. And it did not get any better.

"Dr. Cunningham, this doesn't help," Ernie Lavalle whined every time Cunningham tried to shut him down on getting a student worker.

Robert Farnsworth, the elder statesman of the department and the primary English professor, snoozed through the entire meeting. Fran and I had made sure to sit well away from Eunice and with our backs to her, just to be safe. I fidgeted, making inane notes about the other faculty members. Fred Wirth, a corpulent fellow who taught political science, showed off pictures of his latest grandchild in between wondering why the endowment couldn't do something about the small portions in the Faculty Dining Room. This inspired yet another debate about the endowment and budget and Lester Zaner jumped in, complaining that he and his wife Marianne had been promised new tape cassettes for their various foreign language classes. I have no idea what Eunice was doing, but I saw Cunningham glare at her several times, and heard muffled laughter more than once from Ted Curtis, who was sitting next to her.

Eventually, even Cunningham couldn't find something to complain about, and everyone got up and left as fast as they could. I and a few others weren't quite fast enough.

"Uh, Janet," Cunningham called. "About your Shakespeare outline."

I turned to him and folded my arms across my chest. "Yes, Joe?"

The remaining faculty members stopped their rush to the exit and openly stared at the two of us.

Cunningham swallowed. "Uh. It will do."

"Thanks, Joe," I replied, and sauntered off.

Eunice and Fran were beside themselves with holding in their laughter. Fortunately, they waited until we were outside the building to start whooping it up. Dwight Atwater, a bespectacled psychology professor with a dark beard streaked with gray, came up to us.

"Dr. Mayfield, may I congratulate you on a splendid piece of brinkmanship," he said.

I shrugged. "Ted Curtis told me we were all on a first-name basis here."

That set off a gale of giggles from Fran.

Dwight chuckled. "Well, if he gives you any trouble, I will be happy to support any claim you make. With any luck at all, we'll be rid of him for good."

Eunice drove Fran and me to dinner at Barb's Diner, a traditional kind of place near the interstate. They were still laughing.

"I just hope I haven't gotten myself into trouble," I sighed after we'd ordered.

"You probably have," Fran said. "But with Dwight on our side, maybe we can get rid of him."

"I just want to know how they found somebody with some backbone," Eunice asked.

"She was hired by the chancellor," Fran said.

"That explains it. Joe wouldn't have hired anybody he couldn't control."

"Oh, great," I grumbled. I suddenly realized why I had stood up to Cunningham. It was because I was not hungry for tenure. I wasn't even going to be there that long. I had another life and family that I loved.

"Oh, don't worry about it, Janet," Eunice said. "Sometimes the best way to get what you want is to act like you don't give a damn. Fran, here, is a perfect example."

"It hasn't worked so far," Fran said.

"It hasn't failed yet, either," Eunice said.

Fran didn't seem entirely convinced.

"Eunice, you're probably right," I said. "But it's a very fine line between not caring and shooting yourself in the foot."

Eunice would not be swayed, but we did not argue the point much. Our dinners arrived, and from there we went to a dark bar called The Cider Keg that was near the university. Eunice got a snootful, so I ended up driving the three of us to her house in her car. Fran and I walked to our building from there. It wasn't far, but Fran was more than a little winded as we unlocked the outside door.

"Next time we go out," she said and gasped. "Let's one of us drive."

"Sure, Fran." I laughed and waited while she got into her apartment.

She was in better shape than Eunice, but not by much.

I ran up the stairs, letting the squeaking and creaking go on. It wasn't going to be bothering Fran. However, when I got to my door, my front pants pocket vibrated. I got the powder compact from the pocket. The rim glowed a dull pink. In addition to telling me if anyone was broadcasting on a low-level frequency almost exclusively used by bugs, the compact was connected to the trip wires I'd installed. The pink meant that one or more had been broken, which meant someone was or had been in my apartment.

I swallowed. I had a gun in my purse, a Smith and Wesson Model Thirteen revolver. The last time I'd shot it, less than two months before, I'd killed someone. That it was absolutely self-defense, or actually, saving Sid's life, didn't really help. Sid had saved me, holding me close as I worked through the trauma. But Sid wasn't there.

I shut my eyes. On one hand, entering my apartment without a gun at the ready was asking for trouble. On the other, entering my apartment fully armed and ready to take somebody down didn't really work for my cover as a nice English professor, especially since I wasn't supposed to know that somebody was in my apartment. I settled for slinging the purse over my right shoulder and going in with one hand on my gun.

Inside, the faint light from the streetlights showed the silhouette of a tall man with a pronounced stoop sitting on the couch. I turned on the lights. The man had reddish hair and wore horn-rimmed glasses.

"Good to see you," Dr. Steve Carmona said as I shut the door.

"Nice of you to break in," I said, withdrawing my hand from the purse. I was playing tough. It was what he would expect.

"Sorry about that."

"I'll bet." I dropped the purse on the small table I'd bought and placed next to the door.

"We need to talk."

"And you couldn't have just made a phone call? Left a message for me at the department office?"

He pulled a pack of cigarettes from his shirt pocket. "Mind if I smoke?"

"Yes, I do mind." It was, perhaps, not the nicest thing to say, but I was so glad it wasn't considered rude anymore to say no.

"Oh. Sorry." He stuffed the pack back into his shirt. "I'm here to brief you." He grimaced. "Not that I have much to tell you."

I nodded. In that split second, I decided to drop the defenses. The poor guy was worn out and probably frustrated.

He looked up at me. "I'd heard you and Little Red were assigned to this case."

"I'm Little Red." Which was my code name. I couldn't help feeling nettled. "He's Big Red."

Steve shrugged. "Okay." He looked at me again. "Look, I'm sorry to be such a grouch. But this one has gone nasty.

We lost two students last spring." He paused. "One of them was mine. Brilliant kid. Could have gone far."

I found the chair to my desk and sat down. Steve was a bit of a mess, and it was easy to see why. Technically, in the spy biz, you're supposed to check your emotions at the door, so to speak. I had never been able to, and Sid had hinted over the couple of years that I'd been at the game, that those who could be that divorced from their emotions were not people you wanted to be dealing with.

"Do we have police reports on them?" I asked.

"Yeah. I gave them to Little, I mean, Big Red. He got the apartment on top of mine. Posing as a rich Second Career guy."

"I know. So, why are you talking to me?"

"I'm talking to the whole team. You all are covering different parts of the campus."

He closed his eyes, then opened them with a sigh.

"So, who is this scientist we're trying to protect?" I asked.

Steve let out a sharp bark of laughter. "I have no idea."

"What? Aren't you his handler? You're faculty. I was told the other faculty member on the team was the handler."

"And I am. The guy, or maybe even gal, is spooky as hell. Refuses to complete the job if anyone knows who he is. We've only communicated by notes and phone messages."

"How is the formula being stolen?"

He held up his hands. "I wish I knew. But, like you, I don't know who the developer is, which makes it pretty damned hard to figure out who's doing the stealing."

I groaned and glared at the ceiling. "Okay. What do we know?"

"We've got two dead students. One was a music student. A bomb was planted in her car. The other, my kid, was comp sci. He got injected with some nerve agent. They ID'd the substance as one favored by the KGB. We've got one person who's been confirmed as an agent here in town, and two others suspected of being agents or with ties to suspected agents here on campus, so someone has figured out that our guy is here. But like us, they don't know who he is, either."

"But why kill students? It doesn't seem like they'd be secretly developing some formula."

Steve snorted. "Which is why I believe we're dealing with an amateur under KGB control."

"I'd heard that."

"Nice of them to let you know that much." He yawned and stretched. "I think the music kid got it because I'm fairly sure our developer is someone in the music department. My kid got it because there's probably a connection with the university's computer system. It's a closed system, but some folks modem out to the ARPANET. We don't have a strong science department," He stopped. "I'm talking gibberish to you, aren't I?"

I frowned. "Not entirely. I have a friend who sometimes talks about ARPANET, and I understand that it's a way for computers to talk to each other. But I don't know how that affects the average person."

Steve chuckled. "I suspect it will eventually. People are already using it to send messages to each other. And there's other stuff."

"Which really doesn't have much to do with our specific problem."

"True." He yawned again. "You count as a hub, right?"

"If you mean someone who has contact with our other operatives, then yes."

"You're also covering the Humanities Department. From what I've seen, it's ideal for a hub. Not a lot going on there, but lots of contact across departments. Believe me, if you think humanities gets short shrift around here, you should try being in the math/sciences division. The only reason comp sci gets some respect is that there is some money and art involved in computer games."

"Okay. There's a little internecine skullduggery, too."

He laughed. "Yeah. There's that between departments, but it wouldn't be a university without it."

"True."

He shook his head, then pulled a small piece of paper from his shirt pocket. "I'm briefing each one of the team. I'm covering math/sciences for obvious reasons. You'll figure out the others. Here's what I've been able to come up with on humanities, which is pretty much zilch. Your department chair, Joe Cunningham, is basically a blowhard."

"That much I've figured out."

"Fred Wirth, he's..."

"Political Science." I nodded.

"Tends to slip away from campus at odd times. Might be worth looking into."

"Got it."

"Carson Osgood."

I closed my eyes trying to visualize the person I'd been introduced to. He was Fran's colleague, teaching Communications, that much I'd recalled. I could see his slightly Saturnine face peering at me through wire-rimmed glasses, but little more.

"Okay," I said slowly.

"Has a record as a Communist sympathizer. Then there are the Zaners."

"They teach foreign languages."

"Right." Steve rubbed his eyes. "As far as I can tell, they're not interested in anything outside of school besides their kids, and they're up to..."

"Four, according to what I heard."

Steve raised his eyebrows. "Good work."

"It's not that hard, for Heaven's sakes."

"Maybe, maybe not." Steve squeezed his eyes shut, then opened them and gazed at his paper. "David Watts, one of the other English professors, is married to a known KGB operative. He checks out, though. No suspicious activity. The few times I've talked to him, he doesn't seem to have a clue about what his wife really does for a living."

"Sounds like a great marriage."

Steve chuckled. "Yeah. Finally, Dwight Atwater and Perry Addington, just because they're psych."

"That's evidence that will hold up in court."

"I'm not giving you evidence. I'm giving you places to look." He looked at his paper again. "Atwater can be rather reclusive, though, so think about it."

"Okay. Speaking of reclusive, what about Max Beard?"

"That space cadet?" Steve laughed. "He is brilliant, I'll give him that. But you want to talk about lost in his own little world?"

"I got that impression. Anyone else you want me to look at? Robert Farnsworth? Ernie Lavalle?"

Steve closed his eyes and thought. "At this point, everybody is a possible. But you could probably put them on the bottom of the list."

"Always nice to know," I said.

Steve pulled himself up from the battered couch. "I should probably make myself scarce. Umm. Why don't we, um, you know, meet every now and then?"

"Sure." I shrugged. "You mean, like, we're friends or something?"

"Yeah. That would be fun."

"Okay."

Steve headed for the kitchen.

"The door's that way," I said.

"Yeah. With all those noisy stairs? I'm coming in and out the back, thank you."

"Good point." I followed him to the back of the apartment and watched as he made his way down the wooden fire escape.

I wasn't sure what to make of Steve Carmona. Just because he was supposedly briefing me didn't mean he hadn't sold out. But I didn't get that vibe from him. That he was tired and frustrated, there was no question. It occurred to me that anyone who had not been on campus the previous spring was unlikely to be our thief. But it was not conclusive. After all, we had a poisoning and a bombing, which would hint at two different killers. The trick would be to eliminate everyone who had been on campus the previous spring first, and that was not going to be easy.

I spent Saturday in my apartment holed up with my books, trying to make sure my class syllabi were in as perfect a shape as I could manage. Sunday morning, I had another challenge to face - whether or not I would go to church.

I am deeply religious. Although, if I'm really honest, the reason I'm a practicing Catholic is because that's how I was raised, and for some reason, I didn't do the whole rebellion against my parents and seek out other religions thing. Catholicism works for me. But, as Sid had pointed out the previous summer, it was also one of the barriers between us.

Sid is an atheist and for much the same reason that I'm a Catholic. It's how he was raised. He was taught free love and that sex was about being open and whatever. Me, well, sex is about commitment and lifelong love. It has always been an issue for us, but it had gotten to be a real problem the summer before when Sid asked me to move into his bedroom and offered me a lifetime commitment. I almost went for it. But Sid couldn't promise the fidelity that I really needed.

I was okay with Sid not being able to make that commitment. I really was. I mean, I'd kind of figured the two of us would get together at some point, and I was genuinely in love with him. It would just take time.

That being said, Sid had also, quite accurately, pointed out that my religious beliefs were the glue that held me together and that he didn't want to cross those because it would mess everything up. But he'd also written to me that my beliefs were also the last barrier to our true happiness together, which was also true.

His randiness was a big problem. Sid would pretty much sleep with anyone at anytime, anywhere. I was still a virgin.

Which is the long way around for saying that when I decided that Janet Mayfield should not be religious and go to church, it probably wasn't that I was worried about being religious making me too memorable. I wanted to see if I could get past that last barrier. [Please. You were already past that barrier. I was already past that barrier. It was barely an excuse at that point. I'm just lucky that you were willing to hold out for the right reason. - SEH]

The one thing I did do that Sunday was drive into Madison, the state capitol, had lunch there, then found a pay phone.

"Hello?" asked my sister's voice.

"It's me," I said. "We finally got a couple hours off and I was able to sneak into town."

"So, are you having fun being a ghostwriter?"

That was the story Sid and I had told our friends and family to explain our extended absence. Our work with Quickline is so top secret no one knows about it, including our friends and family. How Sid and I were going to maintain our business relationships as freelance writers worried me a bit. But Sid said they'd found a way to help us. After all, the top brass in the organization had a lot invested in us keeping our real personae viable, as well.

"It's been interesting," I told Mae. "How is everybody?"

Everybody was fine. Mae's youngest kids, Marty and Mitch, a pair of twins, were in nursery school and terrorizing the teacher with their antics. Darby was adjusting well to his new school. Janey didn't like her teacher that year, but was learning to deal with it. Ellen had started first grade reading at a second-grade level. Mae was annoyed because Ellen was supposed to be on an accelerated track, but that didn't mean she was being challenged.

I let Mae's voice waft over me, a touchstone to the things I valued and cared about. I asked about our parents, and they were doing well, as usual.

Mae asked how things were going, and I said they were fine and chose not to elaborate, reminding Mae that Sid and I were under contract not to. She didn't like it but had to agree I had a point.

I hung up a good hour later, feeling somewhat better, and drove back to Appleton. The reality was that I had a life away from Martin U. and I did not have to worry about tenure, department cliques, and interdepartmental skullduggery. I just had to pretend that I cared about all that stuff.

September 17, 1984

Monday morning, I stood outside the classroom across the hall and two doors down from my office and took a deep breath. The note pinned to the bulletin board next to the door said, "10 a.m. - Basic Composition 11, Mayfield."

My first class. According to my course list, I only had twelve students enrolled, even though maximum enrollment was twenty. That had surprised me. Most first year English Composition classes were overflowing.

But the answer to that little riddle was immediately apparent when I walked into the room. Nineteen pairs of eyes were riveted on me, clearly wondering if I was mature enough or disorganized enough to be the teacher. Back when I had been one of them, that had been what I had wondered.

I smiled. Even when I had been teaching, before Sid and Quickline, I'd felt the same things and that was comforting.

One pair of particularly bright blue eyes caught mine and my breath. Yes, they looked at me through a pair of light-colored tortoise-shell glasses rather than contact lenses, but I knew them all too well. He smiled gently. He knew for sure that I was the teacher.

I stepped to the front of the room. Casement windows on one side added light to the fluorescent fixtures above. The chalk board at the head had been freshly cleaned, but there was the odd ding or two that bespoke the years of service. The students had all wedged themselves into the chair units with woefully inadequate little tops that were supposed to provide space to write notes on. There was a desk at the front, on which I dropped my purse, which was still doubling as a briefcase. The worn desk had enough drawers to serve as my office, but I was willing to bet that it was empty. When I was an adjunct at a community college, those drawers had been a lifesaver. But now I had an actual office.

"Good morning, everyone," I said, slightly louder than normal. The students stilled. "I'm Dr. Mayfield, and this is Basic Composition 11. Given that I have twelve of you on my course list and that there are considerably more than that sitting here, I must ask, are you sure you're in the right place?"

There was a general shuffling, nodding, and other indications that said they were all in the right place.

"Then I assume that some of you are trying to add." I could see several faces looking very hopeful, including his. "At this point, it looks like there's room. However, I'm not signing any paperwork until the class is dismissed. After you hear what I've got to say, you may not want to stick around."

I had a feeling that there was little I could say to discourage anyone. Basic Comp, or some variant thereof, was one of those general education classes that everyone hated but that almost everyone had to take. I pulled a stack of freshly dittoed papers from my purse. Fortunately, I had convinced Mrs. Spinetti to run enough copies on the ditto machine for the full enrollment for all three of my Basic Comp classes that morning, pointing out that I would be forced to ask her for more if all three classes filled up.

"This is the syllabus for the course," I announced as I handed a small stack of copies to each person at the head of the five rows of desk/chair units. "While these are being handed around, I'll call roll."

The name he was using was not on my list and he did not answer to any of the others I called. I tried not to keep looking his way. He wasn't a big man, just under average height and very well proportioned. His hair was dark, wavy, and precision trimmed, as was the beard he absently scratched. It hid a decidedly cute cleft in his chin. I couldn't help smiling. He may have carried a navy-blue daypack instead of a briefcase, but even in khaki slacks and a blue polo shirt, he looked dressed up. But then, he would look dressed up in a t-shirt and cut-offs, although he'd sooner be caught dead in that attire. [Damn skippy, I would. - SEH]

"I'll get the rest of your names later," I said, after checking off the names I had. "As you can see from the syllabus, the objective of this course is to teach you how to write clearly and correctly in the English language. If you already know how to do so, then you are in good shape. However, I will venture to argue that just because you think you know how to write does not mean that you, in fact, do. I think all of us will agree that the best way to learn how to write is to do it. This is why you will turn in a writing assignment every time we meet."

A subdued groan rippled through the students.

"You will also be responsible for a twenty-page term paper due before the final."

The groan got louder.

"Don't panic. The paper won't be that bad. There will be progress assignments throughout the quarter, so you won't have to stay up too late the night before it's due. You'll also be graded on a midterm and a final, plus a spelling quiz on Fridays and a grammar quiz on Mondays. All your writing assignments will be typed, or they will not be accepted. I realize that might be a little hard on some of you, but I want to maintain my eyesight and my sanity this term. Any questions?"

Jason de Boeur, a tall, freckled kid with wild brown hair, raised his hand.

"What about absences?"

"Planning on them already?" I shot back. The class laughed. "I do not encourage absenteeism. However, I realize it's sometimes inevitable. I do not grade on attendance, but you still have an assignment due every class period, whether or not you are here. If, for some reason, you cannot make it to class, leave a message at the department office and we will make arrangements. Fair warning. I am not inclined to be lenient. Also, you will get your assignment for the next class at the end of each class period. I rarely give make-ups for quizzes or exams, so if you are not in the hospital, you'd better be here."

I then went over the syllabus, answered questions about how the tests and homework would be graded, what to do if the bookstore was out of the required textbook, and how to find a typewriter (there were plenty in the library).

After all of that, I cleared my throat. "What I'd like now is for all of us to get to know each other. Some of your work will be read to the rest of the class and we will critique it. I'd like that criticism to be among friends. In addition, anything said in this classroom stays in this classroom. Now, why don't we get our desks arranged into a circle and begin?"

I winced at the deafening noise of desks scraping against the floor. Once settled, the students let their stories out. For the most part, there was a sameness to them. They were all arts students, whether from the music, or the theater, or the fine arts departments. Most of them were fresh out of high school and many from different parts of Wisconsin.

Jason de Boeur, for instance, was clearly the resident clown, a declared theater major, and from the nearby town of Combined Locks. Dennis White, by comparison, was from New York, attending Martin because his father had, and a declared animation major, but with a computer science minor. Sherry Van Wettering, whose family name decorated the Fine Arts building, had Brooke Shields hair and the attitude to match. She was a history major - one of the two majors the Humanities Department offered, the other being English.

Then there was Terry Michaels. She looked like she was still in high school, with a waif-like figure and mousy dark brown hair. She barely mumbled her name, said she was a declared Sculpture major, but really wanted to do arts education. It was a little odd that I didn't recognize her because I knew from her name that she was on the Quickline team, and I'd seen pretty much everyone in the organization more than once. We caught eyes for a second and then I let it go.

Then his turn came. He shifted in his desk and scratched his beard.

"My name is Ed Donaldson. I'm a Second Career student. I got into real estate after high school and, fortunately, was successful enough to allow me to quit for a while and get an education. I am enrolled in the Bachelor of Music program with a major in piano."

"When did you get out of high school?" Sherry asked, flashing her huge brown eyes.

"Too long ago," he said with a subtly lascivious gleam.

Finally, it was my turn.

"As you know, I am Dr. Janet Mayfield," I said. "This is my first term here at Martin U., but not my first term teaching. While I love teaching basic composition, my specialty is Shakespeare." I paused as the five theater majors cheered. "My office hours are listed on the syllabus. In addition to that, I hold what I call Off-Campus Office Hours on Sunday afternoons. The idea is to provide a more informal way for you to ask questions and get whatever help you need to pass this course. Or get some free pizza or other food."

I got a few more cheers in response.

I grinned. "Now that we've all introduced ourselves, you're going to do your first assignment right now. This will be the only, and I do mean only, exception to the typing rule. For the rest of the class period, I want you to write an essay on what is your favorite food and why you like it. I'll give you a hint. I'm more interested in the why than the what. Everybody ready?"

"Dr. Mayfield?" Rita Farley, a quiet blonde, raised her hand.

"Yes?"

"All I brought was my steno pad. Is that all right?"

"I have some extra binder paper. Anybody else need any?"

Two other students raised their hands. I handed out the paper. While they wrote, I thumbed through an academic journal. I kept one eye on the students, trying to avoid Ed. I kept catching myself gazing at him. He caught me one time and smiled gently. I blushed and buried myself in the journal.

Ten minutes before class was supposed to end, I called a halt to the writing, then gave them their assignment for the next class. There was a bit of a traffic jam around the desk as students dropped off their work, and those who were trying to add waited for me to sign their forms.

Terry Michaels dropped her paper and left quickly. She was already on the roll.

Ed Donaldson, better known to me as Sid Hackbirn, remained at his desk until he was the last person in the room with me.

"Are you going to add or not?" I asked.

He got up and handed me the form. "I'm adding." He paused. "I like your natural hair color better."

"And you know why it's not," I said, trying not to sound too acerbic.

"I do." He smiled and my heart raced.

"How's it going?"

He winced. "Not particularly good, I'm afraid. I am besieged by the usual freshman woes. I can't tell you how relieved I am to get this class. I spent all this last week auditioning and taking placement tests, and I still had to fight my way into Beginning Theory. Then this morning, I tried to get into three different math classes."

"Did you get in?"

"No. That's why I'm here now. Otherwise, I was going to have to get into your Tuesday/Thursday section. Fortunately, your classes are the only ones that are open, but I didn't want to take a chance on the Tuesday/Thursday being full."

I looked at him. "You don't seem terribly put out by it all."

He shrugged. "It could be worse."

"Hm. I'm guessing that means the women here are to your liking."

"Can't complain." He grinned, but there was something off about it.

"You reprobate." I smiled anyway. "Speaking of, you'd better card Sherry Van Wettering. Something tells me she's still a minor. You don't want that kind of trouble."

"I never want that kind of trouble. But you're right. Extra caution is in order." He looked around, then lowered his voice. "Since I'm here, you got anything for me?"

"Not really. You?"

"Here."

Underneath his essay was a nine by twelve manilla envelope. Sid took a quick look out the door, then pulled out some photos and sheets of descriptions. They were the known KGB agent and the two suspects.

"I've seen her," Sid said, pointing to one of the photos. "Apparently, she's a secretary at one of the paper mills."

"What about the police reports on the two students who were killed last spring?"

"In the envelope." He put the photos and descriptions back. "There's not much there. The only thing the two murders have in common was that they were traps set for the victims."

"Even the kid who got injected?"

"Yeah. It was some sort of spring-loaded ampule. No way to tell who set it."

"Your downstairs neighbor told me it was a KBG nerve agent that killed him."

"That is not in the police report." Sid paused and grinned. "He doesn't waste much time, does he?"

"Broke into my place Friday night." I rolled my eyes. "He's nice enough, and he's really feeling the kid who got poisoned."

"I noticed."

There was a slightly awkward pause. I pulled the papers that had been left on my desk together.

"So, what classes do you have?" I asked.

"This one, Beginning Theory and Analysis, Intro to Communications, and, hopefully, Intro to Calculus, and one and a half hours Individual Performance Studies."

"One and a half? What's that?"

"Private lessons." Sid shuddered. "One hour a week on piano and half an hour on organ, and who knows how many hours practicing my fingers to the bone in the meantime."

"But you're really good. I mean, you play Tchaikovsky and Chopin and all that heavy-duty stuff."

Sid laughed. "I'm not nearly as good as you think, at least not on a professional level. Those private classes are going to be killers."

"Well, save some time for your typewriter. I expect you to work like everyone else. I'm not going to let you slide through for friendship's sake."

Sid's sigh was exaggerated. "I was afraid you'd say that. I suppose it's some sort of compliment that you think I can keep up."

I grinned. "We'll see."

He laughed, then smiled tenderly. "I'm glad I'm here."

"So am I."

I had an hour and a half to visit the Faculty Dining Room for the snack they provided, then eat the lunch I'd brought back to my office. I also started in on the papers I'd collected. Reading the essays, I could already see that I was going to have to be a real hard nose about the typing rule.

My second (or B) section of Basic Comp was not terribly exciting. A young man that I had not seen before identified himself as Tim Hannaford, one of the other Quickline team members. He said he was a freshman majoring in Drawing and Painting, and he certainly looked fresh out of high school, just like Terry Michaels had. I wasn't sure what to make of him, but let it go. I went through the same routine I had earlier, without someone challenging me on absences, and Tim hung around after the dismissal just long enough to establish our team connection.

From class, I went back to my office to grade papers. Back before Quickline, my colleagues had teased me about assigning so much work for the students because of the way it would increase my workload. However, one of my graduate advisors, and then later, my mentor teacher had both pointed out that tenure committees loved the kind of dedication to teaching that grading tons of papers showed. I was no longer, technically, on tenure track, even if I wanted to appear as if I was. The weird thing was, I still cared about the students and wanted to help them learn how to write. I also knew that if I didn't stay on top of the grading, I would be drowning in no time. Even if student evaluations were not a significant concern for me, one thing that would get me blasted in no time was not getting students their work back fast enough.

I was about to unlock my office when I noticed a note on my bulletin board. I unpinned it, shut the door, and unloaded papers onto my desk to grade. Just in case, I looked at the note first. It was from Mrs. Spinetti. Apparently, having students move their little desk/chair combos into a circle was strictly forbidden. I tossed the note into the little trash basket next to the desk and went back to work. I still had several papers from the A section (my first section) of Basic Comp to get through, plus all the ones from the B section (at that point, I decided to label each of my sections A, B, and C).

The work was a little demoralizing. I had already gotten the feeling from the papers I'd graded on my lunch hour that I was going to have to start at the very beginning of the grammar textbook that had been assigned. To be honest, I wasn't terribly surprised. I do not know if writing skills aren't being taught or students just aren't listening (probably a bit of both). Either way, at least three-quarters of my students couldn't construct a sentence correctly, and/or couldn't spell, and only one person out of that three quarters could put together a decent argument.

That person was Sid. Alright, the name at the top of the paper was Ed Donaldson. But it was written in Sid's atrocious handwriting and the words, phrasing, and style were all uniquely his. Sid has an innate ability to think and write in a logical flow. His grammar and spelling are the pits. Given that his visible profession is as a freelance writer, one must wonder how he could succeed. Well, until I became his secretary, he didn't, really. Since then, that business has taken off, but that's because I correct his manuscripts.

I will say this. I knew he had not been taught writing skills. Sid's aunt, who raised him, was a serious radical and had sent him to all sorts of freedom schools (mostly ones where she had taught music). Somewhere in all that development of free expression and creative thought, he had managed to teach himself to read and do math well enough to graduate from a traditional high school, and later, Stanford University with a B.A. in Business. While at Stanford, he inherited enough money, so he didn't have to work and could hire me once Quickline had decided to give him a partner.

Having him in my class meant that I was finally going to have the chance to teach him to do for himself what he'd been burdening me with. But as I read his essay, I could see there were going to be drawbacks. He claimed that his favorite food was fresh fruit in general. That was an out and out lie. I knew darned well that he'd take a mushroom and black olive pizza over fresh fruit any day. His argument consisted of an overly familiar lecture on the benefits of eating properly and keeping fit.

The rascal was not very subtly telling me that he expected me to continue exercising and eating right. I snorted. The last thing I needed or wanted was a watchdog. Sid's healthy (translate finicky) eating habits drove me nuts. In turn, my insatiable appetite drove him nuts. We were always fighting about food.

I spent a good ten minutes thinking up a way to tell him that I was going to eat what I liked and as much of it as possible. Finally, I smiled.

"As you can see from the red marks, your grammar and spelling need a lot of work," I wrote. "Your paragraph structure is quite good, though, and you write in a nice, orderly fashion. However, you did not answer the question, which was why you like fresh fruit, not why you want to stay healthy."

Or, in other words, stuff it, Hackbirn!

With a little flourish, I gave the paper a B, recorded it, and went on to the next paper.

September 18 – 20, 1984

Tuesdays and Thursdays, I had the Shakespeare seminar and the final Basic Comp section (aka Basic Comp C). The Shakespeare seminar had three Second Career students in the class among the eight total. Rick Waters was a small man, with thinning hair and glasses, and a declared playwriting major. An only child, he'd worked at his parents' dairy, taking college classes as he could. Once his parents had both died, he'd sold the dairy and went to follow his dreams. Marge Haver, a real live wire with graying brown hair and a full figure, announced that she was a theater major. She had put a husband through school, raised three kids, been dumped by said husband for a younger model, and had decided it was finally time to do what she'd originally wanted to do instead of getting married.

The third Second Career student, however, startled me. The name that she answered to was Kathy Richards, and with dark brown hair that was feathered in the front and long in the back, she looked like any other college student. Her story was that she'd been taking community college courses until she'd saved enough in her job as an office

worker to go to school full time and was majoring in theater production. I'd met her the summer before as Blue
Shield, and the office she'd been working was a high-level
code breaking and development facility. She'd looked older
then, too.

I gazed at her when I announced Off Campus Office
Hours, and she smiled and nodded. She also stayed after
as the other students sauntered out of the room.

"Good to see you," I said quietly.

"Likewise." She grinned. "I'm guessing you know I'm
here for any code-breaking duties, right?"

"I figured that out."

She glanced at the classroom door. "I just want you to
know that we also got some intensive training."

"We?"

"Me, Hannaford, and Michaels." She rolled her eyes.
"They don't even have code names yet, so they decided
we should just use our cover names. Give us a chance to
get used to them. Anyway, those two may be pretty wet
behind the ears, but there shouldn't be any problems with
any take downs."

I couldn't help laughing. When we'd met the summer
before, it was to apprehend a suspect that had gotten away,
thanks to one of her colleagues.

"That was not your fault," I told her.

"Maybe, but I was embarrassed to death. When I heard
there was going to be field training for this operation, I
jumped on it."

"Oh," I said. "You guys got field training."

Kathy shrugged. "None of us had any field experience.
My crew at the Factory mostly ride desks, maybe a little
courier duty here and there."

"Well, that would explain why I hadn't seen you before last summer. What about the other two?"

"Infants." Kathy rolled her eyes. "Michaels is, obviously, a lot older than she looks, but she's still pretty green. She's in Systems and really wanted to go out in the field, and they really needed somebody who could believably pose as a freshman. Same with Hannaford." She made a face. "Fresh out of college and six months at Langley."

"He's a loaner from The Company?" Or what we called the CIA, when we weren't calling it other, less kind names.

"Not a loaner. He was just trained there. He'll be a permanent courier if he doesn't get his butt killed first. We don't usually pull recruits out of college, so I suspect The Company sent him to us for revenge on somebody."

"That would be like them, from what little I've seen."

"Yeah. Anyway, they could only get one person on faculty, and not too many in the Second Career program, so we're stuck with the infants."

I tried not to sigh.

Kathy hoisted her backpack to her shoulder. "Anything I can give to Little Red tomorrow night?"

"Big Red," I said, frowning. "I'm Little Red."

"Oh. Right." Kathy shrugged. "I can never keep you two straight. You're kind of a package deal."

"Nice to know," I grumbled.

"Well, you are the same address on the line. Do you have anything for him? We'll be catching up at a Second Career party tomorrow. At our orientation, they really encouraged us Second Career students to socialize. They said it helps offset all the discomfort being with kids who are so much younger than us. Personally, I think they want to keep us older folks from leading the young'uns astray."

"Good luck to them." I shook my head. "I don't have anything, but thanks for offering."

"You're welcome." Kathy waved as she left the room. "Ta-ta!"

I waved weakly back. As Kathy left the room, I couldn't help wondering how much "catching up" Kathy and Sid had done. Knowing Sid, the odds were decent that they'd been together. The man was randier than a British royal. It wasn't Sid's fault, I reminded myself. He had been raised to see sex as something to be indulged in, not as something sacred, which is how I saw it. There was a part of me that believed him when he said that other liaisons didn't mean anything, they really didn't. That didn't help. I still felt as if I wasn't enough for him.

I shook my head. That line of thinking was not going to help me function, let alone resolve the impasse our relationship was in.

My final section of Basic Comp was that afternoon, and it was basic. The students were all in one of the arts departments, had little to no interest in writing and were simply suffering through. My mentor teacher had pointed out that some classes are like that and there's little to be done about it. It was almost like teaching Confirmation classes at church back home, where the kids have little interest in learning and are only going because their parents made them.

I wasn't sure if I was glad that the Faculty Dining Room was closed by the time I got that last class squared away. At least, the Commons was fully open, and there were several food stands serving different styles of food, most of it not that good. I'd tried eating a hamburger earlier that day and swore never again. So, I got some insipid macaroni and cheese, and with a nod to trying to eat healthier, a salad of wilted iceberg lettuce drenched in bad blue cheese dressing.

I took my food back to my office and stayed late, grading Basic Comp papers, and reviewing my lecture for the next day. The idea was to solidly establish our covers before beginning any real investigative work, with a focus on behavior that would make it look normal to be doing things like searching offices and stealing people's papers.

That Wednesday, I had all my papers graded and my fingers crossed that I could stay on top of them all. I started the A section of Basic Comp by calling roll, then handing back the papers from the Monday before. I noticed Ed looking at his paper, then smiling softly.

As I handed back the last paper, Jason De Boeur raised his hand.

"Yes, Jason," I said.

"Why do we have to do an assignment for every class period?"

I grinned. "Jason, aren't you an actor?"

"Yeah."

"How do you learn your part in a play?"

His eyes didn't quite roll. "I rehearse it."

"Yes, but how do you rehearse it? Don't you do it over and over again?"

"Oh."

I looked around. "Ed, you're a pianist, right?"

He looked a little startled. "Yes."

"How do you learn a new piece?"

"Well." He shifted and scratched his beard. "I read the music, then play it."

"Just once?"

"No." He smiled as the light dawned. "I play it several times."

"Right." I smiled at Jason and then the rest of the class. "All of you have learned how to do many different things. None of you did any of those things perfectly the first time you did them. Some things may have come more easily than others, but you still had to do things over and over again. Writing is the same thing. You must practice it. And I know, and you know, none of you are going to go out and practice writing correctly on your own. You need motivation. That's what this class is for and that's why you're turning in an assignment every period. Now, will you all open your textbooks to page twenty-three? We're going to start with sentence structure."

I had the class turn in their homework at the end of the period. Ed dropped his paper on the desk and left with the bulk of the group, his daypack slung over one shoulder. But as I stacked the papers together to get them into my purse, a small bit of lined notepaper fell out.

"Point taken," read Sid's handwriting. "But please try to take care of yourself. I only say it because I care."

I held my eyes shut against the tears. He did care, drat him. He cared more than just about anyone in my life. Worse yet, he had a point, at least, about the exercising. At home, we ran every morning except on Sundays. I hated it. Or, maybe, I really liked complaining about it. Either way, I knew darned well it was a necessary part of staying fit, which would keep me alive. Which was why Sid had left his note.

The next morning, instead of sleeping for another hour, then heading to the shower, I got up and put on my running suit and took off. Later, after Basic Comp C, I brought my racquetball racket to the campus sports club and signed in. The amenities were genuinely nice and keep in mind, the club where Sid and I work out at home is pretty much top of the line. Strangely, the place was almost empty.

"I think it's because the students have to pay to use it," said the young blond woman in the weight room who pulled me as her client. "We got a couple faculty who use the facilities, and a few students. But you gotta figure most people aren't interested in keeping their bodies up."

"That's too bad," I said, and shrugged. "At least I won't have to wait in line for a machine."

"And I've got so little to do, I get to coach you directly. I'm Tina, by the way."

Tina turned out to be a great coach and got me through a full-body weight workout in under thirty minutes. I was just sliding off the sit up bench when an all-too familiar voice greeted me.

"Dr. Mayfield!"

I turned and smiled. "Hello, Ed."

"Did you just join?" He was dressed in black shorts and a white warm up top with a sleeveless t-shirt underneath. His fancy special shoes for playing racquetball were gleaming white, and he had his racket in a black gym bag that I knew also carried his eye guards, two towels and several cans of balls.

"Faculty get free memberships." Tina's eyes glowed with lust, but for some reason, he ignored her.

"Oh." He looked around. "You don't happen to play racquetball, do you?"

"I'm not very good," I said.

"Courts are empty," he sighed. "Sadly, there's no one else to play with."

Tina glanced up at the clock. "I'd play, but I've got to lead aerobics in a few minutes. It's the Queen Bee's time, you know."

She hurried off with one last look of longing.

"Queen Bee?" I asked him.

"Dr. Ermengarde," he replied. "She's, uh…"

"Head of the acting department." I quickly racked my brain for what Eunice had said about her at the luncheon. It had probably been something grossly impolite.

"Right." He looked around again and held up his racket. "Wanna play?"

"Sure." I got my racket and eye guards from where I'd left them on the weight room desk and followed him to the courts.

The weird thing about a racquetball court is that it's a completely closed two-story high long room. There's usually a tiny window in the door, but these courts had lights above the doors instead. The walls are concrete, which means you can't hear what anybody is saying inside the court unless the door is open, or someone is really screaming. So, as soon as we closed ourselves into the court, we dropped our covers.

"How about if we just bat the ball around?" I asked, rolling my shoulders to loosen them.

Sid chuckled. "You're never going to get better if you don't play full on."

"Every time I play full on with you, I end up with bruises all over me."

"I'll spot you five points."

"Make it ten and you're on."

Playing with Sid is not easy. He is intensely competitive and insanely good, which is why I usually end up with bruises when I do, and that's with him going easy on me. He even let me serve first. It was the last time I served. Sid had me soundly beaten within fifteen minutes. At least we were both a little winded and sweating.

"Got anything for me?" he asked.

"Not really." I winced. "Kathy Richards said that she'd be catching up with you last night."

"She didn't have anything." Sid sighed. "I'm hearing some jealousy there."

"I didn't say so."

"By now, you don't have to." Sid bounced the ball absently. "Well, you have no cause when it comes to Kathy."

"I know."

"No. You absolutely have no cause. She'd rather be dating you than me."

I had to laugh. "Yeah. I guess so. I'm sorry. I just assumed..."

"It's not like you don't have a reason not to." Sid dropped the ball and whacked it hard with his racket.

The ball flew around the court with its trademark thunk.

"I still shouldn't. It's not fair to you."

He shrugged, then looked at me. "What else is going on?"

"Well." I made a face. "It's kinda stupid, but both Kathy and Steve Carmona mixed our code names up."

"Kathy knows our code names?"

"Kathy's Blue Shield. I met her last summer on that trip to Vegas, so she knows me as Little Red. Only she thought I was Big Red. Anyway, she must have tagged you as my partner because the other two were in training with her, and we weren't. Kathy said we were a package deal."

Sid sighed. "I suppose we are. But why does that upset you?"

"It does, and it doesn't." I made a face. "I mean, I was really looking forward to being on my own, testing myself, seeing what I can do. Only we're getting lumped together again."

"Oh."

"It's not being together with you. That's the nice part." I picked up the ball and rolled it in my fingers. "It's just not knowing how much of us is what you do and how much is what I do. You've had time on your own. You know what you can do."

Sid snorted in a bemused way. "And I've always thought we were both stronger together. But I get what you're saying. Working with me is all you know."

"Exactly." I smiled at him. "You know, I really appreciate how you listen to me."

He smiled back. "That's easy." He frowned. "I am glad we have a team for this one and that we know who they are. I've done a few where I was either the only operative or wasn't but had no clue who else I was working with. Trust me. That's the pits."

"Tell me about it. I was the one who was almost arrested by our own that time."

Sid laughed. "Yeah. That was grim. In any case, you're still going to be on your own a lot. We all will. And since you're the lead on this case, you'll get your chance to discover what you're made of."

"Thanks." I bumped into him, then realized something. "What did you say? I'm the lead?"

"That's what Steve said." Sid pulled back and thought. "Come to think of it, he called you Big Red, and I didn't think anything of it."

"Oh, wait. They must be thinking Big Red is the lead."

"Which makes sense. I've been around a lot longer than you have."

"And if I'm the lead, then I must be Big Red." I laughed suddenly. "Which means I'm now your boss."

Sid laughed, then paused and looked at me thoughtfully.

"Honey, when we get back home, can we ditch calling me your boss? I know that's how we started. But it doesn't make sense anymore. We've been a team for well over a year."

"I guess so with the writing."

"And the spy biz."

I looked at him, puzzled. "Are you serious?"

"Yeah. Just because I take the lead more often, that has nothing to do with your skill level. I simply have more experience. And lately, you're as likely to be running something as me."

"I never really thought of it that way." I blinked. "Are you okay with that? I mean, I'm not the pesky little sister outdoing her older brother?"

Sid laughed. We'd had that conversation before.

"Okay, I have been in sympathy with your sister Mae more than once. But I am not your brother, and that does help. Besides, I love seeing you succeed."

"A team. That has got to be one of the nicest things you've ever said to me." I blinked again.

Yes, he was still sweating heavily, and that usually turns me off. Then, all I could do was slide into his arms and kiss him for all I was worth.

[Yeah, that was the problem with those kisses, however utterly delicious they were. I know we played a while longer, but it wasn't near enough to cool me down. I'd been putting off Tina, the weights coach, part of my grand plan to be what you needed. I couldn't help it. That night, I gave in, and Tina finally got what she'd been angling for since I'd arrived. And I kicked myself for giving in yet again. - SEH]

September 21 – 22, 1984

Friday afternoon, with the weekend ahead of me, I debated taking some time off from grading papers. I'd spent every night that week in my office working. After racquetball the evening before, I had gotten my dinner to go from Barb's and went right back to my office and stayed there past midnight.

Unfortunately, I wasn't the only one who liked to work late. In fact, the only person on the humanities staff who didn't was Joe Cunningham. Fran Mercer and Max Beard were the real die-hards, though. Every night that week, as I finally left my office, lights still glowed from theirs.

So, that Friday evening, I asked Fran why she kept working so late. We were both in a philosophical mood as we sat in her office. I was entering my grades on her computer since it was hooked up to the college system and I still didn't even have one yet. Fran was also grading papers.

It had been a busy, slightly rushed day. After my classes, Fran and I had gone to lunch at Barb's Diner because the Faculty Dining Room was serving fish sticks that day. Apparently, the fish sticks' only virtue was that the portions were so small, you didn't have that much of them to eat.

But lunch out almost made us late to the faculty meeting that afternoon. The good part of the meeting was that I managed to avoid getting Joe Cunningham mad at me, although he was looking my way when he reminded us that we were to enter our grades for the week into the computer system by that night.

"What else have I got to do besides work late?" Fran said in reply to my question. "I don't have much family to speak of. My friends are all here at Martin U., and just as likely to be working late themselves." She seemed vaguely annoyed. "At the rate I'm going, I'll be next in the running for department old maid." Blinking, she shrugged. "As choices go, I've made worse in my life."

There was a knock on the door.

"It's Ted," he called.

"Come in," Fran said.

Ted entered, with Eunice close behind.

"Ah!" He grinned. "You're here, too, Janet. Terrific. Eunice and I have come up with a great idea for our start of quarter get together this weekend."

"It's strictly unofficial," Eunice said to me. "Those of us who are still single usually get together and be social for a day right after the start of the quarter."

"That sounds like fun," I said.

"Ted and I are the committee this quarter and we've chosen to do an expedition down the Crystal River."

"It's a nice little paddle-yourself canoe trip they have," said Ted. "We thought we'd try it while this heat wave is still holding out."

"Heat wave?" I laughed. "The weather has been gorgeous! We haven't had a day over eighty-five."

Eunice shook her head. "Janet, we're in Wisconsin and it's September and the start of fall today, at that. Eighty degrees constitutes a heat wave."

"I suppose," I said, shrugging. "In California, eighty degrees is nice and balmy, and this time of year, we've had at least a couple weeks of hundred-plus temps and might be hitting the low-nineties."

"And speaking of, you poor, benighted urbanite," Eunice continued. "Are you up for this kind of outdoor activity?"

"Of course. I love canoeing."

"I'll be driving," Ted said. "By virtue of the fact that I'm the only one with a big enough car for the five of us. Ernie and I will be at your place, Fran, at seven a.m. Swimming apparel and shorts suggested. Shoes are required. Apparently, the bottom's rather rocky."

"Sounds great," I said.

"We'll see you then," said Fran.

"Can I see you ladies home tonight?" Ted asked.

I thought of the pile of papers in my purse. "Probably not. If I'm going canoeing tomorrow, I should stay and grade papers."

"Oh, tush," Eunice said. "You can do that on Sunday. Seriously, do you want more grades to enter?"

Ted wandered over to the desk and looked at my grade sheets.

"You are crazy, lady! Why are you assigning so much work?"

Fran snorted. "Ted, some of us actually care if our students learn something."

I rolled my shoulders again. Between weight training and playing racquetball, I was a little sore.

"Ted, you'll see them tomorrow," Eunice said, pushing Ted out the door. She turned back. "I'll see the two of you in the morning."

The next morning dawned bright and clear, and it looked like the local version of a heat wave was going to continue. Fran warned me that the rivers in that part of the world could be quite chilly, and I did not doubt it. However, what I did not tell her was that I had grown up in South Lake Tahoe and, having learned to swim in an icy mountain lake, I liked cold water.

Ted and Ernie showed up exactly on time, which, according to Fran, was not all that difficult for them to do. Ernie had an apartment in the tan building to the south of us, and Ted's apartment was in the building immediately to the south of Ernie's.

Ernie, clearly not a morning person, yawned loudly from Ted's front seat. Eunice pulled into the driveway behind Fran's car at almost the same time. The only other single person on the humanities faculty was Max Beard, but Fran explained that he did not attend faculty gatherings of any kind unless they were required, and sometimes not even then.

Fran had a large thermos of coffee ready, along with paper coffee cups and a bunch of single serving creams and sugars. Coffee is not my favorite beverage, but I accepted a warm cup and doctored it heavily.

"Ted, don't forget to pull in to Silverfield's when we get there," Fran called from the back seat where she, Eunice and I were sitting.

"I won't."

"We need snacks," Fran told me.

We'd been on the interstate for less than twenty-minutes when Ted pulled into the parking lot of the small cheese outlet. Ernie, still too sleepy, stayed in the car while the rest of us went into the small store filled with refrigerator cases and shelves stocked with cheese spreads and gift items.

While we were inside and out of the earshot of Ted, Eunice and Fran explained that they only asked Ernie on these outings to be nice, although Eunice insisted that Ernie was not bad company when he wasn't trying to get something started.

Fran looked over the cases with the air of a connoisseur.

"What is this?" I asked, pulling a plastic-wrapped bundle of little orange nuggets out of a case.

Ted, Eunice, and Fran all stared at me.

"You've never had cheese curds before?" Ted asked, almost incredulous.

"I've never heard of them," I said.

Eunice sighed with a great deal of drama. "I am reminded of my ignorant state as a young woman eager to find something she liked about being in the middle of nowhere." She smiled at me. "A decent shot at tenure is one thing. But cheese curds can make a lot seem worthwhile."

"What are they?"

"They're the leftovers from the cheese-making process," Ted said. "After they pour off the whey and pull together the rest of the curd to finish and age, there are these little bits left behind. And while they may be simply green, or unaged, cheese, they are amazing."

Fran oversaw the purchase of several snacks, including a package of cheese curds for me. Back in the car, as Ted drove us onto the interstate, Fran got the package open and handed me one of the light-orange rounded chunks.

"They're good," I said, chewing the spongy snack. "A little on the salty side, but good."

Two chunks later, I was hooked. It was a good thing that Fran had control of the package. I would have devoured the entire package in minutes.

The expedition, itself, was a lot of fun. Eunice and Fran made sure that Ted and Ernie had one of the two-seater canoes. I volunteered to take the single canoe because I had some experience, although both Eunice and Fran did, too. The guys had a lot of trouble shooting the very mild rapids and tipped over twice. Near the end of the trip, they got tired of seeing we women dry, so they dunked us. Eunice objected, with all manner of foul language, to their lack of sportsmanship, but it was all in good fun.

We all returned to our respective apartments to rinse off and get some clean, dry clothes on. I kept wearing my beloved deck shoes, along with the jeans and sweater I put on. The shoes' dirty gray was even more pronounced because they were damp, but they were still the most comfortable shoes I owned. Plus, they had a couple tools hidden along the sides of the soles. I didn't even think about the piece of spring steel I had hidden under my hair clip. As Sid says, you can always hide something.

We took our time with dinner at a restaurant off the interstate, then, when we got back to Appleton, found our way to The Cider Keg, and settled in. Well, the two men stood around the bar, hoping to score, it appeared.

Eunice, Fran, and I found a table in a back corner. There was a bit of shuffling as both Eunice and I tried to get into the seat with our back to the wall. I somehow snagged it. Eunice found the other corner seat, and it turned out we both had an excellent view of the rest of the room. Fran just shook her head.

"Honestly, you two." She sat to the side of the table and could still see the door.

Eunice and I looked at each other and laughed.

A young woman in tight jeans and carrying a tray appeared.

"Oh, hi, Dr. Blakely," she said.

"Good evening, Sara," Eunice said, smiling warmly. "When did you start working here?"

"Last quarter. What will it be tonight?"

"Is Doreen on?" Eunice asked.

"Yeah."

"Oh, this complicates things," Eunice replied. "Tell Doreen it's me. Then, while she's chilling the snifter, have her make a round of Bloody Marys for all of us."

Fran giggled. "I'll have a Seven and Seven after the Bloody Mary."

Sara looked at me.

"I was just going to have a glass of white wine," I said.

"Something you will surely regret," Eunice said. "Have Doreen chill a second snifter and we'll both have the Lagavulin for our second round. But, first, the Bloody Marys."

"You got it, Dr. Blakely."

As Sara went back to the bar, I frowned.

"You know, I don't do a lot of hard liquor," I told Eunice and Fran.

And, in truth, I didn't. When your life depends on secrecy, you tend to avoid alcohol.

"All the more reason to get you drunk, dear," Fran said.

"There she is," Eunice nodded at the bar with an odd sense of reverence.

The woman behind the bar was wearing a bright blue top, which emphasized her cleavage, with white, super short, hot pants and white granny boots. Her impossibly blond hair was piled on top of her head, and also fell about her face in curly ringlets that almost reached her waist.

"She's seventy if she's a day," Fran hissed. "But she makes probably the best Bloody Mary ever made."

"Really?" I was getting excited.

When the Bloody Marys arrived, they were as advertised. Plenty of vodka, the mix was mild but not too tomato-y, and the spicy pickle, instead of the traditional celery, was divine. I couldn't help but miss Sid. He would have loved Doreen's kitsch and the spicy pickle.

Fortunately, I wasn't too absorbed with my drinking buddies to not notice when a woman that I recognized came in. Ted and Ernie were still yukking it up at the bar. I laughed at some tale Fran was telling, even as I watched the room. Sara returned with two brandy snifters of Scotch whiskey, the glass frosted over, and Fran's Seven and Seven.

"I wonder what she's doing here?" Eunice asked, nodding toward the woman I'd been watching.

She was a KGB agent popularly known as Ilona Swedburg Watts and she had shortish brown hair and a slender figure. I had a feeling pretty much everybody in the bar would have been shocked to find that a known Russian operative and assassin was doing the typing at the local paper mill.

Technically, Ilona was a suspected operative, but someone had noticed how bodies filled with nerve agent turned up wherever she'd been. There are those operatives who are known to the other side. Often, a government won't arrest or stop them in the hopes that they'll lead someone to their colleagues. Other times, the operative simply doesn't care if she's been tagged as a spy. Those were the dangerous ones, since their jobs didn't involve ferreting out secrets, but taking out targets. Ilona was the latter.

"Ilona?" Fran asked. "Funny. David isn't around, either."

"David who?" I asked.

Fran turned around to get a better look. "David Watts, the other English professor. They got married last fall."

"Perhaps the bloom is off the romance," Eunice said.

"No surprise there," Fran said. "I've always thought she was rather cold."

It didn't surprise me, either, knowing her real trade.

"Anyway, David is gaga over her," Fran continued. "And she seems happy enough."

"Maybe she's just meeting a friend," I said.

"I think we need another round," Eunice said, signaling Sara.

I declined another drink. Fran got another Seven and Seven and Eunice got another scotch.

"I remember one night," Eunice told us when Sara had brought the drinks. "It was back when I was working on my M.A., I put down three boilermakers and drove home my three drinking buddies."

"What's a boilermaker?" I asked.

"Beer with a shot of whiskey," Eunice replied. "You can drink it as a chaser or just drop the shot right into the beer."

Fran giggled. "Eunice was a wild one before she got her PhD and decided she had to be dignified. At least, by her own accounts, she was."

"I had to do something." Eunice snorted. "I was the only woman PhD candidate at the school. It was bad enough having to work twice as hard to impress anybody." She looked at me. "Those were the bad old days, Janet. We women were expected to produce babies, not dissertations. To get anywhere, I had to prove myself better than the men, and one way I could was to drink them under the table. Which was insanely easy. Thank God we historians are nothing like Indiana Jones."

"He's an archaeologist," Fran said.

"Similar fields." Eunice shrugged.

Fran yelped and laughed. "Oh, my God, I think Ernie is actually scoring."

Ernie had moved off to a standing table near the door, where he had his arm around a woman wearing a University of Wisconsin sweatshirt. Ted had already disappeared.

Behind them, the door opened, and Fran yelped again.

"It's him!" she hissed and ducked her head over her drink.

Ed Donaldson's eyes swept the bar with practiced ease. He looked like he was on the prowl, but something was off. I wondered if he'd been tailing Ilona Swedburg. With a panicked flinch, I looked for her. Somehow, she had disappeared.

"That's right, Janet." Fran looked back at the bar. "You have him, too."

"Oh, Ed. He's in one of my Basic Comp sections. You've got him in what?"

"Intro to Communications. You should see the girls in my class. They are drooling all over him."

Eunice looked Ed over. "Hmm. He definitely has his full mating plumage on."

"What?" I asked as Fran shook her head in warning.

"You are aware, of course," Eunice went on, "that male birds, during their mating seasons, will go through elaborate courtship rituals, and many will grow more extravagant plumage, all in the hopes of attracting a mate. Females, in most species on this planet, usually have the role of selection."

"Janet, I should have warned you earlier," Fran groaned. "Do not ever get Eunice talking about biology and mating rituals. Especially when she's been drinking."

Eunice had long since finished her Bloody Mary and her snifter of Scotch. I, by comparison, still had half a glass of Bloody Mary, and while I had taken a small sip of the Scotch, it had a slightly burned taste (that Eunice said was peat moss) that I didn't care for. Eunice had taken over that glass, as well, and the third glass was half-empty.

"It's how things are continued on this planet," Eunice said.

Fran rolled her eyes. "But we're here to have a good time, not listen to a biology lecture."

Eunice sat up straight in umbrage. "Since when is a biology lecture not a good time?"

I couldn't help laughing long and loud, then sighed as I saw Ed Donaldson pick up the hand of a young brunette and kiss her palm.

"Looks like you might be receptive to the plumage," Eunice said.

I blushed and looked down. "He's a student. I think that means he's off-limits."

"More's the pity," Fran said with a sigh.

Eunice shrugged. "I, personally, have no interest either way."

"You're getting old, Eunice," Fran said, looking around the bar again. "Uh-oh. Look who's back."

Ernie Lavalle wandered back into the bar. Ed, however, had disappeared, and oddly enough, the brunette remained, looking decidedly peeved. [I know I'd told you that things were off that fall. I don't know if I ever told you just how badly they'd gone off. That brunette was hardly the first time I'd started something, only to realize I didn't want to follow through. I had no idea what was happening to me, but it was unsettling. I had no idea you were there, and, yes, I'd been following Swedburg. – SEH]

"Guess Ernie struck out after all." Fran toyed with her drink.

"Or his date was disappointed," I said.

Fran burst into laughter. Ernie spotted us and came over.

"Hello, ladies." He grinned. "The night is young. Who wants to go dancing? Maybe a little parking lot mambo?"

His hips supposedly wriggled, but there was so little rhythm, it looked more like spasms of some sort.

"Ernie, you're drunk," Eunice said, her own voice a little thick, as well.

"Well, that explains the fast turnaround," I told Fran, who laughed even harder.

"Come on," Ernie said, looking directly at me. "Let's have some real fun. We can go back to my apartment, get comfortable."

"Watch things peter out," I said.

Ernie's face fell as Fran laughed some more. I suddenly yawned.

"And speaking of, I think it's time for me to head home." I stretched and stood up. "How much do I owe you, Eunice?"

"You didn't drink anything. It's on me." She got up as well.

Ernie took what little remained of his pride and stalked out of the bar.

"I don't get it," Eunice said as she helped Fran out of her chair. "Obviously, you are talking in sexual innuendos, but I haven't the faintest clue to what you are referring."

I only sort of did myself. "The doorkeeper scene in Macbeth. Drink 'sets him on and takes him off, makes him stand to and not stand to.' In short, guys can't perform when they've had too much to drink."

"Oh." Eunice steadied Fran, who was still giggling. "Well, that might explain my un-breeched state. I thought they just didn't want to. Hmm. Why don't you help me with Fran?"

"Are you safe enough to drive?"

"It's not that far away and I've made it in worse condition."

"Where did you learn to talk dirty?" Fran asked.

"I have a very good friend who does." I took her other arm, and Eunice and I pointed her toward the door.

I was not thinking about Sid, however. My friend Esther Nguyen has possibly the dirtiest mind anywhere. She's been known to top Sid, and he, not surprisingly, can come up with some doozies.

Fran and Eunice managed to walk home with a minimum of staggering. The night was cool and clear, and it helped both Fran and Eunice sober up a little. It was automatic, but I kept an eye out for potential tails or enemies. Twice I saw Ernie Lavalle's slight form behind us. I wondered, but was more occupied with getting Fran and Eunice off the streets.

By the time we got to the house, Fran was, fortunately, sober enough to convince Eunice to stay in her apartment and not drive home. As soon as the two of them went inside, Eunice wondering loudly why what I had said about Ernie was so funny, I made my way up the creaky staircase. My trip wires were all in place, but after I got in and shut the door, I felt a buzzing in my pocket. I pulled out my bug finder, and the compact's rim glowed a faint pink. There was somebody broadcasting something, but probably not in my apartment. The signal was so low I doubted it was in my building.

Leaving the kitchen lights off, I went out onto the back landing and pointed the bug finder toward the building to the south. Wherever the transmission was, it was coming from that direction.

September 23, 1984

My plan had been to spend Sundays as a rest day. But since I'd goofed off the day before, I stayed in my apartment and graded Basic Comp papers. Fortunately, the Shakespeare students were being graded on class participation and exams, with only three major essays - one for each play. That brought down the workload.

The other good thing was that the Basic Comp assignment that had been turned in on Friday was writing sentences, which were easy to grade. The quizzes were even easier since they were shorter and there were few judgment calls on a right or wrong answer. I was thrilled when I marked up my last paper and it was just after two in the afternoon. Off Campus Office Hours didn't start until five. There was a load of laundry in the basement that I needed to retrieve, but other than that, I was free.

I got the laundry, put it away and was ready to go before three. Elation filled me as I stepped out onto the back landing and locked my door. Elation which immediately dissipated when I saw Ernie Lavalle sitting on the bottom of the steps.

I suppose I could have, should have, unlocked the door and gone out the front. But I've never been good at avoidance and there was the slim possibility that I could crack our case wide open with a confrontation. No such luck.

"Ernie, why are you here?" I asked as I came down the stairs.

"I-I wanted to talk to you." He slowly got up.

"Shavings. I'm sorry about last night."

He shook his head. "I'm a big boy. I can take some teasing. Besides, I was joking about doing it in the parking lot."

"Good." Not that I believed him.

"But I would like to get together with you. It would be so nice."

I winced. "Ernie, I'm really not interested. Look, it's not you."

"It never is," he sighed.

I shrugged. "Maybe it's a little bit you. But not in a bad way. We're simply different is all. Political science bores me to tears and I'd hate it if you felt bad because I didn't share your passion."

His eyes rolled. "It's well past passion for me. I can't tell you how many mornings I wake up wondering why I got into this racket. The hours are good, and I can't think of anything else to do, so here I am."

The epitome of the burned out academic and everything I hated about that dark side of academia.

I sighed. "Please, Ernie. You and I are not going to happen. There are lots and lots of reasons. You're not a bad guy, but this is not right. I'm sorry."

I waited, but he didn't leave. I prayed he wouldn't start begging.

"Um, I've got to go?" I said.

"Oh. Okay."

He finally moved out of the way. But he didn't leave to go back to his building. I headed out, carefully checking behind me.

If he followed, he was one heck of a better tail than I'd ever seen. I didn't see any evidence of a team, but took the usual evasive actions as I walked toward the downtown area. It was a pleasant strand of small shops, and I happily browsed the antiques, praying I wouldn't find anything to fall in love with, which would make getting it home tough.

I found a pay phone and called Mae. It was somewhat risky, but I also needed to keep my cover intact at home, as well. Mae kept trying to weasel out of me what I was really doing, but it was rather easy to dodge her questions.

My watch read five minutes to five when I arrived at Giannotti's pizza place and found a good-sized table. I ordered three large pizzas, one with mushroom and black olives, one with everything, and one with just cheese. I decided that if I ended up with a low turnout, I'd have lunch for a few days. Given the Faculty Dining Room, that was possibly one of the better decisions I'd made. I also ordered a pitcher of beer, a pitcher of cola, and a glass of white wine for me. I'd invited Steve Carmona in the hopes that our team members would all be there, and we could map out some strategies.

However, Jason de Boeur was the first to show, followed quickly by Sherry Van Wettering. Dennis White also wandered in, with Tim Hannaford close behind. Ed Donaldson (aka Sid) showed next, then Terry Michaels arrived. Rita Farley showed next. Marge Haver swept in.

"Beer?" she asked loudly. "Oh, may the gods be praised. I have suffered through possibly the worst week of my life. I need beer."

"Then here you go," I said, handing her the pitcher.

Terry winced. I suspected she was, in real life, over-age, but since she was pretending to be underage, public alcohol was a no-no. I had to give Kathy Richards credit. One moment, she was not there, then suddenly she was.

It was a fun gathering. Jason was still complaining about the Basic Comp workload until Ed/Sid pointed out that I had to grade all those papers.

"Who," Marge asked, adding a particularly vile epithet, "decided to study Coriolanus? My god, that play sucks."

I laughed. "I'm probably being far too nice, but it was not my idea. Still, it has its pluses."

Admittedly, I couldn't think of one and Marge, bless her, did not press it. Instead, she did an incredibly funny rendition of Dr. Ermengarde encouraging her students to join her for aerobics classes at the campus sports center.

"Your body is your instrument," Marge declaimed in an eerily accurate voice. "You must ensure its care."

Marge was thrilled that she had been chosen to be included in Dr. Ermengarde's Elect (aka favored students) but was dismayed that being among the Elect included twice-weekly aerobics classes.

Steve didn't show until close to seven o'clock. At that point, Marge, Ed, and Kathy had gone through another pitcher of beer (although I had good reason to believe that Tim had scored some, as well). The fourth and fifth pizzas had been decimated. Most of the civilians had left except Marge and Jason, although Jason took Steve's arrival as an excuse to take off.

For all Marge had proclaimed that she was having far too much fun with the younger kids to spend time with the other Second Career students, I could tell that she really enjoyed being with people closer to her own age. She finally took off of her own volition, and the rest of us sighed in relief.

The music playing on the restaurant's loudspeaker was loud enough to cover conversation, which is why we were there.

"Should we be checking her out?" Tim Hannaford asked. His western shirt hung on a scrawny frame topped by straw-colored hair.

"Possibly," I said. I looked at Steve, then Sid/Ed. "Couldn't hurt. Do you want to do it, Tim?"

Tim sighed, as if such a chore were beneath him, but I let it go.

"Right now," I said. "We're not in full investigative mode. We need to focus on establishing our covers. That being said, do any of you have anything to report?"

"I found a code!" Tim whipped out a piece of paper.

I knew the style of the paper well. It was the lightweight paper that Sid and I used in our dot matrix printer for rough drafts. You could practically see through the stuff and the cuts to separate the pages and the holed edges that fed the paper through the printer were rough and widely spaced apart. Sid also had a letter-quality printer, and the paper for that was heavier with micro-cuts between the pages and the tractor rows on the edges, so you couldn't tell that the printing had been done on a computer as opposed to the individual sheets one would use on a type-writer.

The sheet Tim produced had three columns of numbers and letters all printed out in tiny dots. Each column was evenly spaced and filled with six digits of numbers and letters, although none of the letters went further in the alphabet than F.

Kathy Richards looked at it and frowned. "I've never seen anything like this before."

Terry snatched up the paper and groaned loudly. "Hannaford, you idiot. This is machine language. All you've found is someone's Comp Sci homework."

"Not necessarily," said Steve.

We all looked at him.

"It's how our developer is getting his work to me," Steve said. He picked up the page that Tim had flourished. "As I have told some of you, I do not know who the developer is. It was part of his agreement to work on the nerve gas formula that no one would know that he's doing it." He looked over the sheet. "He... Well, it could be a she. Anyway, I get a message that the next installment is about to be printed. So, I go down to the system printer in the computer center and hope like hell the command went through to that printer. Mostly, it does, and I pack it up and set up a Chicago drop. But the other night, the run went to the Fine Arts department printer, which is where, I'm guessing, you picked this up."

He glared at Hannaford, who nodded.

"That doesn't sound terribly secure," I said.

"It's a lot more secure than you might think," Steve said. "There's no way to tell which campus computer generated the print run, and the output looks like someone's comp sci homework. The problem is, if the computer center printer is busy, the system kicks it to another system printer, usually the music department one. And at least twice the printout got run, the comp center printer was online and free, and it still ended up in the music department."

Sid frowned. "How do you know it's not someone's homework?"

"No headers," Steve said. "Just the printer number and time/date stamp on the bottom. Plus, I only have three students doing anything with machine language."

"So, what happens when the run goes to another printer?" I asked Steve.

"Hopefully, I catch it. Sometimes, someone else gets it off the printer, can't find a name attached to it, and tosses it in the scrap paper pile." Steve shook his head. "There are bits of that formula all over campus."

"Is that how it's being stolen?" Sid asked.

"I don't think so." Steve shifted and frowned. "I'm usually pretty quick to get to the other printers, and if it gets tossed into the scrap, I find pages of it."

Terry's eyes widened. "If you don't know who the developer is, then how do you let him know you didn't get the printout?"

Steve shifted and signaled the waiter. "I post a confirmation code on the faculty system bulletin board." He looked at me. "You should be checking that out, Janet."

The waiter came over and Steve ordered another pitcher of beer and a small cheese and onion pizza.

"All right," I said. "Is there anything else we need to go over?"

Terry dug a small set of nine by twelve manilla envelopes from her pack. "Mail call."

"Isn't that dangerous?" Sid asked, taking the envelope she had.

"It's more dangerous to blow our covers back home," Terry said. "Too many of us have people in our lives who would question it if we don't come up for air every now and then."

Sid glanced over at me. He'd never had that problem before he'd hired me as his secretary. He'd been told that he needed an associate and talked the Powers That Be into letting him recruit someone who could take over the mundane trivialities of life. He'd recruited me after my year of unemployment when we'd met in a bar and I'd ditched my blind date, even though I sorely needed the meal. When I'd gone to work for him, I'd had no idea that he was recruiting me for the spy biz. He'd had no idea how deeply our two lives would become enmeshed. As he'd told me earlier, we really were more of a team than boss and secretary.

Sid perused the small slips containing phone messages, shook his head over one, then looked over the three letters.

"We've got an editor with an emergency," he leaned over and told me softly.

I shrugged. "Unless it's something really easy to turn around, I don't see how we can."

Nodding, he stuffed the letters back into the envelope. "Oh, and the kid would like to hear from you."

The kid was Nick, Sid's belatedly discovered son.

"I'll try to call him tonight," I said.

I sighed as I saw the one message I had. Given what it said, I got the impression we were only going to get the most urgent mail and messages.

"What's wrong?" Steve asked.

"Oh, a friend of mine." I looked up at Sid. "He has AIDS."

Sid put his hand on my shoulder. "I'm so sorry."

He knew which friend it was, although I knew more than one gay man.

"What's AIDS?" Terry asked.

"Oh, I know," Tim said, brightening up. "It's that disease that's killing all the gays."

Well, he used the pejorative term. Tim wilted under both Kathy's and Sid's glares.

"And hemophiliacs," I pointed out. "Not to mention people using needle drugs. But, yes, it seems to be mostly affecting gay men, one of whom happens to be a good friend of mine." I looked away and got my composure back. "All right, why don't we close this meeting? I've got a couple phone calls to make."

Tim left first, no surprise there. Terry and Kathy left together. Sid hung around for a couple more minutes, then took off, leaving Steve to finish his pizza and the pitcher of beer.

"Want some?" Steve picked up the pitcher.

"No thanks. I'm not a beer drinker." I smiled weakly. "I know, anathema around here."

Steve shrugged. "It's whatever you like." He paused as he chewed, then swallowed. "I'm sorry about your friend."

"Thanks." I nodded and folded my envelope into my purse.

"You know, I was pretty skeptical about this whole team thing."

"It's something new for us, too." I snorted. "They're still not sharing as much as they could. I just found out that I'm the lead on the investigation."

Steve laughed and shook his head. "You sound so surprised."

"I'm not used to being lead on anything. Ed usually runs things. I've only been doing this for a couple years, and he's been at it forever."

"That's not the way I heard it."

"Heard what?"

"That case you two ran a year ago last summer when one of your lines went down. You two went rogue, and you, specifically, ran roughshod over a couple of CID's best."

"What?" I gaped. "That's ridiculous. We didn't go rogue. We were supposed to get out of the country, and I didn't ride roughshod over anyone. Where did you hear this? How did you hear this? We're supposedly top secret."

"And that doesn't mean we don't like to gossip?" Steve grinned and took a hit off his beer. "Big Red has had a rep for a long time. None of us knew who you were, but every now and then, we'd hear about how he'd get something done that someone else couldn't. And then Little Red came along…"

"And the stories only grew in the telling." I felt my face getting warm. "This is ridiculous. Look, if I'm any good, Ed is why. He trained me."

"Okay," said Steve.

"Listen, do you mind if I take off? I have those calls I want to make."

Steve nodded. "Be seeing you."

It took a good twenty minutes to get out of town and find a gas station with a pay phone that worked. I called Nick, Sid's son, first. He was so happy to hear from me and chattered about his friends at school for several minutes. I didn't want to put him off, but I still had to call Rick.

I let Nick go for a while, then finally called Rick.

"Hey, it's me," I said.

"Lisa!" Rick sounded rather good. "I'm so glad to hear from you."

"I'm so sorry not to call sooner, but I only just now got your message. This crazy job I'm on."

"Yeah." He sighed.

"How are you doing?"

"Well, it's pretty awful news, but there's nothing I can do about it. Dave's been great. It's been hard on him, though."

"Has he got it, too?"

"Not yet, but he still could. It's just that he's worried about me."

"I'll bet."

Rick and I talked for a good thirty minutes. His health hadn't deteriorated that badly yet, but he'd seen enough of what was to come. Still, he was keeping as positive an attitude as he could.

"'For there's no blue Monday in your Sunday clothes,'" I suddenly sang.

He laughed. "'Put on your Sunday clothes when you feel down and out.'"

The next thing I knew, we both were singing our favorite tune from Hello Dolly at the tops of our lungs.

We'd each been in the show when we were in high school, Rick in his hometown in Nebraska, me in South Lake Tahoe. Rick had played Cornelius, and I'd been in the chorus. Neither of us knew why we both loved Put on Your Sunday Clothes so much, but we'd been known to burst into a chorus or two at the strangest times.

We gasped with laughter and then it was time for me to hang up.

"I'll be praying for you, Rick," I told him.

"Thanks. I appreciate it."

October 2 – 4, 1984

I t was odd how it felt like life had settled into a routine even by the third week of classes. I managed to keep up with grading papers, getting workouts in, and morning running. We had two more faculty meetings, filled with reminders to turn out the lights in our offices when we left, not to move desks around in the classrooms, and getting our grades into the computer system every week.

"It would be a lot easier for Janet to do it if she actually had a computer in her office," Eunice told Mrs. Spinetti the morning of the third Tuesday.

The secretary sighed. "There isn't anything I can do, and you know it. Janet, please remember to keep track of how many copies you're making."

"Just sixteen of them, I promise," I replied.

Eunice looked over my shoulder. "You wouldn't have time before class for a quick walk to the Commons, would you? I could use a cup of coffee before facing the students."

"I think so." I checked my watch. "Yep. Thanks, Mrs. Spinetti."

We walked outside the building as I stuffed the copies into my purse. The morning was gray, but crisp with the early autumn chill. The leaves on the trees danced in the light breeze, and one yellow leaf wafted away, a harbinger of what was coming.

"So, how have your classes been?" Eunice asked as we made our way across the lawn.

"Pretty good so far. Yours?"

"The usual." Eunice pulled her cardigan more tightly around her body. "I've got a few students showing some signs of life, but most of them are just putting in the time."

We nattered on, the subject drifting into campus politics and the ongoing perfidy of Joe Cunningham.

Ernie Lavalle was waiting in line for coffee as we walked up. His smile took on a lascivious twist when he saw me.

"Janet, it's so good to see you." He stepped much too close to me. "What did you think of the faculty meeting yesterday? I think it's truly appalling that we shouldn't be able to get student workers to enter our grades, don't you?"

I stepped away. "I suppose."

Eunice glared at him while the three of us walked back to Lawrence Hall. Once there, Ernie headed upstairs.

"Why don't you send him on his way?" she asked me as I emptied my faculty mailbox.

"I have," I said. "He hasn't gotten the message."

"Ernie's not usually that persistent."

"That's interesting." I looked over a note from Steve Carmona, inviting me to dinner that Friday night, then checked my watch. "Shavings. I'd better get running."

I probably should have been bracing myself for the Shakespeare Seminar. Marge Haver had already freaked Rick Waters out with her assertion that Coriolanus should have ended two acts before it did, while there was still some sympathy for the title character.

"And the resolution is a joke!" she'd proclaimed the week before. "How could anybody possibly believe it when Aufidius, after he has gotten the conspirators into a murderous frenzy, suddenly turns around and less than two speeches later, says, 'Gee, I'm sorry, he was an okay dude after all.' It doesn't work!"

Rick worshiped Shakespeare and was convinced that the Bard could do no wrong. Every time Marge made a point with her more, shall we say, realistic take, he looked like he was going to cry.

That Tuesday, I was about to pour gasoline on the fire.

As the class settled, I handed out the copies I'd made.

"How many of you are familiar with Thomas North's translation of Plutarch's Parallel Lives?" I asked.

"What's Plutarch's Parallel Lives?" Linda Powell asked. She, too, was a theater student, and while a junior at the university, she was able to stand up to Marge.

"The Parallel Lives are a series of biographies written in ancient times of Greek and Roman heroes," I explained. "Plutarch matched a Greek and a Roman, contrasting and comparing their characters as people. In 1579, Thomas North translated the biographies, and it was a pretty popular work. One guy we know really liked it."

Jeff Lindsay, another acting student, grinned. "William Shakespeare."

"Right. And one of the biographies in Plutarch is Marcus Coriolanus. What you have in front of you are sections of North's translation of that chapter. On the other page are speeches from the play. I'd like you to compare the cuts from the chapter to the speeches."

There was a brief silence, then Marge screeched with laughter.

"Hot damn! Shakespeare just put this whole speech into blank verse. It's almost word for word."

Rick sighed deeply, but had to admit that The Greatest Dramatist of All Time was a plagiarist. That's when I explained that copyright and literary ownership were unheard of in Shakespeare's time and what the Bard did was, in fact, quite common. From there, the discussion covered what made Shakespeare so great. I couldn't help smiling. Even Rick was thinking.

As the students left, Kathy slid up to my desk.

"Good one, professor," she said, laughing. "I didn't know about that translation."

"I appreciate the compliment." I focused on gathering my notes together.

Kathy looked around and sighed. "Has Tim come in with anything on Marge?"

"Hasn't said a word." I looked at her. "Why?"

"No reason. But you asked him to check her out two Sundays ago and we've gotten bupkes. I know we've had to focus on establishing our covers, but still."

"I know. I'll talk to him tomorrow."

"He is going to be trouble."

"He's just green."

"Like we need that." Kathy snorted. "Oh, and you know that one KGB suspect that's a janitor here?"

I stuffed my papers into my purse. "Yeah. John Timorivich, right?"

"Yeah. Every time I go by the computer center, it seems like he's hanging around."

"Hm."

The next day, Basic Comp A was as challenging as usual. A debate broke out over Sherry Van Wettering's term paper topic, which was looking at chauvinistic male attitudes toward women as exemplified by the miniskirt. Ed, curiously, stood with the boys in the class, pointing out that most women didn't have the legs to wear them, only to be bombarded by young women exclaiming that was exactly what being chauvinistic was.

"Enough, please!" I finally broke in. "Sherry, I think you've certainly chosen something controversial. Do you think you can get at least ten sources to support your thesis?"

She frowned. "I think so."

"Why don't you give it a shot? Who else has a subject to share?"

Ed left with the rest of the class, and with a short sigh, I went back to my office, got my sandwich, and went to the Faculty Dining Room to eat and relax for a few minutes before my next Basic Comp class. Wouldn't you know, Ernie Lavalle was not only in the Dining Room, he also made a point of standing far too close to me in line for the small lunch.

"Ernie, I'm not interested," I told him firmly even as he began to speak. "Back off. Please."

Ernie swallowed and stepped back. I took my tray and looked around the room. Lester Zaner waved at me from a table not far away. He had dark brown hair with a pleasant face and glasses. I had to admit he was one of the better-looking men in the Humanities Department. We both watched as Ernie took his tray out of the dining room, and, presumably, back to Lawrence.

"Did I just see you give Ernie the sendoff?" Lester asked with a grin.

"I hope so." I sat down. "Maybe this time it will take."

"That's strange," Lester said. "Ernie isn't usually that persistent." He stopped and flushed. "I don't mean to imply that you're not attractive."

"No. I get it. Even if I was a raving beauty, guys like Ernie give up sooner or later."

"Well, I hope it's sooner for your sake." Lester looked down at his plate. "Maybe if you gave him some competition. You're not dating anyone, are you?"

"No, but mostly because I don't want to be right now." I unwrapped the sandwich I'd brought from home and bit into it.

"Oh? Why's that?" Lester's eyebrows rose, then fell. "I apologize. I shouldn't ask such a personal question."

I smiled. "It's all right. Let's just say I'm not ready to get out there again."

"Ah. Well, when you are, feel free to let me know. Marianne and I would love to have you over for dinner, and we do know some really nice single men from our church."

I knew I should accept the invitation. It would give me a chance to check out the Zaners firsthand.

"Thanks, Lester," I said, finally. "It's sweet of you to offer. But I really don't feel like dating right now."

Still, when I got back to my office, there was Steve's note on my desk. I pushed it aside and got my notes together for Basic Comp B.

The class was barely interesting. Tim Hannaford livened things up a little with his term paper topic: Nudity in Art.

"Just remember, you need ten academic sources," I told him. "And it will make life a lot easier if you have a thesis for your paper."

I held Tim back as the rest of the class left.

"Believe it or not, I've done the paper before," Tim said with a smirk.

"Actually, I do believe you." I double checked the open door and lowered my voice. "You got an assignment two Sundays ago. Have you found anything?"

He shrugged. "She's clean."

"And you're basing that assessment on what? Field reports? Continual surveillance?"

"Just a feeling I get."

"Feelings can get you dead."

"I got good instincts."

"Instincts are good. But you need to back them up. I'm not seeing that here." I glared at him.

Tim swallowed. "Yes, ma'am."

"I want a full report on Haver on Sunday."

"Yes, ma'am."

He left, and I shook my head at his attitude. Still steaming, I went back to my office for another round of grading papers. I finished around four, then decided to head over to the sports club and bat a racquetball around. At the courts, Sid saw me and waved.

"Hi, Ed," I said, walking over.

"Wanna play?"

I shrugged. "Sure."

Once inside, however, I asked Sid if we could just bat the ball around.

"Why not?" Sid bounced a ball onto the floor, then grinned at me with a mischievous twinkle. "It's the only chance you'll get to serve."

"Very funny."

"I thought so."

We played hard, nonetheless. Every so often, Sid would send the ball whizzing around the court at bullet speed while I cowered.

"Come on," he teased. "If you'd face it head on, you might get a point."

I glowered at him, but served, then braced myself. Sure enough, the ball came right at me at full speed and hit me in the right arm.

"Ow!" I yelped.

"Sorry." He wasn't.

I looked at the bright red welt on my right bicep. "See, this is why I cower. It's easier not to get hit."

He looked a little abashed. "I suppose."

I couldn't help smiling at him. "You got anything?"

"No." He made a face.

"I might have a couple of things for you." Still breathing heavily, I leaned against the wall. "I had to give Tim a bit of a dressing down today. He eliminated Marge Haver simply based on instinct."

Sid wiped his forehead with the hem of his muscle shirt. "That kid is going to be a liability."

"He's just green."

"Yeah, and this is not the sort of job to cut your teeth on."

"I know, but he's what we've got." I blew out a breath. "Why don't we try to find a way to mentor him? I know. Kathy told me she's seen our suspect janitor, Timorivich, hanging around the computer center a lot. Why don't you and Tim team up and tail him here and there? Obviously, you can't follow too closely, but there is a chance you might catch something."

Sid grimaced. "It does not sound like a lot of fun, but you've got a point. All right."

"Also, please keep an eye out for Dr. Ernie Lavalle. He's five-ten, bad dye job on the hair, glasses. I've been told by two different people that he's being unusually persistent in his pursuit of me."

"Not to imply that you do not warrant the interest, but that is curious."

"I've told him flat out that I'm not interested. I don't know what it's going to take."

Sid shrugged. "Well, self-defense classes are all the rage these days. You can always break his fingers."

He bounced the ball on the floor with his racket. From the grim set of his mouth, I almost believed he wanted to break Ernie's fingers, himself. [I would have settled for fingers, but his nose and a few other parts of his anatomy would have been better. - SEH]

"I'll keep that in mind," I said, rolling my shoulders. "And I'll see if Steve has anything for me Friday night."

"Why?"

"He invited me out to dinner."

"Oh. Good." Sid smiled at me. "Are you going to go?"

"I kind of have to, given the case." I fidgeted with my racket.

"Why don't you want to go?"

"Oh, I just don't want to date right now."

"It's just going out, having a little fun. It'd probably do you some good."

"Possibly." I looked at him. "Probably." I grimaced. "But you know how these things usually end up. At some point, he's going to want sex, and I just don't want to."

"You don't want to? Huh." Sid looked away.

"Kind of an issue? Remember?"

"I think I do." He grabbed the racquetball and tossed it at me. "Come on. Let's play."

[It wasn't that you didn't want to have sex with Steve. That was a gimme. It's that you'd never phrased it in quite that way. Always before, you didn't want to because of your religious beliefs. This time, it was that you simply didn't want to. I probably shouldn't have, but I found that incredibly encouraging. - SEH]

After playing, I showered, got some dinner from Barb's Diner, and headed back to my office to finish typing up the exam on Coriolanus for my Shakespeare seminar the next day. As I got to the head of the stairs, I could have sworn I saw Ted Curtis coming out of my office. I pulled back and waited to see if it was him (it was), and what he'd do next. He glanced back my way, but I don't think he saw me because he turned back toward his office. I went the rest of the way up.

"Hey, Ted," I called.

He jumped, then turned. "Oh. Hey, Janet. You startled me."

"Sorry about that." I smiled. "Say, you got a second?"

"Sure. What can I do you for?"

"I've got a student doing a term paper on the impact of male chauvinism on fashion."

"Ah. The rise and fall of the hemline." Ted laughed. "You have Sherry Van Wettering, too?"

"Another student doing double duty with the same term paper."

Ted laughed again. "Can you blame them?"

"Not entirely," I said, smiling. It wasn't as though I hadn't done the same. "Anyway, I'm requiring ten different sources. If she comes up short, I was hoping you'd have some to suggest."

"I might, but I don't have a minimum requirement on sources. I'm looking at the quality of the sources and what the student pulls from them." He thought for a second. "Eunice might be able to help you, though. She's into that whole feminist thing."

"That's right." I ignored the dig at feminism. "Thanks for the idea."

I watched as he unlocked his office door and went in. While shifting my purse and my dinner around in my hands, I looked at my doorknob. There were no obvious traces of someone breaking in, but that didn't mean Ted hadn't.

I hadn't put any trip wires on my office because I didn't want to chance anyone finding them. My apartment was different in that I needed at least one place I could count on to be safe, and it was relatively private. But the office was in far too public a place and I didn't want to risk it.

After checking my compact to be sure that nothing was broadcasting, I looked around the office. Nothing had been disturbed. I could tell.

How do I explain this? It's like being followed. If you're not expecting anybody to tail you, chances are you will not notice it if anyone with some skill does. On the other hand, if you're expecting the tail and are looking for it, it's going to take a highly trained crew of people to have a hope in Heaven of successfully following you.

The same with searches. A decent professional can search a place in a remarkably short time, but cannot possibly do it without leaving something not quite in the same place it was. If you're not expecting someone to search your home or office, you probably will not notice. If you're expecting it, you'll spot the search immediately. I always laugh when I read a book or see a film where somebody leaves a hair or a thread in such-and-such a place, so they'll know the place has been searched or not. Trust me. You don't need a hair.

So, assuming that Ted had been in my office, even if he were a spy and using his soft appearance and jovial attitude as his cover, he would have left traces that I would have seen. My gut instinct said that Ted had been in there, though how he'd gotten in and why he hadn't searched anything was beyond me. But, as I told Tim, I needed something more certain to back that feeling up.

I put Ted out of my mind and focused on questions about Coriolanus.

The good thing about exam days was that my Shakespeare class that Thursday got out early. As each class member dropped the exam on my desk, I looked the papers over and went back to picking spelling words for the Basic Comp quiz and refining my notes on Julius Caesar. By the time Jeff Lindsay finally finished his exam, there were still forty minutes left in the two-hour class period.

From force of habit, as I started out of the classroom, I glanced out the doorway at the hallway, expecting it to be empty. What I saw was Fred Wirth, the other political science professor and proud grandpa, slipping furtively down the stairway. I followed. Even though he could have easily gone past the department office without anyone questioning it, he paused to peek in and make sure that Mrs. Spinetti was fully occupied before slipping past the open door. I continued behind him out of the building to the faculty parking lot. Given how late I'd been staying most days, I'd gotten into the habit of driving to the campus. Besides, it had rained that morning.

I followed along, as if I were headed for my car, myself, pretending to be absorbed in a paper in my hand. Fred rushed to his car, not noticing me at all, and took off. I tailed him to the outskirts of town. Less than an hour later, I returned to my office feeling as though I needed a shower and certain that Fred was not the big family man he made himself out to be.

Admittedly, Sid and I had gotten somewhat intimate in various attempts to avoid capture, but not as intimate as Fred had gotten. Having an affair while claiming to be devoted to one's wife was bad enough. The seedy motel where he was doing it was even worse. I got a couple good looks at his paramour and didn't recognize her. It was possible that Fred was still exchanging secrets with her, but I doubted it.

That night, just to be certain, I searched Fred's office. I can't say that what I found didn't belong, but the collection of pornography and sex toys didn't really fit in with Fred's family-style image. I checked, and the nasty stuff didn't appear to be hiding anything else.

As I locked Fred's office, I noticed a light on in Max Beard's office two doors down. I put my ear to the door, hoping he wasn't still in there. Seconds later, I pulled away, blushing. Max had come out of his own little world long enough to invade some other woman's. I couldn't tell who she was, but I heard her gasp Max's name. There was no mistaking his happy groan, either. I prayed that I was not going to be doomed to perpetual voyeurism on this case.

October 8, 1984

"Okay, everyone," I told Basic Comp A near the end of the period the following Monday. "Today's assignment is to put each of this week's spelling words into a different grammatically correct sentence. Don't forget, your midterm is on Friday. If you have been doing your homework, you should have no problem with it. Finally, you may want to review all the spelling words we've had so far this quarter. I've got a little surprise for you on Wednesday."

"Dr. Mayfield?" Jason's hand went up in the air. "Why do you want us to memorize so many spelling words? We can just look things up in the dictionary."

"And they always tell you to look it up in the dictionary," Sherry Van Wettering added. "If you don't know how to spell, how are you going to find it?"

"That's why we memorize so many spelling words," I said. "The dictionary should only be a backup. If you have good spelling skills, you'll have an idea of where to look for a word you're unsure of. If you're using the dictionary as a crutch, you're wasting a lot of time. You'll get a lot more sleep the night before the term paper is due if you don't have to stop every five seconds to look something up.

Oh, and one more thing, just so you're thinking about it, a week from this Friday, your assignment will be a piece of creative writing. It can be a short story, poetry, anything you like on a topic of your choice."

"How about a scene?" Jason asked.

"As long as you write it, sure." I looked around. "Are there any more questions? No? Then I'll see you all on Wednesday."

Ed Donaldson stayed behind as the others left, then yawned and stretched once we were alone.

"Beard still bothering you?" I asked.

"Itches like hell," he said. "It will be the first thing to go once I get home."

I smiled. "I kind of like it."

He just looked at me.

"Okay, I like your dimple better."

He grunted, then looked at me. "I didn't get a chance to get to Office Hours last night. Did Hannaford cough up a report?"

"Yeah. I'm looking it over, but it seems that Haver's story checks out. He not only got her academic record, he pulled the divorce records, and he somehow got a copy of her driver's license history."

Sid's eyebrow lifted. "Impressive. He's been surprisingly good at the tailing thing. I don't know how he does it, but it's like he just fades away and disappears."

"Maybe there's hope for him."

Sid smiled. "We'll see."

"So, how are your classes going?" I sat down next to him.

"Going." He made a face. "Piano is hell. Reinhold keeps telling me I don't practice enough, and I'm already practicing more than the two hours a day he requires. Communications is okay. Calculus is okay, just a lot of work. Theory is scraping the pits, though. I like theory, but Deutsch is possibly the most boring human being alive. He talks in this soft, low-pitch drone, and the class is right after lunch, and I'm having a hell of a time just staying awake."

"You could try sleeping at night," I said with a giggle.

He rolled his eyes. "I mostly do."

"Things not going well in that department?" I watched him carefully.

"It's going well enough." He smirked.

"Then if your sex life is in order, then why are you so down?"

He looked away. "I miss you."

My breath caught. "Yeah. I miss you, too." I swallowed and got up. "Listen, um, I'm supposed to have dinner tonight with two of the other humanities professors, and our department chair just made a big speech about reaching out and building relationships with the Second Career students."

"Gee, I wonder why." His eyes glittered as he grinned. "Could it be that most of us have money?"

I put my hand to my chest. "Could it really?" We both laughed. "Anyway, why don't you meet us at Barb's Diner? I'm sure I can talk them into letting you join us. Fran is already a fan of yours."

"Fran? Dr. Mercer?" Sid chuckled.

"Yep. Steve said he might come by, too."

"How did that go on Friday?"

"It didn't." I shrugged. "Steve got a message that another print run was due, and he stayed in his office all night. He can see the computer center printer from there, apparently. And he wasn't at Office Hours on Sunday. I think he took the run directly to Chicago himself."

"Yeah. Now that you mention it, I was wondering where his car was the past few days."

"He's back now, thank God. Another reason for you to come to dinner."

Sid chuckled. "Enough with the arm twisting. I'll be there."

I told him what time, and he slowly got up and left the classroom.

Fran drove me and Eunice to Barbs' directly from Lawrence Hall. It was raining again, and temperatures were dropping into the low fifties. In the back seat of the car, I snuggled into my favorite Shetland wool sweater. Back home, I didn't get to wear it too often because it was so warm and while the weather in Los Angeles can get chilly, it doesn't get that chilly, and I had made the sweater for snow.

Ed Donaldson (aka Sid) showed up at the diner just after Eunice, Fran, and I had.

"Hi, Dr. Mercer, Dr. Mayfield," he said, his blue eyes glittering with a less than innocent gleam. "What brings you here?"

"We're having dinner with Dr. Blakely," Fran said, smiling back. "Eunice, this is Ed Donaldson. I have him in one of my intro sections, and, Janet, he's in one of your classes, too, isn't he?"

"Basic Comp 11," I said.

Eunice gave Ed the sort of appraising look that would have quailed a lesser man.

"Good to meet you, Dr. Blakely," Ed stuck his hand out and she took it.

"Good to meet you, Ed."

Fran smiled. "Ladies, would you like to have Ed join us if he's free?"

"I don't mind," I said. "Eunice?"

"Oh, I think that might be nice," Eunice said, although her eyes looked Ed over again, as if she wasn't sure he'd be able to keep up.

Ed smiled. "I'd love to join you. Thanks for the invite."

We had just gotten seated in a booth near the back when Steve Carmona walked in and waved at us.

"Steve, why don't you join us?" Eunice called. "We're having dinner."

"Sounds good," he said as he made his way around the other tables.

Fran re-introduced Ed, then laughed when Steve pointed out that Ed had the apartment above his.

We ordered, then Eunice zeroed in on Ed.

"You're obviously a Second Career student," she said. "What's your first career?"

"Real estate," said Sid. "I started out as a broker's assistant, then worked my way up to sales."

"Am I to guess you got drafted, and that's why you didn't get your education earlier?"

Ed cleared his throat as I held my breath.

"Yeah. I did." He was telling the truth.

"'Nam?"

"Yeah. I don't talk about it, though."

"Understandably." Eunice gave him an odd, penetrating look. "At least my brother was able to finish his education. But they caught him once his deferment was up and sent him out."

"Did he come back?" Steve asked casually.

"Not in any meaningful way," Eunice said.

"I knew a few guys that happened to," Ed said, which surprised me.

"Have you heard from him lately?" Fran asked, reaching over and holding Eunice's hand.

"No. He left the latest home a couple of months ago. We don't know where he is." She sighed. "And Mother was so glad that he didn't come home in a box."

"I'm sorry," Steve said. "I shouldn't have asked. So many of my friends, you know."

"You didn't go?" Fran asked.

"I was four-F." Steve pointed to his shoulders. "Scoliosis."

Given that I'd seen him more than once standing perfectly straight, I wondered how true that was.

"Well, hardly the sort of conversation to induce relaxation," Eunice said suddenly. She chuckled. "But more interesting than university politics."

We laughed at that. Our dinners arrived, and we talked about everything but university politics. Eunice talked to Ed about real estate. Ed held his own in the conversation, which didn't surprise me because he is interested in the subject. Nor, really, was I surprised that Eunice was knowledgeable about the subject as well. I was beginning to see that her interests ran far and wide.

I wasn't quite finished eating when Fran and Eunice decided to head back to the university.

"I can give Janet a ride back," Steve told them.

"Great. Thanks, Steve," Fran said.

"Fran, before you go," I said. "Can I use your computer tonight? I'd like to get some grades entered."

"No problem. I'll leave the key in your box. Please put it back in mine."

"Will do."

Eunice got up and looked piercingly at Steve. "Steve, do you think you can find a way to get Janet a computer and hook it up to the university system? It's ridiculous that she should have to bother Fran all the time."

"It's no trouble," Fran said as she scooted herself out of the booth. "It really isn't, Janet."

"I'll see what I can do, Eunice," Steve said with a chuckle.

We watched them go.

"You know, it would be pretty easy to wire your office," Steve said.

"Any reason you shouldn't?" I asked.

"I hear Joe Cunningham is balking on it."

I laughed. "As if I cared about Joe Cunningham."

Sid/Ed shifted. "Using your colleagues' computers, though, does give you a good excuse to get inside their offices."

"Only Fran's," I said. "Frankly, I'd love to do an end run around Cunningham. If you think you can, Steve, please feel free. Eunice will be thrilled."

Steve winced. "About her."

"What?" I asked.

"She's been turning up in some pretty interesting places since last spring," Steve said.

I groaned. "Not Eunice. I adore her."

"I get it." Steve waved his hand, then shook his head. "I like her, too, and I haven't gotten anything solid on her. That story about her brother checks out." He shrugged. "That's one of the things I picked up in Chicago over the weekend. I'd ordered a dossier on her. No KGB connections of any kind. On paper, at any rate, she looks like what she is. But she's been a little more interested in the university's computer system lately than she has been before."

"Why is that suspicious?" I asked. "If the formula is going out on paper, she'd have to be stealing it some other way, wouldn't she?"

Steve frowned. "I don't know. That's what bugs me. The system is secure. We use passwords on everything. We're not the Pentagon, for crying out loud. We're an arts school. But it's secure enough. The only reason we have computer science classes is that the university needs the computer system to function. So why not offer comp sci as an elective or a minor? Keeps the parents happy that their precious little darlings might have some usable skills after they leave here."

Sid grinned. "It sounds as if you actually care about the students, Steve."

"Oh, I do." He sighed and leaned back in his seat. "If this case ever ends, I think I'm going to let my bosses know that I want to keep this cover and stick around. I really like it here. And I like what I'm doing." He sat up. "However, I have noticed a certain John Timorivich hanging around a lot. I'm not sure what he's doing, but when the print run came through Friday night, he didn't even seem to notice it, and I was watching him."

"Well, Hannaford and I have been running a loose tail on him every so often." Ed scratched his beard. He glanced at me. "That's where I was Sunday. It's mostly to give Hannaford some practice."

Steve nodded. "My god, he's green, and cocky."

"Yeah, I know," Sid said. "But he's not bad as a tail, I have to say. Sadly, we haven't gotten anything on Timorivich."

"Okay." Steve glanced at me. "Janet, I just now thought, if we get you a wired computer, it will be easier to check the faculty bulletin board, and I can leave messages for you. I've got an even better idea. I'll set up a bulletin board just for the three of us."

"Will that be safe?" I asked.

"Sure. There are dozens of them on the system. I have students set them up as an assignment and usually forget to take them down." Steve got up. "Come on. We're all paid up. Why don't we go do it now?"

"I have grades," I said, getting up as well.

"You can enter them later," Steve said. "On your new computer. Let's go."

Sid followed us back to the campus in his car, and I rode with Steve.

"By the way," I asked. "Why do you think the developer is in the music department?"

"Because that's where Timorivich has been hanging out, mostly." Steve kept his focus on the road because the rain was coming down hard. "Also, there's Arlen Deutsch."

"The theory teacher. Ed had some interesting words to say about him, but nothing related to the case."

"The Monotone, himself." Steve chuckled. "But he's also one of those guys who's seriously eclectic, kind of like Eunice is. He may seem pretty sleepy, but he's one of the smartest men on campus."

I sighed.

Steve glanced at me. "Look, I'm sorry about pointing the finger at Eunice."

"Don't be. You have to. I just hope it isn't her."

Sid was waiting for us outside the back entrance to Petrie Hall. The lights were on in the computer center because it was open until ten most nights. A student aide was snoring at a desk near the front of the room filled with rows of desks with wires sprouting out the backs of the carrels on top of the desks. The monitors on the putty-colored computers were all black, although Steve cursed when he saw one with a green cursor blinking. He switched the monitor off, snarled at the student aide, and sent him home.

He beckoned Sid and me into the office at the back of the room. It wasn't nearly as big as my office, and the walls were lightweight prefabricated panels, blue on the bottom and glass on the top. Steve settled into the chair behind the desk that was overflowing with green and white printout paper, books, his ashtray, stacks of dot-matrix paper, some that still had the tractor holes, some with the tractor holes torn off. The waste can next to the desk had fallen over and the strips of tractor holes that had been torn off spilled out.

"Sit down," he gestured at the two chairs in front of the desk.

I coughed lightly and Steve, who had been reaching for his cigarettes, suddenly pulled his hand away from his chest pocket. I was glad. The place reeked of cigarette smoke. Sid noticed Steve's hand and lifted an eyebrow.

It didn't take long for Steve to get the bulletin board set up. Sid and I each selected a phony username and a real password. Steve's username was MPWilkins. Several minutes later, we were ready to go. Steve said that he had to wait to lock up and asked Sid to walk me back to Lawrence Hall.

"You can just go home if you want," I told Sid crossly once he and I were alone.

The rain had stopped, but Sid had his umbrella ready.

"No point," he said.

"You know how I feel about being protected."

"I do, indeed, and I know how well you can handle it if there is trouble. However, I think this time let's just call it maintaining appearances."

I sighed. "Fair enough."

As we came up to Lawrence, I stepped sideways and looked up at the windows. Fran's office lights were on, as were Max's, Ernie's, and I thought it was Carson Osgood's office at the end on the third floor, but it could have belonged to Perry Addington, the second psych teacher. Either way, the lights were on.

"I've got to go upstairs to Fran's office," I told Sid as I unlocked the front door to the hall. "If she's there, she's probably expecting me. But if she isn't, we can hang out together for a little bit."

I got the key from Fran's mailbox, just in case she was in. I didn't really need it. Sid followed me silently up the stairs to the third floor. I knocked first and got no answer. I opened the door. Fran was long gone and had left her lights on again.

"You sure she's not coming back?" Sid asked as I ushered him inside and shut the door.

"Her purse, her briefcase and her coat are all gone. And she didn't have her briefcase when we left for dinner, so I'm fairly sure she won't." I slid into the chair behind her desk and flipped on the computer. "So, what do you think?"

"Nothing to think about. That bulletin board should come in handy, though." He settled his seat on the desk next to me.

"Yeah. I think I'm going to log in," I said.

I did. Steve had already left a short note. I replied, then exited the bulletin board. I looked at the computer.

"You want to try?" I asked, getting up.

"That's actually a good idea," Sid slid into the chair.

"I'll start searching," I said, going to the bookshelf.

I heard Sid's fingers clicking the keys.

"It's not coming up," he said.

"What do you mean? I just opened it myself a few minutes ago." I came around to the desk and looked over his shoulder.

"It keeps saying there's no Catalog84." He pointed to the spot where he'd entered the name of the bulletin board.

I sighed. "That's because catalog is spelled C-A-T-A, not U."

"Oh."

I went back to searching. "You'd better brush up by Wednesday."

"So, what is your little surprise, anyway?"

"If I told you, it wouldn't be a surprise."

I looked back at him as he read the screen. He nodded, then his fingers rattled across the keys at lightning speed.

"Can I ask you a question?" I said.

"Sure." He looked up at me.

"Why did you hire me to do your typing when you can type faster than I can?" It was not the first time I'd asked.

"Because I hate re-typing something I've handwritten."

"Oh." I went back to looking through books. "Did you learn to type in college?"

"Nope. 'Nam."

I looked at him and waited.

He took a deep breath. "I taught myself how to type because I wanted off the lines. I was supposedly there to spy on my fellow soldiers, but there really wasn't anything going on that way. So, when a clerking position came up in Saigon, I and pretty much the rest of my unit all said we could type. They knew we were all lying, but I snuck into the unit office and taught myself how to type in two evenings. I was the only one who passed the typing test, then passed it again later against all the other unit guys. They had to give me the job whether they wanted to or not. Colonel Landry, the SOB who got me into intelligence, was furious, but there wasn't anything he could do."

"Why did they get you into intelligence in the first place?"

Sid chuckled. "What I usually got into trouble for. The base commander in boot camp had an eighteen-year-old daughter, and we got caught. Colonel Landry made a deal with the commander, and I accepted it. It was a good thing for Landry that I was hung over when he told me I'd been transferred to Quickline." Sid looked at me. "I'd just gotten discharged and when I got home, I spent three solid days drinking. Then Landry showed."

"You don't normally talk about this stuff."

"I don't know. Maybe I should." He looked at the keyboard. "It may have been Dr. Blakely tonight. Or just the way I've been feeling being here. It's a lot like when I started Stanford. Thanks to the war, I was light years older than people my own age and starting school with kids who were already years younger than I was. Being around here reminds me of that lost feeling I had." He looked up at me. "One of the reasons I don't like talking about those years."

"I can imagine." I set a book back in its place and went over to him.

He took my hand. "I don't want you to misunderstand. I've always appreciated the way you listen to me. But the big reason I don't talk about the war is that most people don't really understand what I went through, what all of us went through. You, on the other hand, have been through enough to maybe have an idea. That's why, after you shot that man last summer, I was there for the nightmares."

"You'd had them too."

He nodded. "Still do, sometimes. Anyway, it's getting late. Have you found anything?"

"Not yet. I did go through the desk the other night and there wasn't anything there." Well, I had found a few condoms, but didn't see any reason to mention those.

"Why don't we take off then? I should probably walk you to your car. Gives me a reason to be here in the first place."

I sighed. "Okay. Let me get Fran's key."

But before we left the office, Sid stopped me. He held me for a minute, then dipped his head and softly, gently, kissed my mouth.

October 9 – 14, 1984

I wasn't entirely sleepy and stupid the next morning, but I wasn't all that chipper, and overslept on top of things. Fortunately, I had all the Shakespeare exams graded and with me, in fact, those were the grades I was going to enter the night before. I went straight to the Shakespeare Seminar from the parking lot, just barely registering that Steve Carmona was chatting with Mrs. Spinetti in the department office.

When class was over, I went to my office. Dennis White was inside, sitting at my desk and playing with a brand, spanking new computer sitting on my desk. He scrambled to his feet as he saw me.

"Hi, Dr. Mayfield. Your computer is all set up for you." He smiled ingratiatingly at me.

"Thanks, Dennis." I came over and looked at the screen. I wasn't sure what the game was, but it didn't matter. "That was fast."

"Dr. Carmona asked me to come over first thing today. Along with Tad Murphy. He also said I should show you the hardware."

"No problem, Dennis. I've worked on computers before, and I've been using Fran's."

"Yeah, but this one is a Macintosh." And he launched into an extended speech on all the wonderful things this new machine could do, most of which went right past me. "See, here's the mouse."

He pointed out a small oval-shaped object that had a long wire attached to the machine. He moved it around, and the cursor on the screen moved with it. I smiled. Late the previous winter, Sid had accidentally killed my computer. My friend, Esther Nguyen, who is an electrical engineer, had seen to getting us new ones, and they had been the same model as the one that was now on my desk. I didn't use the mouse much. I'd spent too much time learning the commands on the old computers.

"Can I get onto the university system with this?" I asked.

"Sure. We've got it all set up." He launched into another speech, showing me what commands I needed to get the computer to log into the university's system.

"But this office isn't wired to the university system," I said.

Dennis laughed. "Yeah, it was. They probably wired it up when they wired all the other offices. Tad and I found the wires in no time."

"Oh, really." I grinned, but there was a part of me that felt nettled about it.

Still, that wasn't fair to Dennis, who was still going on about the virtues of my new computer.

"You really seem to enjoy this," I told him, after logging into my university account and logging out.

Dennis rolled his eyes. "I love computers. I always have. I wanted to go to Caltech or MIT."

"Why didn't you?"

He sighed. "My dad is an artist. I mean, he doesn't mind that I like animation, but he totally does not get me liking computers. And he's paying for this, so this is where I am. At least I can get a minor in comp sci."

"And there's always graduate school," I pointed out. "But you should be able to be able to get some sort of scholarship for that."

Dennis grinned. "Thanks, Dr. Mayfield. That's what Dr. Carmona says. I sure hope so."

I couldn't help smiling as Dennis left my office. He was a nice kid.

After that, it took me all of one minute to call Fran and Eunice and invite them both to my office at four-thirty that afternoon.

Fran appeared first outside my door.

"No," I said. "I want both you and Eunice to see this together."

Fran blinked and glared at me. "Honestly, Janet, what is so exciting?"

Eunice showed at that point, which saved me some explaining.

"I want you both to witness this," I told them, then opened my office door and pointed to the desk. "Behold, Eunice has prevailed, and Steve Carmona has delivered."

"A Macintosh," Eunice gasped. "How did you rate a Macintosh when the rest of us are forced to deal with a Two-E?"

"I have no idea," I said. "But I can't say I'm not grateful. Here's the kicker. You know how Joe has been going on about how we can't afford to wire this office?"

Both Fran and Eunice nodded.

"I found out today that the office has been wired all along." I told them. "In fact, it was probably wired to the university system at the same time all the other offices were."

Eunice cursed Joe Cunningham out with an amazing combination of swear words.

"I'm not surprised," Fran said. "The question now is what we do about it?"

"Don't say anything!" Eunice snapped.

"I have to agree with Eunice," I said. "This will be our secret. If either of you wants to use it, I'm happy to let you."

Eunice snorted. "I have a Macintosh at home. Fran?"

The smaller woman sighed. "I really don't care. My office computer works fine." Fran looked at me. "But I have to say, it sure looks like Dr. Carmona really likes you."

My heart stopped beating. That really hadn't occurred to me, but once Fran had said so, I had to think about it. I didn't want to. I did like Steve, but there was no question my heart was centered elsewhere. I couldn't tell Eunice and Fran that, however.

"Whatever," I said, then realized I'd used one of Sid's token responses. I blushed.

That evening, I took advantage of the new computer and entered all my most recent grades into the university system. I didn't think it was going to appease Joe Cunningham, assuming he heard about my new computer, but there was a definite moral victory in knowing that I was following his dictates.

As I looked around for something else to do, I marveled at how I'd been able to keep up on the grading. That had been a major challenge when I'd taught before. I looked at the clock and suddenly realized how I'd stayed caught up. I'd been working late almost every night so that I could search my colleagues' offices.

Max Beard's office was at the top of my search list because his was going to be the toughest to get to. The man worked insanely late hours, judging by how late his office lights were on.

That night, between correcting quizzes and checking note cards, I listened for movement in the hall. Max and I both had offices on the second floor of Lawrence Hall. Right before midnight, I heard a door closing and being locked. I peeked out my door. The light still shone underneath Max's office door.

I slid down the hall and stood before Max's office. The problem was, I wasn't entirely sure that it was Max that I had heard. Just my luck, one of the campus security guards ambled up at that moment.

"Something wrong, Dr. Mayfield?" he asked kindly.

"Um. Well. I was working late, and I heard somebody leave," I said. "But then I saw that Dr. Beard's light was still on. I was afraid that something was wrong."

"I doubt it." The guard rattled the door. "Dr. Beard?"

There was no answer. The guard pulled out a key chain loaded with keys. Somehow, he found the right one and opened the office door. The office was empty of life.

"I thought so," said the guard, turning out the light. "Dr. Beard always forgets to turn off his lights."

"Oh." I made a face. "I didn't think of that."

"Well, it never hurts to check." The guard smiled at me. "We had an old guy kick a few years back. He only had Tuesday - Thursday classes. He died on a Thursday night, and we didn't find him until the next Tuesday."

"Dr. Pendergast you mean."

The guard grinned. "Yeah."

"I've got his office."

"Yeah, I know." The guard laughed.

"Didn't they smell anything?"

"Oh, yeah. But they thought it was a dead rat. We get those every so often."

"Charming," I said.

"Are you ready to leave now?"

I sighed. "Yes. Do you mind if I get some paperwork from my office first?"

The guard was kind enough to walk me to my car. He was very nice and a complete nuisance. An observant security guard was the last thing I needed.

The next morning, the students in my Basic Comp A section were a touch livelier than normal. I wouldn't call it excited, but they were curious, which I thought was a good sign.

"So, what's the big surprise?" Jason de Boeur asked as I handed back quizzes and note cards.

"You'll see. Mark Ayers, Leslie Whiting, Jason..."

I finished handing back papers and stood behind my desk.

"All right. In an effort to put a little life into our spelling drills, I have decided that today we are going to regress into our childhoods and have an old-fashioned spelling bee."

"I told you," Sherry Van Wettering said to Jason.

Terry Michaels looked panicked, and Ed Donaldson shifted in a way that should have told me something. The rest of reactions varied between moderate pleasure and looks that indicated that they were too old for spelling bees.

"I am changing the rules a little. Instead of this being an elimination competition, you'll just go to the end of the line when you miss a word. If you spell it correctly, you get to keep your place in line. Now, everybody, line up against the walls."

"Where's the head of the line going to be?" Jason asked over the noise of nineteen students getting up.

"I'll tell you when you get lined up." I grinned. "Let's make sure all the crib sheets are covered up."

Someone booed. They settled into place, with Jason at one end. About a third of the way down the line, Ed, Sherry, and Terry stood next to each other.

"Okay, Jason," I said. "I guess I can let you be the head. I don't know how else you're going to get there."

"Hey, I am going to stay." Jason grinned.

"Right. Spell turkey."

"T-U-R-K-E-Y."

The class cheered and Jason held up his hands in triumph. When I got to Ed, I gave him the word catalog. He smiled, his bright blue eyes catching mine, then spelled the word correctly. I wasn't cheating. I was giving everyone a word I knew they could spell for the first round.

Terry nearly choked when she got her word, but she finally got it out, and flushed with joy that she'd been able to overcome her shyness.

It was a fun class period. Even the students who'd thought they were too old had a good time. By the end of class, Terry was at the head of the line, Jason was in the middle, behind Ed, who had survived Mississippi and psychology to bomb out on banana. Sherry spent most of her time at the end.

Ed took his time leaving.

"Have fun?" I asked him.

"Yeah." He was a little surprised.

"You did pretty well."

"Especially considering that I'd never done one before."

"I had a feeling." I smiled. Sid's education before high school had been unorthodox. "Got anything for me?"

"Nope."

"See you Friday, then."

"See you Friday." Ed paused, then left the room.

I collected the homework papers together, then decided to grab something from the Commons and the snack from the Faculty Dining Room, then eat in my office. It was another thing we were not supposed to do, but we all did anyway.

I was surprised to see Max in the Faculty Dining Room. Sitting very closely next to him was Dr. Ermengarde.

"My darling Max," she said, her voice carrying through the room. "You know I only have your best interests at heart, and that is mystery meat. It is poison, and your body is a veritable temple."

"Yes, Thalia," Max said, smiling at her.

"You deserve better, my dearest."

"We both do, darling."

I got my sliver of meat loaf and left, wondering about the night I'd heard Max and some woman making love in his office. Max and Dr. Ermengarde weren't acting like lovers, more like old, very comfortable friends. Although, I had heard that old friends often make the best lovers. It was hard to say what was going on, and I wasn't entirely sure I wanted to know.

Thursday and Friday, all three sections of Basic Comp were given over to the midterm. Friday afternoon, Steve invited me out to dinner. I thought it was about getting some information, but Steve told me he just wanted to have some fun. The nice thing was, we did, until he pulled his car up outside the house where Fran and I lived.

"Um," Steve began slowly. "I've been getting some odd signals from you and Ed. It seems like you two have a thing for each other, but Ed was quite clear that you two are not a couple."

"We're just really good friends." I said, my stomach turning over.

"That's good to know. I was wondering how you dealt with all his running around."

I bit my lip. "We're not a couple. That's how." I opened the car door. "Anyway, thanks for dinner. I had a really nice time."

I unlocked the front door, went in, locked the front door, and made my creaky way up the stairs. No vibrations in my pocket. The trip wires were sound.

It had been a nice time with Steve. I wasn't sure if he'd bought my lie about how I was dealing with Sid's extracurricular activities. It didn't matter. If Steve was thinking about me as anything other than a colleague and friend, he was bound to be disappointed.

I spent the next day cleaning my apartment and grading papers. Sunday, I drove out of town, called Nick, but had to leave a message, then called Mae and let her talk for an extended time.

When it came time for Off Campus Office Hours, we had a good crowd from the A section of Basic Comp. Kathy Richards from the Shakespeare Seminar showed up with Marge Haver close behind. Sid/Ed was missing. Steve showed up as most of the kids left, except for Terry and Kathy. Marge winked at Steve, then took off, herself. That's when Sid and Tim finally arrived.

The only good thing, for me, about dealing with Sid when he is really, really mad is that I usually am, too. Tim, on the other hand, was the focus of Sid's wrath and not dealing well with it. Sid shoved Tim into a seat next to Steve.

"What's going on?" asked Steve.

"This idiot!" Sid snapped, adding a nasty curse word between this and idiot. "He blew my cover."

"What?" I asked amid the horrified chatter from Terry, Kathy, and Steve.

"He handled it okay," Tim whined.

"We were tailing Timorivich," Sid said.

"He'd made you, man," Tim said.

"So what?" Sid glared at him. "You don't go up to your partner and ask, 'Why are you following that guy?'"

"You what?" Steve bellowed at Tim.

"He handled it!" Tim cried. "He said, 'Following who?' I knew he would."

Steve cursed loudly.

"We ought to ship your ass back to Langley," Sid snarled.

"Hold on!" I almost yelled. "Kathy, that includes you."

Kathy lowered the fist that had almost hit Tim.

"All right." I took a deep breath. "Ed, you did handle it right. It's possible that your cover isn't blown. It doesn't look good, but it's possible. If we ship you out now, it for sure will be. We need to think about damage control." I glared at Tim. "First things first. Tim, both you and Ed are not to do another thing related to the case. Ed, I'm sorry."

Sid glared at Tim. "You have nothing to apologize for. You're right. We're both tainted now."

"He'd been made," Tim said again. "I had to do something."

"No," said Steve. "You should have hung back and let the more experienced agent handle it. We've all been made on tails. It's one of those things that happens. That doesn't mean our covers get blown."

Sid put his face really close to Tim's. "I have never blown my cover in my life. Never, do you understand? I am alive now because I have never blown my cover or had it blown. You have not only put this entire case in jeopardy, you have put me in the KGB's crosshairs, and possibly yourself. Do you understand that?"

I put my hand on Sid's shoulder. "Ed, you're right, but he is green."

Sid snorted but pulled back. "You'd find a way to forgive Hitler."

"That's neither here nor there." I sat back and looked at the little group in front of me. "All right. Terry, you're a sculpture major, right?"

"Yes," she said softly.

"You're going to have to cover the drawing and painting staff as well." I pressed my lips together. "Have Tim update you on any searches he's done, then finish up on the rest of the staff."

Terry looked a little worried, but nodded.

"Kathy, do you need help with the theater department?" I asked.

"I've got it," she said, looking like she still wanted to hit Tim.

"Don't bite off more than you can chew," I told her. "If you need help, let me know."

"I won't say it will be easy," Kathy said, throwing another glare Tim's way. "But I think I can handle it. If I can't, I will make a point of asking."

I bit my lip. "Our biggest problem will be the music department, but I think I may have a way around that. Tim, you leave now and make sure you head straight to where you're living, or I will let Kathy follow you."

Tim bolted out of the restaurant.

Kathy sighed. "Are you sure I can't have a piece of him?"

"Some other time." I took a deep breath. "Yes, he has messed things up badly, but that's inexperience. We've all been there. Crucifying him, no matter how much he deserves it, is not going to help. What we need to do now is figure out how to work around the damage." I closed my eyes, trying to visualize the campus staff. "All right. I've got humanities. Steve, you do have one problem with math/sciences. These are people you've been working with for some time, and some are probably friends."

Steve sighed. "You're right. Why don't I bring you my assessments and you can farm out any searches to Terry and Kathy."

"Or take them myself," I sighed. "Also, we have one most likely suspect for the developer in the music department." I looked at Sid. "Ed, your theory teacher."

"Deutsch?" Sid made a face.

"He's pretty eclectic," Steve said. "And I have reason to believe he likes science enough to be a possible."

"You can check him out, Ed," I said. "If he's the developer, he's on our side, so the cover thing is less of an issue."

"If they don't put a team of tails on me," Sid grumbled.

"It's better than doing nothing," I said.

Sid looked like he was about to get angry again but backed off. Shortly after, Terry, Kathy, and Steve all left. Sid was still sulking in the chair across the table from me.

"Are you going to be okay?"

"Possibly." He sighed. "Probably." He looked at me. "You were that green once, but you never did anything that stupid."

"I had you training me."

Sid snorted.

"It's not good," I said. "But it's what we've got. In some ways, this is how we show Tim how the experienced pros make it work. We've seen worse and pulled it off. Besides, we don't know for sure that your cover was blown. How about if we give it a couple weeks? We should know by then. Just keep plenty of distance from anybody who might have an injector and nerve agent."

Sid rolled his eyes, then looked at me. "Are you going to be okay?"

"I don't see why not. Steve and I did the date thing Friday night, so we're covered. We've got Off-Campus Hours. I think I'll be okay. I'll keep my eyes open as well."

He nodded, then smiled at me. "I'm really proud of you. You're doing a terrific job."

"Thanks." I smiled, then watched sadly as he got up and left the restaurant.

October 18 –19, 1984

The rest of the week was quiet. Steve got me his list of his colleagues, and I searched a few of their offices, but found nothing. As for Tim, he was avoiding me. I'm fairly sure he thought I was still mad at him, which was rather astute on his part because I most certainly was. Sid was dancing around contact with me, trying to find the balance between normal contact with a teacher with whom one was friendly and anything suspicious.

The campus trees had turned a riot of fall colors, and the wind blew leaves everywhere. There had been showers dampening things here and there, but on Thursday, the sky was perfectly blue with a few puffy clouds here and there. I filled my lungs with the fresh, nippy air and felt surprisingly good, considering how the case was going.

I lost that feeling about twenty minutes into the Shakespeare seminar. Joe Cunningham slid into the classroom through the back door.

"Can I help you?" I asked him.

"Oh, no." Cunningham said with a fake smile. "Just ignore me. I'm only here to observe."

"Good to have you," I said with my own fake smile. "Please, have a seat." I turned to the rest of the class. "Linda, you had a comment?"

"Well, it's just that if we're going to be down on Cassius because he seduces Brutus, we can't let Marc Antony off the hook, either." Linda leaned forward. "Come on, he totally seduces Caesar into going after the crown and doing exactly what has Brutus all ticked off. And then Antony goes and dumps on Brutus to the crowd with a wink, wink, and a nudge, nudge."

"That's an excellent point," I said. "Anyone have a counter to that?"

Cunningham loudly cleared his throat. "Why aren't you lecturing?"

"This is our discussion period," I told him. "It's clearly listed as such on the course outline that I gave you. Rick, what do you think?"

Rick mulled it over. "It's true that Antony is being manipulative, and if we look at the original monarchistic context of the play, one could argue that he's encouraging Caesar to be what he should be - a king."

"But even Shakespeare understood the concept of the Roman Republic," Marge cut in.

"Excuse me," Cunningham said, getting up. "I'm afraid you are all missing the classical understanding of this great work."

He glared at me, then went to the front of the room and proceeded to lecture us on a classical understanding that had fallen out of favor in academic circles before I'd started school. I waited to cut in until he'd gone on for a good half hour, and even Rick Waters had gone to sleep.

"Well, thank you for your perspective." I turned to the class. "I think that wraps it up for today. Please remember that your exam on Julius Caesar will be next Thursday, and you've got an essay due on Tuesday. Thank you."

The students got up quickly.

"What an asshole!" Marge's voice boomed from the hallway.

"I wonder if he's even read the play," Rick said.

I pressed my lips together as Cunningham glared at me.

"It would probably help your students if you were a little more professional," he said, drawing himself up.

That did it. I turned on him.

"You come into my classroom and undermine me in front of my students, and you are calling me unprofessional?" I slammed my notes onto the desk. "I think I'm going to have to file a complaint with the provost's office."

He winced. "You may want to consider what that will do for your chances of achieving tenure here."

"If this is how you treat your staff, I may not want it," I snapped. "Good lord, no wonder you guys have a problem keeping faculty."

He turned white briefly, then left the room. Trying to calm myself, I began pulling together my papers. Fran slid into the room.

"Was that Joe Cunningham that you just yelled at?"

I blushed. "You mean you heard me?"

"The entire floor heard you."

I moaned. Just when I most needed to be circumspect.

"I'm sorry. He just got me so mad."

"Some of the students said he took over your class with a really bad lecture."

"And then called me unprofessional when Marge Haver left, calling him an asshole." I looked at my watch. "Listen, I've got to get to the provost's office before my next class and file that complaint."

Fran sniffed. "Janet, please don't."

"Why not? Someone should have written him up years ago."

"But I'm afraid you're going to leave us. We need you, Janet."

I looked at her. "If it's that awful, why are you staying?"

"I love—" She blinked rapidly. "I love Eunice, and everyone else."

Eunice arrived in the classroom.

"Oh, great," I said. "You've heard."

"Yes, and I've come to celebrate with you."

I laughed. "Can we wait 'til tomorrow night? I've got to get to the provost's office to file that complaint."

"Perfect." Eunice's eyes lit up as Fran tried not to cry. "You definitely must. The more, the better, and from someone besides me. I'm there so often, Dean Lacey says he can write the complaints up for me."

"But, Eunice..."

"Tush, Fran. It will be all right. Janet filing that complaint will be the best insurance against her leaving. With someone besides me complaining, they'll have to take notice and send Joe on his smarmy little way."

So, I spent my lunch hour filing a complaint, then stuffing my sandwich into my face before Basic Comp C. That evening, I only worked late enough to make sure the larger part of the faculty had gone home. Cunningham had left hours before. The trick was going to be searching the office without any lights showing through the windows. Fortunately, Joe had the blinds pulled on all his windows, including the one on the door to the department office. So, I used my small flashlight. It was unlikely the tiny beam would be seen under the door. I was extra thorough. I felt a little guilty that it wasn't because I had any real reason to suspect Cunningham. I was just still mad and hoping that this would be one of those rare occasions when the real jerk happened to be the bad guy.

I mean, people who engage in international espionage aren't generally what you'd call nice people, especially KGB or CIA assassins. But they're not unnecessarily mean. In fact, they're mostly business-like. They have a job to do, and they do it, no matter what I or anyone else might think about the ethics of it. Jerks, on the other hand, are far more common, impossible, and unpleasant to deal with, and far too often aren't guilty of anything worse than being jerks.

I didn't find much. There was a thick file filled with the print outs of the formula code, or what looked like it. More suspicious and very odd were the two cheap paperback novels I found underneath the paper. They were a couple of romances from one of the lesser romance publishers, the kind that are cranked out under contract to specific formulas. The author was Leticia Petrie.

I fanned through the two books. There was nothing stuck between the pages or written anywhere. It was possible that Cunningham was using the books as a way of hiding stuff for another courier or as the key to a code. Or it was possible that he simply had lousy taste in recreational reading.

By the time I finally finished and got back to my apartment, it was almost one-thirty. The next morning, I overslept badly and had to scramble to get to Basic Comp A. I was profoundly glad that the Creative Writing unit was one of the easier ones to run. I read off the spelling words, then blinked, trying to wake up.

As soon as I'd read off the last word, I had the students pass the pages forward and yawned.

"Sorry, gang, I was working late last night."

"I'll bet," someone sniggered.

As I looked around the room for the person who'd said that, I caught Ed/Sid's beautiful blue eyes. Playing on his lips was an all-too familiar, but special smile. I caught my breath because that smile meant he was thinking about making love to me. I blushed, then swallowed.

"Enough nonsense," I said. "I'm not going to do a lecture today. As I pointed out last week, the point of this exercise is to understand when and how to break the rules of grammar appropriately. All right. Who wants to read their paper first?"

"Can Sherry and I do my scene?" Jason asked.

"Sure."

It was a cute little scene and rather funny. The class laughed appropriately. Then Rita Farley read her short story, and we discussed that briefly. Then Terry Michaels put up her hand. That surprised me.

Terry, it turned out, really was incredibly shy and not just using that as her cover. But, as she'd told me the previous Sunday, she wanted to work on coming out of her shell. That day she not only came out of her shell, she might as well have been buck naked. The poem she read was incredibly erotic. Every boy in the class was drooling, including Ed.

"Um, those are some interesting images, Terry," I said when she'd finished.

"It's about dancing," she said, then flushed a deep red as it suddenly occurred to her how the rest of the class was interpreting it. "It really is about dancing."

"I can see that," I said. "Why don't we move on to the next paper?"

Mark Ayers read his paper with one eye on Terry. I saw Ed, who was sitting next to her, slip her a note. I couldn't help thinking he'd be sure to take advantage of her first. It wasn't a worthy thought, and I knew darned well that Ed would treat her better than anyone else in the class. Still, it hurt.

After class let out, I hurried to the Commons to get something to eat. I'd never seen Sid/Ed there, probably because they didn't serve anything healthy enough for him. That was fine with me. The last thing I wanted to see was Sid with Terry. I skipped the Faculty Dining Room because they were serving fish sticks again. At least I was awake enough to do that. I ended up buying two of those horrible hamburgers that they served, along with a couple tacos. I'd been avoiding trying the tacos, not expecting to find decent Mexican food in the heartland of America. I took everything back to my office. Surprisingly, the tacos were not half bad. Either that I was so upset I'd lost my sense of taste.

After Basic Comp B, Tim Hannaford stayed after.

"I want to apologize," he said, softly.

"Good move," I growled. "But I'm not the one who needs one."

"Well, I can't just go up to Ed. He'll kill me."

I had to concede his point. "All right. I'll see what I can do."

Eunice was waiting for me at the door to my office.

"What's up?" I asked, opening the door.

She followed me inside. "I thought we might go over some strategies in case Joe gets petty at today's faculty meeting."

"He is already getting petty." I dumped my purse on the desk and sank into my chair. "I did not get notice of this meeting."

"And Joe called it this morning." Eunice plopped down on the couch next to the desk. "Even Bob Farnsworth was pissed, and he usually supports Joe."

"I'd say this day couldn't get any worse, but you know what happens when you do." I propped my elbows on the desk and sank my head into my hands.

"It gets worse." She paused. "I do have one favor to ask you."

"Sure."

"I want to lose my virginity this weekend."

"What?" I gaped at her.

"I've been thinking about doing this for a while now. I'm fifty-two years old. I've never been with a man before. I think it's time I found out what all the fuss is about."

"Eunice, that's, that's nuts!"

She shrugged. "That may be. Still, I'd like to do it with Ed Donaldson, if possible."

The bottom dropped out of my stomach. "He's a student."

"He's not my student, and he's older, not to mention experienced and apparently quite accomplished." Eunice got an odd smile on her face. "And I like him. Although I don't think there will be any issues with having to maintain a relationship."

"I agree on that last point." I sighed. Sid's girlfriends never lasted more than two weeks. Even our good friend Angelique Carter was more of a repeat live-in than an actual steady.

"Anyway, I'm hoping you have some way of contacting him for some time this weekend. I'm between exams right now, and if it gets any later in the quarter, I'll also have term papers to grade."

"Are you sure you want to do this?"

"Of course. Why wouldn't I? And don't worry if you can't get him to cooperate. I'll find somebody."

"No!" I gasped, Sid's various warnings ringing in my ears. "You can get really hurt that way." I took a deep breath. "I'll see what I can do. I'll get his phone number from the class list."

"Good. Thank you." Eunice got up. "And I see that it's just about time for the faculty meeting? Shall we go confront Professor Petty?"

"Sure," I said in a small voice.

The meeting hadn't started when we got there. Eunice went to her usual place at the conference table, and I pulled Fran aside.

"What's going on?" Fran asked.

"Eunice wants me to set her up with Ed Donaldson so that she can lose her virginity this weekend," I whispered.

"Oh, she's finally going to do it." Fran shuddered and let out a curse word. "She's been talking about it for months now. I told her I did not want anything to do with it."

Unfortunately, that's when Cunningham walked in. The look of surprise on his face when he saw me would have been a lot more gratifying if I'd been in a better mood. As soon as he'd called the meeting to order, he went on about how some of the faculty were getting lax with the rules, particularly leaving the lights on in their offices.

"Some of us are working late," Fran objected.

"That's what you say," said Ryan Martin with a rather yeasty guffaw.

"What are you saying?" Fran held herself upright in high dudgeon.

"That you're doing a little twilight two-step in your office after hours." Ryan laughed loudly.

"I am not!" Fran shrieked, and with a liberal assortment of curse words, continued shrieking that Ryan was a mean-spirited, filthy-minded jerk.

"It was just a joke," Ryan said.

"It was not a joke!"

I looked over at Eunice as Fran continued dressing down Ryan and mouthed, "It got worse."

She nodded. There seemed little likelihood that Cunningham would re-gain control of the meeting, so he adjourned. There was darned near a stampede to get out the doors of the room. Eunice and I waited for Fran, who had collapsed in tears.

"What's going on?" Eunice asked soothingly.

Fran sniffed and began blinking back her tears. "I do not want to talk about it. I absolutely do not want, under any circumstances, to talk about it."

"Very well, then." Eunice gently helped Fran to her feet. "Come on. Let's get some food in our stomachs. I am assuming you skipped the fish sticks today. It's not good to go to a faculty meeting on an empty stomach."

Ted wandered back into the room. "Hey, Fran. Are you okay?"

Fran sniffed one last time and wiped her eyes. "Okay enough. I'm sorry, Ted."

"We're going to get something to eat," Eunice told him. "Why don't you join us?"

"Sure."

"Janet, are you coming?"

"Uh, yeah." I grabbed my purse and followed them out.

Eunice insisted that we needed stronger reinforcements than usual, so we went to the Whistling Cow, the steak house that Ted had brought Fran and me to the night I'd arrived. The steaks were still phenomenal, and Fran visibly calmed down as soon as she'd had some food.

"I get emotional when my blood sugar gets low," she said.

We all agreed that Joe Cunningham and faculty meetings were not to be faced on empty tummies.

Having been well fed, I was in a somewhat better frame of mind myself. But as I mounted the stairs to my apartment, I knew that the very last thing I wanted to do was set Sid up with another woman. It was part of our original agreement when he first hired me that I would not be involved in his fooling around in any way. But Sid had told me any number of times that good sex didn't just happen, that it was a skill, one that too many guys thought they had.

Once inside, I decided to get the dirty deed over with. My watch said that it was a quarter to ten. There was a chance that Sid was still up. I dialed the phone. It rang three times.

"Hello?" asked the familiar, but sleepy voice.

"Who is it?" asked a breathless female in the background before I could say anything.

I hung up. It was the coward's way out, but I just couldn't help it. I was tired, but I didn't feel sleepy. I prowled the apartment, looking for something to do. The broom beckoned. I got out a dust rag, too, and dusted and swept the entire place. It was after midnight at that point. I got ready for bed, but sleep would not come. So, I scrubbed the sink, counters, and the floor in the kitchen. By two-thirty, I was still awake. I scrubbed the bathroom, even getting up the hard water stains on the bathtub floor.

At three-fifteen, I realized I had cleaned the entire apartment. There was nothing left to do except grade papers. I pulled the Basic Comp papers from my purse, got out my red pen and grade book, and took everything to my bed. I arranged the pillows so that I could sit up comfortably and looked at the first paper in the pile.

It had Ed Donaldson's name at the top and was titled "The Virgin."

I didn't recognize the exact story, but I certainly recognized the high school setting. Sid had changed his name and set the high school in Chicago, but I realized after a couple sentences that he wasn't writing fiction.

It was his junior year. A new girl had arrived at the school at the same time two of Sid's female classmates decided that they needed to get him back for something. So, the two girls talked about how loose the new girl, Denise, was within earshot of Sid. Sid asked her out, and it turned out that Denise was a nice girl, bent on behaving herself. But because Denise let it get out that she'd gone on a date with Sid, the other guys figured she was as loose as Sid was. In desperation, he'd given Denise his class ring, the ring he'd practically sold himself for getting the money to buy it.

"Wear this outside your blouse," he told her. "Tell all the guys we're going steady. Tell the girls what Mia and Nancy did to you."

It worked. Denise had been protected. Right before Sid left for Vietnam, she gave him a double-tailed quarter for good luck. Sid got the ring back after he'd been back home for about six months. Denise's husband found him. Denise had finally taken the ring off, at her husband's request, only to be killed in a car accident three months later.

I couldn't help sniffling. It was so typically Sid. As much as I resisted him protecting me, he had always been there when I'd needed him. The few times I'd had to walk out on a date, he'd come right away. He'd even had a girlfriend over one time and walked out on her to go get me. Protecting me was how we met. I'd ditched a blind date and had to go wait in the restaurant bar until my sister and her husband came home. Sid sent my date on his way and bought me dinner.

And there was another woman in his bed, even at that moment. That hurt. I had to figure it was Terry. Sid talks a lot in his sleep, and he'd agreed that he wasn't going to bring anybody back to where he was staying just in case. Terry was one of us, so she was safe. And her own safety, I suddenly realized, was also why she was there. Okay, there was sex going on. I wasn't that naïve. But Sid hadn't reached out with his note to get first in line. He'd reached out to protect her because that's what Sid did.

I looked down at the story. It was bare of red marks, and I knew it needed them. A teardrop left a big wet spot on the page. I brushed it away, but more were falling.

October 20 -21, 1984

T ippy-tap, tippy-tap. It thundered through my brain, but all I could see was the splatter of bright red blood against a white interior wall. My stomach roiled, and I heard myself crying.

A second later, I awoke. The tapping sound was still there, but in the fuzziness of waking, I was able to identify it as rain beating down on the roof above me. The window was light enough that I knew the sun had risen. Papers were scattered all over the bed and my red marking pen had left large round stains on the comforter.

I gasped, still shaking from the nightmare. The clock on the nearby dresser said eleven-oh-five.

"Crap!"

Which is about as foul as I get. It's probably my mother's fault. There were few things Mae and I could do that would get our fannies tanned faster than uttering a naughty word, and keep in mind, even "stupid" and "darn" were asking for it.

I blinked. I had fallen asleep crying over Sid's short story.

"Crap," I muttered again.

I had made up my mind that I was not going to suffer over the man. However difficult things were because of his fooling around, our relationship was still strong enough that it was worth staying around. I stumbled out of bed, gathered all the papers together, and staggered out to the living room, where I had a small desk. That's where I put the papers.

It was almost noon by the time I'd showered, dressed, and eaten breakfast. My heart thudding in my chest, I made the phone call. He picked up after two rings.

"Hi, it's me," I said.

"Hey, good to hear from you. What's up?"

"You sound cheerful."

"Uh, let's just say I had a decidedly good night."

"Yeah. I figured."

He chuckled. "Hey, I got laid in my own bed for the first time in weeks. Yes, I am a happy man."

"Terry, right?"

"You know that I am nothing if not discreet."

"Shavings. Is this going to cause trouble on the team?"

He paused. "I don't think so. I was clear on the expectations, and she was happy with that. In fact, she said further encounters would only cause trouble for her back home."

"I'm not sure I wanted to know that much." I blinked. "Anyway, the reason I'm calling... Well, this isn't easy for me, but, um..."

"What?" He sounded very hopeful.

"Not me," I snapped, then drew a deep breath. "It's one of the other faculty. Eunice Blakely."

"Oh. I liked her."

"Yeah, well, she wants to lose her virginity this weekend and asked me to set the two of you up."

Sid laughed. "Really? I'm honored."

"She's fifty-two years old."

"A first-time experience at fifty-two? That sounds like a blast."

I couldn't help groaning. "Only you."

"Why don't you have her meet me at The Cider Keg at, say, seven-thirty?"

"Okay."

He sighed. "I am detecting a strong note of jealousy there."

"I don't want to talk about it."

"I'd still rather be sleeping with you."

"I know." I bit my lip. "I just don't want Eunice to get hurt. By the way, she is not looking for a relationship, so you should be clear on that end."

"That's good news. Don't worry about it. Let her know about the meeting spot and I'll take it from there."

"Thanks." I swallowed. "You know, I appreciate that. My conscience is really screaming at me right now."

"Well, you know how I feel about it, but I understand. It's a little hard for you. You did the right thing."

"I'm glad you think so. Anyway, I'll talk to you later."

"Can't wait."

I hung up with a half-hearted sigh, then dialed Eunice. She seemed quite pleased with the arrangements. Hanging up again, I looked around the apartment. It almost glowed, it was so clean. I groaned. I couldn't believe I was upset enough to clean. I hate housework.

Hanging around the apartment was only making things worse. I stuffed the papers and grade book into my purse and took off on foot. The skies had cleared, and it was chilly. But in my Shetland wool sweater, I was just warm enough.

The downtown wasn't that far away, and I went there first, ambling around looking at the shops. I found a yarn shop offering some nice worsteds on sale. I sank my hand into the balls, enjoying the feel of the wool. They'd been dyed the full range of colors, but I couldn't help being attracted to a combination of two blues, a white and a light gray.

The next thing I knew, I was going through the pattern rack and found the perfect one: a man's V-neck pullover with an argyle pattern. Sid loves sweaters, usually wearing them tied precisely about his shoulders. I looked back at the worsteds that had called me into the shop. The blue would play off his eyes beautifully. I slammed the pattern back onto the rack.

I did not want to be thinking about Sid. I forced myself to look at another pattern, but that argyle kept whispering to me.

I tried to tell myself that knitting a sweater for Sid could be a dangerous hint that I wasn't who I claimed. After all, when you're undercover, it's those little details that can give you away. But that was ridiculous because my cover did include a family with male relatives back home. Nor did anyone have to know who I was making the sweater for. It could even have been for me. I'd certainly knitted up menswear for myself before.

The worst of it was, I knew I needed a project. Back home, I sew and knit all the time, and I make most of my clothes. I call it my therapy, and at that moment, I realized that having something to work on would probably help my mood. Sid was still my best friend, and Christmas wasn't all that far away.

So, I picked up the pattern, bought all the balls I would need, plus a little bit more, needles, stitch markers, and a couple of other tools. I left the store feeling much lighter in spirit while thinking of a way to explain why I hadn't brought any knitting with me. Of course, the easiest answer was the best one. I'd already told Fran and Eunice that I'd left a lot of my books and furniture in storage back home until I knew where I wanted to land. Why not my knitting and sewing?

I headed back to the university. There was a hint of smoke in the air, and I realized someone was burning leaves. That was the one downside of living in Los Angeles. You didn't get a real sense of the seasons changing. Sid disagreed. He said the changes were simply more subtle. Perhaps, but I loved spring and fall back in Tahoe.

In my office, I got my papers out and set to work. The creative writing assignment was one of the easier ones to grade, too. Unless someone made a major boo-boo and it wasn't obviously intentional, then he or she got full credit. Aside from exposing the students to different forms of writing, the assignment also gave most of them a boost.

I worked away happily, entering my grades into the computer as I marked the papers. No re-typing them. That was going to save a lot of time. Until I got to Ed Donaldson's story. My gut still twisted as I looked at it. There was no way for me to look at it objectively. I'd always enjoyed Sid's stories about his high school days, and I wondered if that had been why he'd chosen this particular one to write about. [Sort of. Mostly, it was that I couldn't think of anything else to write. - SEH] There were a couple minor misspellings and one sentence where the grammar was a little rocky, but it certainly qualified for full credit. So, I put an A on the page and into the computer and moved on.

It only took a couple more hours and the spelling quizzes were done and entered. The light from the windows grew orange with the sinking sun and the hall outside my office was in shadow. The light shone underneath the door to Max's office. I knew that didn't mean he was inside. I thought of a good excuse to bother him if he was there, put on my leather gloves, and knocked on his door.

No answer. I knocked again more loudly. Still nothing. Satisfied, I slipped the passkey into the lock, opened the door, and slid in.

Max Beard looked up from his desk at the other end of the room and blinked.

"Max!" I yelped.

"Why are you here?" he asked, his voice sounding more curious than angry. "The door was locked."

"I know." I swallowed, feeling my face grow red.

Max stood up and came around to the front of the desk.

"How did you get in?" He was still more curious than anything, but I began to get a weird feeling.

"My key," I said, lamely. "Um, you're not going to believe this." Smiling awkwardly, I moved toward the desk. "I think they gave me a passkey. I was going to Fran's office the other day to enter grades and got in, then found out I didn't have hers. I'd used mine. I hope you don't mind. I thought you were gone, so I figured I'd just try it and see. I did knock first."

He shrugged. "I don't always answer because I don't always want to be disturbed."

"Oh." I shifted, trying to subtly get a look at the papers on his desk. "Well, I'm really sorry." I headed for the door. "And, uh, could you not mention the key? I don't want Joe Cunningham to get mad at me again."

"Wasn't planning on it." Max watched me leave.

I was trembling a little as I stood in the hall. Max had a computer on his desk, and the back looked like it was wired to the university system, but I hadn't been able to tell if it was on or not. I got my breath back and debated going home and getting dinner. But then I remembered that Ernie Lavalle had gone home for the weekend to Indianapolis to visit his mother. He'd been complaining about it all week.

I went upstairs to the third floor and found Ernie's office. It was dark. I listened extra hard, but there was silence within. It was also empty when I opened the door. I made a point of pulling all the blinds and got out my small flashlight. The books were empty, his papers strictly related to his classes. I found a couple of small, empty syringes in the top drawer of his desk, which was a little odd. I looked through the trash can. There were no syringes among the scraps of paper and candy wrappers.

I went back to my office to get my purse, then went home. As I was coming in through the front, Fran came out of her apartment and invited me to have dinner with her at her place. We both agreed that we did not want to go into town and chance running into Eunice and Ed. Fran had rented Romancing the Stone and Splash from the video store and we watched both, munching on popcorn and eating ice cream.

By Sunday afternoon, I had recovered from my night of no sleep and my bad mood. I drove south this time and called Mae first. Then I called Nick. He sounded so down.

"Everything all right?" I asked.

"I'm okay. When are you and Dad getting back?"

I sighed. "We don't know. As soon as we can, of course."

"Okay. It's just that…"

"What?"

"I'm having bad dreams."

"Oh, no! What's the matter?"

"I had them when Grandma died and now they're back."

"What are you dreaming, honey?"

Nick paused. "It's just the one dream, but I keep having it. I'm all alone, like I'm the very last person on the earth. And I'm running around trying to find somebody, but everybody's gone."

"That one. You poor thing. Oh, honey. I'm sorry that I can't be there in person. But you know what? I'll always be around for you, one way or another."

"Are you and Dad getting married?"

I rolled my eyes. "We'll have to see."

"I wish you would. Or just move into his bedroom. I don't care."

"I wish it were that simple, kiddo. I know it's not the way you want it. It's not the way I want it, either. Life is like that sometimes. But we get through it and we're better and stronger for it in the long run."

"I suppose."

"I know it's hard to see it, but it's true. Trust me." I couldn't help smiling, grateful that he couldn't see me.

Nick was utterly impulsive and only eleven years old, at that.

"Okay."

"I'll call you next week, my sweet guy."

"Okay."

I hung up and drove back to Appleton, thinking hard about Nick and Sid. I made it to Off Campus Office Hours almost an hour early.

Kathy Richards arrived early as well.

"How are you doing?" I asked, keeping an eye on the door so that we could change the subject if needed.

"Great!" Kathy said. "I swear, it is so wonderful being out of the closet."

"What do you mean?"

"Not having to pretend I'm straight. We're an arts school and a theater department. Trust me, the concentration of lesbians and gays is way higher than normal. Nobody cares if I like girls, and several of them like me." Kathy made a face. "I love the Code Factory, but I think when this is over, I'm going to ask for a transfer to San Francisco. Or maybe New York."

I smiled. "I hope you get it."

Then Rita Farley showed up, holding hands with Mark Ayers. The two of them practically glowed.

"Hi, everyone!" Mark announced. He was a slender young man with dark hair and big, round brown eyes. It was easy to see why Rita was so taken with him.

"Looks like you two have had a good weekend," I said.

"Yeah!" said Rita. "Where's Terry? I want to say thank you."

However, Ted Curtis was the next to show up.

"Hey, Janet, what are you doing here?" he asked.

"Off Campus Office Hours," I said. "It's a more casual way for students to get help."

Ted nodded and grinned. "What a great idea."

"Good," I said, grinning myself. "Then you can buy the next pizza."

Terry and Steve both showed up at roughly the same time. Ed/Sid came in shortly after that, along with several kids from the other two Basic Comp sections. Marge Haver and Rick Waters, from the Shakespeare seminar, showed up around half an hour late. Tim Hannaford did not show.

It was a lively meeting. Terry accepted Rita's and Mark's thanks, blushing furiously. But she, too, had acquired a new confidence.

"Cover me," she whispered at one point.

I wasn't sure how or why, but then noticed some beer foam on her upper lip. Ed left with the other Basic Comp kids. Marge and Rick soon left, as well, leaving half a pitcher of beer on the table. Ted and Steve had gotten into some extended discussion about something or other. I figured if it were important, Steve would tell me. The two of them left together and soon the only people left at our table were Kathy, Terry, and me.

"Is there anybody here who knows us?" Terry asked.

"Nope," said Kathy, after looking around the restaurant.

"Good. I need a drink." Terry grabbed one of the few empty plastic glasses and the beer pitcher and poured herself one. "That is the worst part of pretending to be eighteen. Sneaking around for booze."

"It's the details that will get you killed," I said, smiling in spite of the grim words.

"We'll pretend this is Kathy's, then, and I'm stealing it."
Terry took a long swallow. "Oh. Nirvana."

"I've tasted better," said Kathy.

"You haven't been forced to be underage," Terry said.
She wiped her mouth. "I've got mail call. Lisa, can you get
the guys theirs?"

"Sure," I said.

Kathy swore. "Terry, why did you just call her Lisa?"

Terry and I just looked at each other and groaned loudly.
I couldn't believe I'd just responded to my real name.

"Terry?" I asked, my heart about to pound out of my
chest.

Terry melted into herself. "Kathy, do you mind taking
off?"

"No problem." Kathy grabbed the manila envelope Terry had given her and hurried out of the restaurant.

"How do you...?" I looked at her.

"Know your real name?" Terry winced. "I'm systems.
My job has been setting up payroll, things like that. I know
everyone's real names and their addresses." She grinned.
"He called me the most dangerous woman in Quickline."

I winced at the name. "He would. Okay. But you just
slipped. Do we need to take you off the case?"

Terry blinked and sat up straight. "No. I think there's a
reason I did. It was Friday night."

"I do not want to know about Friday night."

"It's okay." Terry smiled warmly and gently grabbed my
hand. "Look, I know you two are not technically a couple.
He made that clear."

"As he should." I tried not to start crying. "We're not."

Terry snorted. "He loves you."

"So?" I was working hard at being casual, but every bit of my insides was squeezing the breath out of me.

Terry gaped. "You haven't told him how you feel."

"It doesn't matter how I feel," I said, then regretted it. I took a deep breath. "Look. In many ways, we have told each other how we feel. Maybe not in those specific words, but we have. Terry, there's more going on than you could possibly know. This isn't a freaking romance novel, where we say we love each other, and everything becomes moonlight and roses. I'm not going to say more because it's none of your damned business, let alone, any Need to Know."

Terry shrugged dismally. "I know. It's just that…" She sighed. "I don't know how to say this, because I don't want you to feel like I got something you didn't. But he gave me an amazing gift Friday night. Trust me, that's all it was. I don't want anything more. I really don't. I just want to say thanks by helping him to what he really wants, and what he really wants is you."

I squeezed my eyes shut. "I know. I wish it were that simple." I opened my eyes and looked at her. "And I appreciate that you're trying to help. I really do."

"I told him to tell you he loves you."

I sighed. "Thanks, Terry."

The poor kid. Part of me wanted to pound the living daylights out of her for interfering. The other part of me couldn't help but feel warmed by her desire to help, no matter how ineffectual it was.

"Seriously," I said. "It's sweet of you to put your hand in. But we'll all be better off if you leave it out."

She shrugged and handed me two manila envelopes. One had some mail for both Sid and me. The other had a letter for Tim Hannaford.

I got up, paid the bill for the pizzas and drinks, and left the restaurant.

Poor Terry. She had no idea. I looked back at the restaurant. Maybe part of the problem was me. Maybe holding out for fidelity was asking too much. There was no easy answer to that question, and for the moment, I wasn't entirely sure I needed one. But I did need Sid. That much I knew.

[As I needed you. When Terry told me that I should tell you I loved you, I was not happy, to say the least. What really killed me, though, was that I later tried and couldn't. - SEH]

October 22, 1984

T he read-out on my alarm clock read eight twenty-three. The phone had already rung twice. I do not wake up easily. I picked up the phone.

"Hello?" Okay, it was more of a grunt than an actual greeting.

"Janet, it's Steve." His voice sounded worried. "Ed has picked up a tail."

"Huh?"

"When he went running this morning, there was a team on him."

"Oh." I did feel like cursing. I must concede that much.

"You need to stay away from him. You don't want anyone questioning you."

"He's my student," I muttered. "But yeah. I'll do what I can."

I hung up, then got up and went running. If there was anybody tailing me, they did an amazing job of it. It wasn't likely, but I wasn't about to take a chance on changing my routine.

In Basic Comp A, Ed/Sid seemed to be taking the tail philosophically. He participated in the discussion on footnotes and bibliographies by asking how one cites an interview in an academic paper. I handed him our mail when I handed back his story, and he casually slid the papers into his daypack. He smiled when he saw the grade. He smiled again as he turned in his homework. I noticed that there was a small piece of paper on top of the page containing his thesis paragraph.

I palmed it, gathered the rest of the homework together, then went back to my office to read the note.

"I've got company, but can't miss our court date. See you there. Your ever-loving Proteus."

I couldn't help but laugh at the signature. Sid had taken me to see Two Gentlemen of Verona the previous spring. He'd thought the character of Proteus was unnecessarily fickle, then laughed when I'd launched into a lecture on changeability as a theme in Shakespeare's comedies. [Of course, we didn't know at the time that you'd be teaching it that coming fall. But stuff like that was why I wasn't worried about you posing as an English professor. - SEH]

As I ripped the note into tiny pieces, I thought about what Steve had said about staying away from Sid. The problem was, as Sid's note indicated, too many people had seen us playing racquetball, usually on Mondays. Sid did not want us deviating from any of our established routines, and he was right.

I went to the Faculty Dining Room, as usual, but when I got there, I wondered why I had. They were serving some insipid slop called Chili Con Carne that had more beans than anything resembling meat. Several of my humanities colleagues were slurping it up.

I sat down next to David Watts, took a bite, and made a face.

"I don't know why I bother," I said.

"Come on," said David. "It's the same reason we all do. It's free."

"There is that." I sighed and took another bite. "I don't see you here too often."

"I'm playing bachelor this week." He grinned. "My wife's traveling."

"What does she do?"

He shrugged. "What everyone around here does. Works at the paper mill."

"Oh. I heard you haven't been married that long."

"A little over a year." He sighed happily. "Best year of my life so far. Ilona is wonderful. I really thought I was going to be a bachelor. But now 'Let them signify under my sign, Here you may see Benedick the married man.'"

I chuckled. "You do remember that he's saying he doesn't want to get married in that speech?"

He laughed. "Shakespeare's your thing, not mine. Now, Victorian poets, I'll go toe to toe with you on them. But I am so glad you took over that Shakespeare seminar. All those crazy acting students."

"They're fun."

We chatted as I finished the small cup of pseudo-chili. I bought some tacos from the Commons and brought them back to my office to eat. They weren't the best tacos I'd ever eaten, but they were surprisingly edible, and compared to most everything else at the Commons, rather tasty.

During my office hours, after the B section of Basic Comp, I paced the floor of my office. No one showed, and I knew I should have been grading quizzes and thesis paragraphs. But my mind kept flitting back to Steve and what he'd said about David Watts, and what Steve had said about staying away from Sid. He did have a point, but he should have known that Sid and I couldn't change any patterns we'd established. I began to wonder if there was an ulterior motive behind Steve's suggestion.

As soon as office hours were up, I hurried to the Sports Center. Tina coached me through my weight routine, then grinned salaciously. Ed/Sid had arrived.

"You guys going to play racquetball?" she asked him.

"I suppose." He looked at me.

I shrugged. "Sure. Let me get my racket and stuff."

We closed ourselves into the court and began playing. Well, we didn't keep score. That was pointless. [On your part it was. - SEH] Sid signaled the rest first, though.

"How are you doing?" I asked softly.

He wiped his brow with the bottom of his muscle shirt. "Oh, fine. I was expecting it. It just probably took them some time to get the team together. I've tagged three of them, including Ilona Swedburg."

"That's interesting." I told him what David Watts had said.

Sid nodded. "That's right. She's married to him. And he thinks she's traveling? How does she think she's going to get away with it?"

"I have no idea. She must have some way. And David is not the most alert person I've ever met."

"Have you told Steve about this yet?" Sid adjusted his eye guard.

I shook my head. "Not yet. I was debating calling him later."

"He and I are supposed to have dinner together tonight to talk things over. Our friends can't get inside the house where we're living, which means they can't tell if I'm in his apartment or he's in mine, so it's safe. Why don't you come over?"

"I should probably check with Steve first."

Sid laughed. "Why? I'm the one making dinner."

"Oh." I smiled. "That sounds nice. I suppose I can for a little while. I've got papers to grade, though."

"Yeah." He grinned. "Thanks for the A on the story. That's the first one I've gotten from you."

I blushed. "I'm a hard grader." I swallowed. "It was a cute story."

He looked hard at me. "You're really enjoying the teaching, aren't you?"

"Well, it was kind of my life plan." I smiled at him. "I was good at it, too."

"I can see that." He bounced the ball. "Would you rather still be doing it?"

"What do you mean?"

"As opposed to writing and spying."

I laughed. "Actually, no. I like my life back home. What I've been doing here has been fun, but I don't think I'd last very long at it." I scrunched up my face. "The academic politics are pretty rank and I'm not exactly putting up with it. Besides, I'm teaching CCD classes at home, so I haven't given up on teaching completely."

Sid shook his head. "There's got to be a difference between teaching college students and a bunch of teens who don't want to be taking CCD."

"Not really." I shrugged. "Trust me. Nobody takes Basic Composition because they want to, and most of the kids in my classes aren't that much older than the kids at home. I will admit that this has been fun, kind of like the best of all my worlds. And it is nice to see that I've still got it. But

I can also see that I'd get really bored with it after a couple semesters." I smiled at him. "I guess you can say this is no longer my life plan."

"Well, you've always liked being in the spy biz more than me."

"I did have some pretty romantic notions, didn't I?" I frowned. "Are you saying you don't like the biz?"

"I've never really thought about whether or not I liked it." He bounced the ball some more. "It's what I did, what I had to do. I resented the hell out of being put in intelligence, and even more that I wasn't done with it when I got out of the Army. But I kept doing it and, really, it was probably a good thing that I did have something to focus on once I got back. And then last week. Funny how not being able to do my job put a whole new perspective on it." He looked at me. "I've really missed working with you, but I've missed working a whole lot more. Play?"

"Sure."

As it turned out, I didn't need to just show up to dinner. When I checked the computer bulletin board right before leaving for the day, I saw that Steve had already invited me and had sent the address. I drove straight there. It had just gotten dark when I pulled up in front of the old Victorian mansion. It sat on a corner, with a huge lawn in front and hedges along the back edges. There were three stories, at least that's what it looked like based on the turret that took up one corner of the house. I later learned that it had been divided into six one-bedroom apartments, two on each floor. Sid, Steve, and the landlady, Mrs. Bielke, lived on the side with the turret. Steve's apartment was on the second floor, and I went there first. Steve grinned as he ushered me into the wide living room. A dining room table sat in the alcove formed by the turret, with a large brass light fixture suspended from the ceiling above it.

I coughed. The place reeked of cigarettes. Ashtrays overflowed on the beat-up filing cabinets, what not tables, and the coffee table in front of an overstuffed and beat up sofa. The dining table was littered with reams of printouts, and Steve had his computer set up there, as well.

"We're gonna go upstairs," Steve said as he turned off his computer. "I was going to bring in some hamburgers, but Ed said he'd rather cook for us."

"I'm sure he would," I said, trying not to cough again.

I was glad we left. It was getting hard to breathe in Steve's place.

Sid's apartment had the exact same layout, and he'd also put a dining table in the alcove where the turret was. But his furnishings were of better quality than Steve's and better cared for, as well. Sid had gone with the Victorian style to match the house, except for an upright piano that had been backed up on the wall next to the door. Sid's daypack sat next to it on the floor.

"Why don't you drop your purse on the end of the couch?" he asked, as he let us in.

He was dressed in a light green polo shirt and very tight jeans and had a linen kitchen towel in his hands. Next to Steve's shabby long-sleeved striped dress shirt and tan chinos, Sid looked completely gorgeous. The wind whistled outside the windows, but inside, it was nice and warm. I had to take off my sweater and dropped it next to my purse.

Steve started to bring up the case, but Sid called a moratorium on work talk until after we'd eaten. The table, covered by a white linen tablecloth, was set with china decorated with tiny blue flowers, silverware that had the subtle glow of age, linen napkins, and cut crystal wine glasses. Lucy in the Sky With Diamonds played softly in the background from a reel-to-reel tape deck attached to an expensive stereo system in the living room.

"So, what's for dinner?" Steve asked.

"I thought we'd start with a nice little green salad," Sid said. "Followed by Sole Meuniere, prepared table side, and served with fresh broccoli and potatoes gratinées."

Steve looked a little perplexed. Me, I worked insanely hard at not laughing. Eunice's comment a few weeks before about full mating plumage ran through my brain. I could not figure out why Sid was acting like a very classy buck in full rut, but the results were quite nice. [Oh, dear God, you couldn't? - SEH]

I was a little shocked when Sid prepared the floured white fish (real sole, by the way) with clarified butter. He sautéed it in two copper pans on a little gas burner that he'd set up on a cart next to the table. It was incredibly delicious, too, as were the broccoli and potatoes. Even Steve noticed how good it was.

Then Steve decided to assert himself, and as we finished, pointed out that we were there to work on the case.

"Unfortunately, the timing of when the team appeared does point to Eunice," Steve said.

"Why?" asked Sid. "I slept with Eunice on Saturday. The team showed up on Monday. It takes more than two days to assemble a decent team."

"But why would a virile young buck like you be sleeping with an old broad like her?" Steve demanded.

"A lot of reasons," I jumped in loudly. "None of which are relevant."

Steve glared at me. "Are you sure about that?"

"Sure enough," I said. "I know how that little rendezvous happened." I glared at Sid. "That being said, if someone was watching Eunice, I can see how he might see something weird about it."

Sid rolled his eyes. "You're right, Steve. We have to keep an eye on Eunice. But there are other suspects."

Which is when I told them about finding Max in his office, with his strange blocking of his desk, and the two syringes in Ernie Lavalle's desk. And I also remembered to comment on Joe Cunningham's odd paperbacks. Steve glared at me.

"So what?" he asked. "People leave all sorts of weird stuff in their desks."

"Yes," said Sid. "But weird stuff is what we're looking for. It could be meaningless. It could be what breaks this case wide open."

Steve turned his glare on Sid. "Do not tell me how to run an investigation."

"Both of you!" I snapped. "Cut it out."

At least Steve and Sid had the grace to look abashed.

"I'm sorry," said Steve. "I shouldn't be so twitchy. I just do not want another dead student."

"And I'm not happy about enforced inactivity," Sid grumbled. "So, I'm sorry, too."

"All right." I looked at both. "We need to come up with some next steps. As much as I don't like it, we should search Eunice's office, and maybe her home."

"I'll take care of that," said Steve.

"Why?" I glared at him. "I'm in the building all the time, and that is my area to cover."

"But I'm in and out of those offices routinely, and if I accidentally barge in on someone, I have a reason to be there," Steve countered.

"In the middle of the night?" I folded my arms across my chest. "Let's face it. Neither of us can search offices during the day. It's too risky to do it when they're in class because classes let out early sometimes. Not to mention the odds of being seen going into an office. Then there are our own classes, office hours, and the fact that when people aren't in class, they're usually in their offices. It's hard enough to do searches at night, with the way people work late around here."

"But, Janet, you're lead," Steve said. "You can't afford to take too many risks yourself."

I was glad that Sid didn't audibly groan, but he knew Steve had slammed into one of my sore spots big-time. I pressed my lips together. There was no point in yelling at Steve, especially after I'd just yelled at him for squabbling with Sid. Besides, Steve didn't know better, and he did almost have a point.

"I don't need protecting," I told him quietly. "Why don't you hold off on the house until I've had a chance to go through her office? I can do it in the next few days. Depending on what I do or don't find, then we'll see if it's worth searching her house later. After all, none of us needs to be exposed to the level of risk that entails."

Steve nodded sullenly. After that, there wasn't much more to discuss.

"Well, it's probably time to head out," Steve said, getting up. "Janet, you want me to walk you to your car?"

"Steve, we've got some home-related business to cover," Sid said, which was good because, by that point, I was ready to let Steve have it.

Steve looked at us sadly, then nodded. I walked Steve to the door as Sid began clearing the table.

"You're not a couple, huh?" Steve said softly as the tape deck started playing some early Rolling Stones.

"No. We're not. Just friends."

He looked back at Sid, then at me. "Okay. See you whenever."

He left. I shut the door, then went over to the dining table to help Sid.

"Did all this stuff come with your apartment?" I asked him, as I carefully picked up the cut crystal glasses.

"Nothing in here did." Sid finished putting all the dishes on the cart and began pushing it into the kitchen. "You want to dry?"

"I prefer washing. And you know where everything goes."

"True." Sid pushed the cart next to the sink.

The kitchen was modern, but had almost no counter space. There was a dish drainer and drainboard set up next to the sink, which left only one other space between the stove and refrigerator. I turned on the hot water, found the dish detergent under the sink, and put in the plug.

"Anyway," Sid said, answering my earlier question. "I rented the furniture. As for the rest of it, I've been using going antiquing and estate sales down near Madison as my excuse to get out for phone calls. I've been finding some great stuff, like the dishes and flatware. I got those glasses here in town for a song. Weekend before last, I picked up the stereo, along with a load of tapes. The guy had an incredible collection of albums he'd recorded and the tapes sound like they were made from first plays."

"What's a first play?"

"The first time you play a vinyl record is supposedly the purest sound." Sid got another towel from a drawer. "Reel to reel fans would record that first play, usually off someone else's record. You got the best sound, and it was a hell of a lot cheaper."

I started in on the dishes. Sid rinsed and dried almost as fast as I washed.

"You okay?" he asked after a moment of silence.

"Yeah. Just bugged."

"Well, I'm very proud that you didn't bite Steve's head off."

"I wanted to."

Sid looked at me thoughtfully. "Why are you so touchy about that? He was just showing concern."

"Was he?" I glared at Sid. "I don't know. It just seems like every time I want to go out and confront the evils of the world, there's always been some man in my way, trying to protect me. First, my daddy, almost all my boyfriends, George, and sometimes even you."

"I don't want to see you hurt any more than you want to see me hurt."

"Yeah, but I'm the one who gets walked to her car, just in case." I scrubbed one of the copper pans with more vigor than necessary. "I am so tired of the assumption that just because I'm a woman, I'm going to automatically attract more bad guys, not to mention, won't be able to handle it if I do."

"There is that." Sid began wiping down the cart and checking the little gas burner. "But it's not what I'm saying, especially about not being able to handle it."

"Well, that's the way it comes off."

Sid thought it over. "You know. You're right. I'm sorry. I never meant to imply that."

"I know." I unplugged the sink. "You can't help it, really. It's what Ted Curtis calls primary socialization. You and all the other guys are trained to do it. The problem is, to quote Dorothy L. Sayers, in the voice of Lord Peter Wimsey, 'nine-tenths of chivalry is the desire to have all the fun.' In other words, it's probably about control."

"And we both know how much I don't like not being in control." Sid sighed suddenly. "Do romantic gestures count as protective/controlling behaviors?"

"What?"

"I was going to make us some dessert."

"Dessert? You?"

He smiled. "For you. I can bend occasionally, you know. Plus, this should be fun."

"Okay." I smiled, too.

"Why don't you go back to the dining room and get settled while I get everything together?"

I went and sat down at the table and a minute later, Sid brought the cart out again. He dimmed the light fixture over the table, then set one of the copper pans on the burner and turned the burner on. While he waited for the pan to heat, he set small, chilled bowls of vanilla ice cream at our places.

"I know I'm going to hear about this eventually," he said, his eyes glittering.

"In profound gratitude, I will try not to."

"Fair enough." He poured more clarified butter into the pan, waited a moment, then dumped some cherries in syrup in and sautéed them. Then, he added a solid splash of Grand Marnier. "Sadly, I had to use frozen cherries, but it should be okay. You ready?"

I laughed. "Yeah."

"It's show time." With a deft twist, he tilted the pan and ignited the sauce.

"Oh, my god. Where did you learn to do that?"

"My errant youth." He laughed as he spooned flaming cherries over my ice cream. "When I was sixteen, I lied about my age and got a job at a fancy French restaurant. I spent about six months bussing tables, then worked as a waiter apprentice, then finally worked as a full waiter for about five months before they realized I wasn't eighteen yet."

"They believed you about the age thing?"

"Must have been the mustache." Sid had grown a full Sergeant Pepper mustache when he was in high school. "Not many kids my age could grow one." He slid into his seat and looked expectantly at me. "Well?"

"Oh!" I picked up a spoon and took a taste. "Oh, my god, it's delicious! Thank you."

He smiled warmly at me. "You're very welcome."

He ate, mulling something over. [I was thinking that it wasn't fair that I'd never done the flambé thing for you. I'd done it for lots of other women, but never you, who truly deserved it. - SEH]

"About the business from home," I asked.

"Partially a ruse, but I did want to touch base with you about Nick. How did he sound when you last talked to him?"

"Pretty down. He'd been having nightmares. Why do you ask?"

Sid nodded and sighed. "I don't know what Rachel's game is, but Nick really wants to come live with us."

Rachel was Nick's mom. She had not been the easiest person to deal with. She'd never told Sid that she had gotten pregnant, then suddenly introduced Nick to Sid the previous spring. Sid had been pretty angry, but he and Nick had eventually gotten close since then.

"I'd love to have him," I said, my eyes filling. "But it's not the best idea."

"I know. If it weren't for the business, I'd take him in a New York second." He sighed. "I just don't want things with Rachel to get so bad that we're the lesser of two evils. Thanks for keeping up on the calls, though."

"Oh, I don't mind. You know how much I love him."

Sid paused. "Yeah. And I appreciate that, too."

After that, we finished dessert talking about little things. It was cozy and warm, and I did not want to leave.

I sighed as I noticed the time. "Oh, dear. I still have papers to grade. I'd better take off."

"Good enough."

I got my purse and sweater. He walked me to the door, then slid his hand onto my cheek and kissed me warmly and passionately. I fell into the embrace. Grading papers suddenly lost its importance, and I couldn't help continuing to kiss him.

October 23 – 24, 1984

S adly, I did not grade any papers that night. I did get home at a reasonable hour, but was so exhausted and elated at the same time that all I wanted to do was sleep. I got up an hour early, got my run in, then hurried over to the campus where I went to work, getting the bulk of the papers done between classes and the faculty meeting at five that afternoon.

I briefly considered searching Eunice's office instead of going to the meeting, but wasn't sure how long the meeting would last, not to mention it was expected that I would attend and probably raise eyebrows if I didn't.

At least Cunningham convened the meeting on time.

"It turns out," he grumbled. "That the Provost's Office wants us to participate in a workshop on Ethical Practices at the University."

"Are they going to cover sexual harassment?" Eunice asked.

Cunningham cleared his throat. "It will cover harassment of any student or colleague. It will also cover academic integrity and NCAA recruiting."

"We don't have any sports teams here," Ernie Lavalle said.

"It's a national program," Cunningham said. "Apparently, the trustees want to show that we're a progressive institution or some such nonsense. What we must decide is whether we will all go at once, or force one among us to go and then repeat the material for the rest of us."

"I think we should all go," said Eunice. "That way, we'll be better prepared should we be expected to answer for our various indiscretions, youthful or otherwise."

I had no idea what she meant, but Cunningham, Ernie, Max, and Ted all squirmed uncomfortably. Since my back was to her, as usual, I couldn't tell which of them, if any, she was looking at. Fred Wirth and Ryan Martin both chose to ignore Eunice.

Fortunately, the meeting adjourned quickly, despite the extended debate over whether we'd all go or send a representative. I was not surprised that it was decided to send a representative. Cunningham nominated me for the task, but Eunice volunteered. I was grateful and told her so when we went out to Barb's Diner with Fran for dinner.

We returned to campus after eating, each of us heading to our respective offices. I worked away, listening for the footsteps of departing colleagues. By ten-thirty, I was feeling rather smug. I had not only finished grading the homework and quizzes from my Monday classes, but the Tuesday ones as well. There was silence in the hall. I went to visit the restroom and noted that both Eunice and Max were still in their offices. I heard Max pacing in his.

Back in my office, I pulled out my yarn, needles, and pattern, and cast on the stitches for Sid's sweater. As I knit, I scanned an academic journal, wondering if I really needed to. I was hoping that the case would be wrapped up by the time the quarter ended, the week before Thanksgiving, but I knew I couldn't count on it. The journal article was as dry as dust, too, which didn't help.

Finally, shortly after eleven, I heard a door in the hallway open. I went to my door and peeked out. It figured. Max was the one locking the door of his office and moving toward the stairs, briefcase in hand. It wasn't the way I wanted it, but there is that old adage about gift horses and mouths. I went back into my office and got my gloves.

Max had, again, left his lights on and the blinds were drawn over the windows, as they usually were. I thanked God for that and went to work, starting with his desk. Except for the computer and the blotter pad on the top, it was bare. The drawers were neat and sparsely filled. The file cabinets were mostly empty except for notes on various articles he had written. It was annoying. Papers had been strewn across the surface of the desk when I'd seen him that Saturday. Where were they?

I checked under the cushions on his couch, in all the books, everywhere. There were no papers of any kind. I sat back down at the desk and looked under the blotter pad, and under the sheet of blotter paper the pad held. Nothing. But then I saw something on the blotter sheet and ran my fingers over it. Faint ridges, as if Max had pressed down really hard as he wrote. I found a pencil and a blank sheet of paper. Gently, I laid the paper over the pad and shaded over it. As if by magic, little white lines appeared. When I saw what they had formed, I smiled.

It wasn't the evidence I needed, but it was going to make life a lot easier. The question was, who would I tell that Max Beard was developing a chemical formula for, presumably, some sort of nerve gas?

The next morning, I handed Ed/Sid a note along with his homework asking him to stay after class.

"Can't stay long," Sid muttered as the other students left.

"I found the developer," I said softly, then looked around again. "It's Max Beard."

"Are you sure?"

"Yes. I'll explain later."

He thought for a second. "Why don't you come visit Steve tonight and I'll fix us dinner? I'll set it up with him."

"Thanks."

I knew I should have stayed in my office and graded papers during the break between my Basic Comp sessions, but my stomach was growling loudly, and I was so excited by my find that I just could not bear the Commons. It had been raining all morning, so I ran for my car and headed out to Barb's. I'd just parked and was about to go in when I thought I saw Ilona Swedburg. Or maybe it wasn't. I debated following her, but Ted Curtis came up behind me.

"Janet, what are you doing here?" he asked, looking around nervously.

"Getting lunch," I said.

"Oh. Great. Let's eat together."

We got a table near a window but couldn't really see outside since the rain was coming down so hard.

"So, how are you liking it here?" Ted asked after the waitress had taken our orders.

"Fine. Are you okay, Ted?"

He sighed. "I'm just worried about that Academic Ethics Workshop."

"Oh, dear," I said as soothingly as I could. "Eunice hit a little too close to home with her youthful indiscretions remark?"

His face went pale. "What do you know about that?"

"Nothing," I said with a laugh. "You're just really upset. I didn't mean to hurt your feelings. I'm sorry."

"No. It's okay." He smiled weakly. "It really is. I mean, yeah, there might be a little fudged data in my background. But I fixed it soon enough. It's just that you know how tenure committees are."

"You don't have tenure?"

"No. I haven't been here long enough," Ted said.

The waitress arrived with my hamburger and fries and a chef's salad for Ted.

"I didn't know that," I said, grabbing a French fry and eating it.

"I've only been here five years. Fran's next in line. That's why I'm helping Eunice. The sooner Fran gets tenure, the sooner I will. If they pass her over for me, then two-thirds of the female faculty at the entire university will be screaming discrimination and burning Joe Cunningham in effigy."

"I sure hope so." I wiped my mouth. The hamburger was good and messy. "At least, you haven't been teaching for twenty years and still ABD."

Meaning All But Dissertation, as in doing all your course work, but never getting around to finishing the final part of your doctoral degree. It doesn't happen often, but there have been people who have had long careers without anyone realizing that they never finished.

"That's Ernie," said Ted.

My eyes flew open. "Really?"

"Well, it's technically a rumor." Ted munched on his salad. "The story goes that his dissertation didn't pass, but he'd already been teaching here for five years, so Joe let it slide as long as Ernie kept trying to re-write it."

"I find it hard to believe Cunningham being that nice."

Ted snorted. "Joe didn't do it to be nice. He did it so that he can keep Ernie in his back pocket."

Well, Ted did use a much cruder term.

"Wow. I had no idea."

We nattered on for several minutes more, and Ted seemed more relaxed. Still, when I checked my watch, I'd been gone longer than I'd intended.

"I've got to scoot," I said, wiping my mouth one last time. "How much do I owe you?"

"I'll buy this time." Ted grinned jovially.

I paused. "Okay. Thanks."

At least he hadn't offered to walk me out to my car.

I got back in time to get my notes together for the Basic Comp B section and ran off to class. When I got back to my office from class, Eunice was waiting at my door.

"What's up?" I asked as I unlocked it.

"Let's talk inside," Eunice said.

"Okay." I let her go in first, then shut the door. "What's going on?"

"I can't say yet." Eunice looked a little agitated. "I'm having a small meeting at my place tonight at ten. Can you come by?"

"Sure, but why?"

"I'll let you know then." She sighed. "Let's just say that decisions have to be made."

"Okay."

Eunice left the office.

I tried not to think about it. I had two sections' worth of homework to grade, plus notes to go over for the next day's Shakespeare seminar. I did check the computer bulletin board, and both Steve and Sid had posted a dinner meeting at their place for that night. Which meant I'd better stay focused on getting the grading done or I'd be a mess in no time.

When I got to the Victorian mansion that evening, the rain had stopped. I went straight to Sid's. Steve was already there. The table had again been set with the china, burnished flatware, and crystal wine glasses.

"We're having chicken stew tonight," Steve whispered to me as Sid went into the kitchen to fetch it. "Thank God, no girly food."

I sighed and decided not to remind him that I was not only a girl, I also liked really gourmet cooking.

The stew was gorgeous, and Sid served it with a lovely Burgundy. I do need to point out that it wasn't an American wine labeled Burgundy. It was the real thing from Burgundy, France. Where he'd gotten it, I did not know. [I'd found a way to get it shipped to me. - SEH] I do not know why or how the competitive thing had died down between the two men, but I was grateful.

However, as we finished eating, Steve looked at me.

"I hear you've found our developer," he said.

I got the piece of paper I'd taken from Max's office from my jeans' back pocket.

"I'm pretty sure," I said, spreading the paper on the table. "I got this off Max Beard's desk. It was pressed into his blotter pad. I can't figure out why else a history professor would have chemical formulae on his blotter pad unless he was working on them."

Steve cursed as Sid laughed.

"You did it!" Sid chortled.

"Yeah, you did," grumbled Steve. "Who would have thought Max?" He looked up at me. "You know, this doesn't exonerate Eunice. If anything, it implicates her."

"How so?" I asked.

"She and Max have been buddies for years. Even before Fran joined the department." Steve also frowned. "And she is a lot better at computers and systems than you would think. I'm not sure how she's getting the formula, but I wouldn't put it past her."

"So, why does she want me at her place tonight?" I asked.

"She asked you to be there?" Steve's eyebrows rose. "At ten p.m., right? She asked me, too."

"Yeah." I frowned. "She said decisions had to be made."

"I suspect a trap." Steve looked at Sid. "Think you can hide in the bushes long enough to cover us?"

"I don't think that's a good idea," I said. I looked at Sid. "You could probably do a good job, but is it realistic to think you can get out of here without your tail spotting you?"

Sid glared at me. "Possible, but not likely."

Steve swore. "We need backup."

"That would be nice," I said. "But we're not getting it, so we'll make the best of what we have."

Steve shifted unhappily. "I was told you two could be real cowboys."

"We don't get backup," Sid said softly.

"We'll be okay," I said, looking at him.

Sid nodded. Steve was not satisfied and continued to argue that we needed Sid there. Finally, it was close enough to ten that Steve and I would have to leave to get to Eunice's in time. As Steve left the apartment, Sid held me back.

"Can you sneak back here after the meeting?" he asked. "Or call me. I just want to know you're okay."

I smiled and kissed him. "Sure. No problem."

I kissed him again and hurried out to my car.

I was a little surprised to see that Fran was already there when I parked my car in front of Eunice's small house. It was made of the same light tan brick that I'd seen everywhere, and rather boxy. But it had a nice, raised porch in the front and a door with a stained-glass window at the top.

"Do you know what this is about?" Fran asked me as I came up the walk.

"I have no idea," I said.

"Oh, hi, Steve," Fran said.

I turned. Steve walked up the front walk behind me.

"Hey, Fran!" Dwight Atwater appeared on the sidewalk. "Oh, Janet, good to see you. Hey, Steve. So, what's going on?"

"We don't know," Fran said. "And worse yet, I knocked, and she didn't answer."

"She didn't?" Steve looked quickly at me.

"Maybe she's waiting until it's exactly ten o'clock," I said.

We waited another five minutes, debating what Eunice wanted us there for, then knocked again. There was no response. I tried the door.

"It's unlocked," I said, opening it.

"That's strange," said Fran. "Eunice is almost compulsive about locking up."

Fran crowded behind me as I went into the small living room. The place had been tossed. Furniture was overturned and out of place, papers strewn all over. I saw a pair of legs near the desk on the side wall and went to look, my stomach doing three kinds of flip-flops. I shouldn't have. I barely saw Eunice's wide-eyed stare and the cord around her neck before I ran from the room and heaved onto the bushes underneath the porch.

It was that thing with dead bodies I have. I had never been good with the idea, then got totally traumatized that first few months I was working for Sid. And, yeah, it is a problem, but prior to that night, I'd always had Sid nearby to run interference for me.

"Are you okay?" Fran asked as I caught my breath.

"I don't know. Is she?"

Fran began sobbing. "Yes."

I let myself break down in sobs, too. Dwight came up and put his arms around both me and Fran and held us gently.

It didn't matter. I remained in a fog and wasn't exactly conscious when Sergeant Renecke, of the Appleton PD, approached me.

I told him the simple truth of what Eunice had said to me, assuming she'd said the same or something similar to Dwight, Steve, and Fran. I don't know how I was able to drive back to the Victorian mansion, but Steve had somehow beaten me there. I saw his car in the driveway.

I climbed the stairs to the third floor, feeling each step in every fiber of my being. I barely knocked and Sid was there, enfolding me into his arms and whispering encouragement.

He shut the door and held me as I sobbed. Finally, I was able to catch enough of my breath for Sid to lead me to the couch.

"Are you going to be okay?" he asked gently as he sat me down.

"It's bad enough losing Eunice," I said. "But I feel so stupid, upchucking all over the front bushes. This is terrible. You'd think I'd be able to handle myself better after all this time."

"It hasn't been that long, honey." Sid sat down and pulled me close to him. "And you manage."

"I've always had you around to help me."

"Well, you managed without me tonight, and you'll manage it without me again sometime."

"I'm glad you think so. And Eunice. I really loved her."

"I know. I liked her a lot, too." Sid kissed the side of my head. "But Steve called when he got home. We need to conference. I told him I'd call if you came here. Think you can handle it?"

I sniffed and sat up straight. "I have to."

Steve appeared moments later while I was in the bathroom trying to wipe off the streaks of mascara running down my cheeks without disturbing too much of the contouring that I did with my makeup.

"Hey," Steve said as I came into the living room. "Good cover with the barfing."

"Thanks," I said, trying not to shudder.

"You okay?" Steve came over and gave me a hug.

I coughed at the smell of cigarette. "Well, I'm upset. Eunice was becoming a good friend."

"I know." Steve sighed and began pacing. "But why kill her?"

"I don't think it was because she was stealing the formula," Sid said.

"I found a KGB nerve agent ampule taped next to the light switch on her desk lamp," Steve said. "And all her floppy disks were gone."

"But if Max is still working on the formula, why take her out?" I sank onto the couch. "That doesn't make sense. Besides, there's what she told us today. There were decisions to be made. She invited me, you, Fran, and Dwight. I think she found something and wasn't sure what to do about it."

"She didn't invite Max," Steve said.

"We don't know that she didn't," I said. "He may simply not have shown."

"Decent odds on that." Steve pawed at his shirt pocket, then shook a fist in frustration.

Sid sighed. "Look, I don't think we're going to get any further on this tonight. Let's get some sleep and we'll try and post something on the bulletin board tomorrow."

Steve and I agreed, and I let Steve walk me out to my car. It was probably good for my cover, too.

October 25, 1984

I was up by eight that next morning, though not by choice. My sleep had again been shattered by dreams of bright red blood on a wall. I put my running suit on more out of habit than any real expectation that I'd actually run. Fortunately, Fran saved me by knocking on the front door to my apartment and calling out.

"Coming!" I called back right away.

As I went to the door, I realized her car had not been in the driveway when I'd gotten home the night before. I wondered where she had been.

"Hey," I said gently. "Come on in."

"Thanks." Fran wandered in with a blank look on her face.

"How are you doing?" I asked.

"Terrible." Fran sounded as if she were about to break down, but then she pulled herself together. "She was my best friend. I can't believe that she's gone. And in such a horrible way. I tell you, when I saw her, I almost up-chucked, too."

"At least, you didn't." I felt my face growing hot.

"Anyway, I just got a call from Mrs. Spinetti. All humanities classes are canceled today, and Joe Cunningham has a faculty meeting scheduled for three o'clock. Dwight Atwater called Joe last night. He also said he'd take care of notifying Eunice's family."

"That's a blessing."

Fran sat down on the couch. "I just can't stop wondering who would do such a thing, and all I can think is that it must have had something to do with that mysterious meeting of hers."

"Did you tell anyone else about it?" I sat down next to her. "I don't think she told us not to."

"No." Fran frowned. "Come to think of it, I didn't. I thought it was something she wanted to keep between the two of us, maybe some plot to get Joe Cunningham in trouble. I was surprised to see you and Dwight, and then Steve Carmona. Do you think Dwight or Steve may have said something?"

"I went over to Steve's for dinner." As I thought, I pulled my legs up under me. "I told him I had to leave early to go to Eunice's, and he said he'd been invited, too. He thought she wanted help with her computer, so I don't think he would have said anything. He couldn't figure out why she'd asked me to be there. She told me there were decisions to be made."

Fran blinked. "That's what she told me. But what could it mean?"

"I haven't the faintest idea."

Fran looked me and frowned. "And you and Steve were together the whole evening."

"Yeah. Come to think of it. What about you?"

"I, as they say, have no alibi." She sank down into herself, vainly trying not to weep. "I was in my office grading papers. In fact, I waved at Dwight in the parking lot as I got into my car to go over there."

I reached over and hugged her. "Fran, you had no reason to kill Eunice. I know cops say they need to suspect everybody, but they usually have a fairly good idea of who killed a person. I'm sure they're making an arrest even now."

Fran nodded, and my stomach gurgled loudly.

"I'm sorry. I haven't eaten yet. Have you?"

"Come to think of it, no."

"All right. Why don't I change clothes real fast, and we'll go get something to eat?"

"I don't know if I can."

I sighed and got up. "I know what you mean, but you need to get something on your stomach."

"You're probably right."

"I'll be right back."

I drove. The two of us went to a coffee shop near the edge of town. It was part of a national chain, and the food wasn't particularly good, but neither of us wanted to go to Barb's Diner, where we'd eaten with Eunice so many times.

"Why us?" Fran asked as she sipped some coffee and picked at a bowl of fruit.

"What do you mean?" I was busy shoveling in eggs, bacon, toast, and hash browns.

"Why did she invite the four of us? I mean, I'm kind of obvious. We're best friends. She liked you a lot, even though you're new. And you've been feisty. So, if the meeting was about getting Joe Cunningham, that would make sense. Dwight, she trusts, too. He's been a good ally over the years. But Steve? Why him? I mean, they're friends, but it's mostly about computer stuff."

"Maybe her little plan had something to do with computers." I chewed a bit of bacon, thinking and trying not to think. I'd been asking the same questions all the night before and hadn't come up with anything that made sense. "And why wasn't Max there? He's one of her friends."

"I don't think she asked him." Fran frowned. "He didn't know about the meeting."

"You talked to him already?"

Fran nervously stabbed a bit of sliced banana. "This morning. He's pretty upset."

Her gaze drifted off toward the door, as if she were trying to make sense of something.

"It had to have been what got her killed," she said, finally. She sniffed, then pressed her lips together. "You know, I can't get her face like that out of my head."

"I can't, either." I swallowed down the lurching in my stomach.

"It was so horrible. Dwight took me outside. Steve had to call the police from her bedroom phone because the one in the living room..." Fran swallowed. "It was that cord. It took the cops forever to show, and they're usually pretty prompt."

Which meant that Steve had taken his time calling them. No surprise there. I knew he'd done a sweep of the place.

Closing my eyes, I tried to subdue the whirl of emotions in my gut. However upset I was, I still needed to work this case, and do it quickly before someone else got killed. Like Sid. I gasped, then my brain finally began to settle.

I debated calling in a request for the police reports on Eunice. Terry could do the pickup. Or maybe Tim. And somebody would have to search the house again. I'd have Kathy do that as soon as the cops were done. At least, she wouldn't have to worry about Eunice coming home and surprising her.

"What if it was a burglar?" I asked suddenly. "Maybe Eunice surprised somebody breaking into her house and that's why she was killed. Maybe the meeting didn't have anything to do with it."

Fran nodded. "I guess. But what would Eunice have to steal?"

"I don't know." And I really didn't. Her floppy disks were gone, but Steve hadn't said whether anything else was missing. There was also that ampule set up on the switch to the desk lamp. Steve hadn't said whether it had been sprung.

I picked up the check, and we decided we should go to school. I offered to drop Fran off at the apartment house so that she could get her car, but Fran said she'd walk home if I wasn't ready to go when she was.

"Do you want me to stay with you?" I asked.

"Thanks, Janet. That's awfully sweet of you. But I think I need some alone time, if you know what I mean."

"Yeah, I do."

But we were not to get it. As soon as Fran and I entered Lawrence Hall, Mrs. Spinetti haughtily insisted that we go to the conference room to talk to Sergeant Renecke. Dwight Atwater was already there.

"All right," said the detective. He was around average height, but built like a bull, with full shoulders and small hips. His blond hair had thinned so much the top of his head shone in the fluorescent lights of the conference room. He wore a tan polyester suit and had laid a yellow vinyl raincoat with a police insignia on it over one of the chairs at the end of the table. He yawned. "I want to talk to the three of you about this meeting Dr. Blakely had set up."

"I thought you were supposed to interview us separately," Fran said.

Renecke chuckled. "Usually, but I did that last night. Besides, Dr. Carmona confirmed that you and Dr. Atwater were signed into the university computer system from before the time Dr. Blakely was likely killed."

"The coroner was able to determine it that fast?" I asked.

"Oh, hell no." Renecke scratched the back of his neck and sat down. "They can't pinpoint a time of death like that, anyway. Her neighbor talked to her at eight-thirty last night. You found her at ten. You two, Atwater and Mercer, were signed into the computer system until right before ten o'clock. You, Dr. Mayfield, were having dinner with Dr. Carmona. Which means you guys are not suspects and there's no reason to talk to you separately. Now, about that meeting."

"But she didn't tell us anything about it," Dwight said. He thought. "She seemed a little nervous, maybe worried about something. But I have no idea what it was about."

"The only thing I can think of was something to get rid of Dr. Cunningham," Fran said. "Janet and I have been talking it over, and that's what makes the most sense. Although, I don't know why she'd want Steve Carmona there, unless her scheme involved the campus computer system."

"Did any of you tell anyone else about it?" Renecke asked.

"I just told my wife that I was working late," Dwight said. "She asked about it and I told her that Eunice had something she wanted to discuss with me later. My wife said to tell her hello."

I nodded. "I only mentioned it to Steve when we were having dinner because I had to get over there, and it turned out he'd been invited, too."

"And I thought it was about Joe Cunningham," Fran said. "So, I had no reason to say anything to anyone."

"About Cunningham." Renecke said. "There was plenty of bad blood there, and I was told by someone else that Dr. Blakely had made him and some other fellows a little anxious at a faculty meeting the other day."

Dwight laughed. "Eunice did that on a regular basis."

"She implied that some of us had committed unnamed indiscretions," Fran snorted. "Joe, Ernie, and Ted were the ones who reacted."

"Any of them have a secret worth killing for?" Renecke asked.

I looked at Dwight and Fran, who both shrugged.

"I've heard rumors that Ernie is still ABD," Dwight said. "But to the best of my knowledge, he finished his dissertation several years ago."

"Could it have been a burglar?" I asked. "Maybe she surprised him."

Renecke shifted. "We have reason to believe it was not a burglar." He looked at the three of us, and I got the funny feeling he wanted to tell us about the ampule of KGB nerve agent just to see how we'd react, but he couldn't because, well, that was top secret. "Do you know if Dr. Blakely had any connection to Marina Swanson or Reed Dupont?"

"Who are they?" I asked, even though I knew.

"Those were the two students who died last spring," Dwight said. "There was some explosion in her car, and I think Dupont got sick suddenly."

"Well, you must have checked Eunice's class lists," Fran said. "Did she have them for any classes?"

"No," said Renecke. "But they each had classes with Max Beard. Swanson was a Second Career student. Dupont was majoring in drawing and painting with a minor in comp sci."

"That's not surprising," Fran said. "Max usually teaches three sections of lower-level history in the spring, and he is fairly popular with the students."

But Fran did not know what I knew about how those students had really died. Again, I got the feeling from the way Renecke was watching us that he was looking for a reaction that did not belong. I wondered what he knew. Which meant that requesting the police report on Eunice was no longer a matter of debate. I needed the report and to send a report upline as well. I hadn't sent a report yet because I hadn't had anything to report, although Sid had mentioned somewhere that he'd checked in occasionally.

Renecke let us go back to our offices after that. I immediately signed into the computer system and the special bulletin board. Steve had already posted his interview with Renecke, who had asked pretty much the same questions. He had also asked Steve why someone would steal Eunice's floppy disks. Steve was a little worried that Renecke might getting too close to our investigation, and with good reason. The formula and Max were super top-secret.

I posted what Renecke had told Dwight, Fran, and me, as well as my plans to have Kathy and Tim search Eunice's place as soon as the cops were done with it, to phone in the request for the police report, and then send a report upline.

I wondered about adding a thought I'd had as I'd gone back to my office. Eunice's comment had startled not just Ted, Ernie, and Cunningham. It had also startled Max. Now, if Max was developing the formula, then it would make sense that he'd be worried that Eunice might know what he was up to. But he'd also have the least reason to kill Eunice unless she was the thief. But if she was the thief, and that's why Max had killed her, why was there a KGB ampule rigged to her desk lamp?

If Joe Cunningham was up to no good, then he'd have a reason to be worried about Eunice's little joke, especially since Eunice was clearly trying to rid the university of him. But physically, he didn't seem up to strangling a tall woman like Eunice.

Ted, on the other hand, was big enough and probably strong enough to do the deed, but he had the least reason, as far as I knew. Some fudged data that he had promptly fixed many years ago might make getting tenure a little harder, but hardly insurmountable, and not nearly hard enough to kill someone over it. Plus, he'd told me about it.

If Ernie hadn't completed his dissertation, letting that out could cause him a lot more trouble. Still, he was so burned out, he might find getting fired a relief. Or he might fight tooth and nail over it. Killing someone, how-ever, seemed far-fetched.

I got lunch at the Commons, more out of desperation than anything else, and ate it there. Kathy Richards came by the table, and I asked her to contact Tim and search Eunice's. By the time I got back to Lawrence Hall, it was time for the faculty meeting. I was a little surprised to see Renecke there, sitting quietly in the back of the room.

Ernie was fretting and whining about how terrible it was and none of us were safe in our own beds, and, really, the university needed to do something to ensure the safety of its faculty. Most of the rest of the group was somber, with an extra layer of tension enveloping us. Fran's eyes were reasonably dry, but it didn't look like that would last. The only two missing were Max and Ted.

Cunningham was nervous, too. But I realized why when he looked directly at me shortly after opening the meeting.

"Losing Eunice has been a significant loss for our department," Cunningham began sonorously. "However, as I'm sure she would have agreed, life does go on and we do have students to tend to. I have hired an adjunct professor, Dr. Littleton, from UW Madison, to take on Eunice's World History classes. However, there remains Eunice's Elizabethan England seminar. Janet, I have decided that since your Shakespeare seminar has only eight students, and Eunice's class has only nine, to combine the two classes. There's certainly enough overlap with the history, don't you think? I'm assuming you're up to the challenge, of course."

I smiled, trying to think of Shakespearean insults to toss his way.

"Well, one doesn't want to go rushing into these things," I said slowly, trying to buy time.

I had two options. I could give him hell and complain to the provost, which he would interpret as me not being up to it (which I had to concede, I possibly wasn't), or I could accept the challenge and let him wade in his victory over me. But then a third possibility occurred to me.

"I'd have to re-do the course outline," I said, as if I were thinking aloud. "And you know, the play Titus Andronicus, that's set in the classical period, and the histories are a little early for the Elizabethan period. I've got it. I'll teach Merry Wives of Windsor instead of Titus. The play is strongly associated with Elizabeth I, which is, I believe, the subject of Eunice's seminar. What a great idea, interlacing the history of England's greatest queen with a play by England's greatest dramatist. Joe, you're a genius."

"But, eh... But..." Cunningham gaped.

I noticed several shoulders in the room shaking with suppressed laughter. Sadly, so did Cunningham.

"Janet, we do want to be conscious of maintaining decorum," he said, finally.

"Of course," I said. "'If I were disposed to stir your hearts and minds to mutiny and rage, I should do Brutus wrong.'"

Cunningham looked at me strangely. I decided to help him out.

"The second half of Antony's eulogy over Caesar, act three, scene two," I said quickly.

"Oh! Of course. Nice quote."

Still, I didn't miss the glare he shot my way just before clearing his throat and gathering his notes together.

"We also have the matter of Eunice's memorial," Cunningham continued. "I have reserved the campus chapel for a service on Sunday afternoon at two o'clock. I have asked Max Beard to conduct it, as he was Eunice's good friend."

Fran blinked and glared at Cunningham.

"Finally, we have as our guest today, Officer Renecke, of the Appleton Police Department. I know he has talked to several of us already, but I would appreciate it if you all cooperate fully with him."

Odd. Cunningham's eyes landed on me at that moment. Renecke cleared his throat loudly and stood up.

"First up, I'm *Sergeant* Peter Renecke," he said. "I know this murder has come as quite a shock to you all, and I respect that. However, I'm also sure that you want this cleared up as badly as I do. So, if any of you has any information that you think might be relevant, I want you to call me. It's my job to decide what is relevant and what isn't. So, even if you only think you saw or heard something, I want to know about it. Thank you for your time. Dr. Cunningham?"

"I think that will be all for today. Let us adjourn the meeting." Cunningham all but ran from the room. The others filed out, but first Dwight patted my shoulder, then Fran gave me a hug.

I noticed Renecke watching me and waited.

"Julius Caesar, right?" he asked.

"Yes. I'm teaching it this quarter."

"Yeah. I heard there was a dust up between you and Cunningham over that."

I pressed my lips together. "He took over my class, and I had to file a complaint with the provost."

Renecke nodded. "He's not the one who's dead."

"I know." I shut my eyes to keep from crying.

"Good thing. I'd have to be looking more closely at you." Renecke laughed. "So why the fireworks between you two?"

I shrugged. "He's into power games? I also heard that the Chancellor hired me over his head, which probably didn't help."

"You were friends with Eunice Blakely."

"I was." I blinked again and a couple tears escaped after all. "I didn't know her very long, but I'd really come to love her."

"I'm hearing that you're the odds-on favorite to take up her mantle in the fight against Cunningham."

"I have nothing personal against Joe Cunningham per se," I said. "I just don't like bull puckey."

"And he's full of it." Renecke laughed again. "By the way, the quote?"

"Yeah, from the 'Friends, Romans, and Countrymen' speech."

"'I come to bury Caesar, not to praise him.'"

I found myself smiling. "Very good."

"Funny what sticks with you." He shrugged. "It's been a while since I was in high school, but I seem to remember that speech was about Marc Antony turning everybody against Brutus."

"Exactly."

"So that line you quoted, even though he's saying he doesn't want to do Brutus wrong, that's exactly what he's doing."

"Yes."

Renecke nodded at the door. "You think Cunningham got that?"

"I have no idea." I looked at the door through which Cunningham had fled. "I'll try to be charitable and say he did."

"He and Dr. Blakely did not get along."

"Eunice ran circles around him. She wasn't about to put up with his nonsense, and, surprise, surprise, he didn't deal with that well."

"Hm." He, too, looked out the door thoughtfully.

"You don't think...?"

"There's some other stuff." He looked at me. "I can't talk about an open investigation." He patted my shoulder. "But thanks for talking to me."

He walked out the door.

I didn't want to assume. As I had told Tim Hannaford however long ago, assumptions can get you dead in no time. However, I had pointed out that instinct does have a place, and at that moment, my gut instinct was screaming that Renecke liked Joe Cunningham for the murder. If he liked Cunningham, there had to be a reason, perhaps one I should be looking for, as well.

I went back to my office. It looked like everyone, including Ted, had gone home. I got my leather gloves and searched Eunice's office. It was relatively easy, as the lights had been left on. There was nothing there I wouldn't expect, although I pulled her syllabus and notes for her Elizabethan seminar. She had several floppy disks for her computer, all neatly labeled, but all of them were related to coursework or journal articles. I took them just in case. The only odd thing I found was a copy of a Leticia Petrie novel. The interior had been marked up heavily, but not in any way that made immediate sense to me. I took it, too, and left the office, turning out the lights as I did.

October 27 – 28, 1984

F riday, most of us stumbled through our classes. I'd gotten my report done and slid it to Terry with her homework. Terry looked a little worried and stayed after to make sure she understood. I told her to make the pickup on the police reports when those came through. I also got an interesting invite from Steve.

He picked me up that Saturday morning at close to eleven.

"So, what have you got for me?" I asked as he pulled the car out of the driveway at my apartment.

"Absolutely nothing." Steve grinned nonetheless.

"Then where are we going?"

"On an old-fashioned picnic."

"What?"

"Look. We have been beating our heads against this wall for days, if not weeks. It's time to do something strictly for the fun of it and relax a little."

"And hopefully, our subconscious minds will come up with a solution." I sat back in the car seat with a satisfied smile. "Thanks. That's a great idea."

I rolled the window down a crack, despite the chill in the air. Steve's car had been cleaned, but the stench of cigarette was still under the reek of the artificial sweetness of a chemical air freshener.

The park was small and mostly deserted. No surprise. Dark clouds covered the sky, and the temperatures were in the low fifties. Steve had picked up a cue or two from Sid, because he covered the picnic table with a red-checked cloth tablecloth, and there was a decent bottle of cabernet sauvignon in the basket. Sadly, the menu also featured peanut butter and jelly sandwiches and Twinkies. Not that I don't like either, but not with a good, solid red wine.

I let it go. Steve and I ate and talked about university politics and the generally hell-bound state of the world. He told me about all the cool things I could read on the ARPANET, and I had to admit, that was fascinating. But then I spotted something. I jumped up and ran to the playground.

"What are you doing?" Steve yelped.

"Swings!" I ran over and slid onto one and started pumping. "I love swings."

Steve laughed, but still looked perplexed. "Aren't you afraid some student is going to see you?"

"Who cares? I hate teachers who can't be human."

The chain was jerking as I soared higher and higher. I eased off and let the swing carry me back and forth until I decided to jump off it.

"You're nuts, lady," Steve said.

I couldn't tell if he was amused or appalled, or both.

"It's who I really am." I said.

Steve looked at me and smiled. "Yeah. I think I get that. That first night when I broke into your apartment. You were cool, like you should have been, then, I don't know. You saw something in me and became all nice."

I shrugged. "Also, who I am."

Steve stepped up closer to me. "I'm starting to see that. I gotta tell you, I'm really liking what I see."

I stepped back. "Steve, we're friends."

"Yeah. Like you're friends with Ed."

I flushed. "That's different."

"How? You guys keep saying you're not a couple, but it sure doesn't look like that."

I closed my eyes. "The problem is we're not. It's complicated. We're probably headed that way. We're just not there yet."

"Because he keeps running around."

"Which he's probably doing because I won't sleep with him." I blinked back tears. "It's all about our values. They just don't mesh right now. We're getting there." I looked at him. "I'm sorry. You and I, all we'll ever be is friends. I really like being friends with you. You're a really great guy."

"But there's this other guy, who's acting like a complete ass and breaking your heart—"

"He's not!" I looked Steve in the eyes. "He really isn't. Neither of us can help being who we are. He was raised to believe in free love. I was raised to believe in marriage. Yeah, things are at an impasse right now." I took a deep breath. "The funny thing is, I'm happier with the impasse than I am being without him. I've really thought about it. I've had to. He's my best friend. And he's more than that."

Steve looked away. "I was hoping I could be more than that."

I chuckled sadly. "I'm sorry. I do like you. It's just that someone else beat you to me. Not much consolation, I know. But it's the best I've got."

A big, fat raindrop landed on my nose. More followed within seconds.

We ran for the picnic table. The drops turned into a downpour.

Steve swore. "I can't do anything right!"

"It's okay," I yelled.

I moved the basket and the bottle of wine aside and gathered everything else on the table into the center of the tablecloth and gathered it together.

"It's freezing out here!" Steve said.

"I'm fine." I laughed.

"What are you laughing at?"

"This would be insanely romantic if I were actually in love with you."

"What's romantic about freezing our asses?"

"Which is the inherent difference between us."

It was. Sid might not have been excited about being so cold, but he would have laughed and maybe even been charmed that I found it romantic. Steve very clearly did not get that.

I told Steve he could drive us back to his place. He wasn't thrilled but did, anyway. As we struggled into the hallway of the mansion, he held me back.

"You know. For a while there, I thought this nerd had a shot at the gorgeous girl."

I put my hand on his face. "Maybe not this girl, and I am very honored that you think I'm gorgeous. But you've got more than a shot at the next one. You're a great guy, Steve. Really."

I kissed his cheek and ran all the way up to Sid's apartment. I had no reason to believe that he was home and couldn't help being gratified when I heard the piano music coming from the other side of his door. I knocked, then knocked again, a little more loudly.

The music stopped. I could almost feel him checking me out through the peephole in the door, and then he opened it.

"You're wet," he said.

"Yeah. Steve took me on a picnic. Can I come in?"

"Uh, yeah. Let me get a couple towels."

The apartment was nice and toasty, and Sid's towels were very fluffy and nice.

"What the hell happened?" Sid asked as I blotted my clothes off.

"Steve wanted to do something relaxing and took me on a picnic. It was, alas, a gesture doomed to failure and not because of the rain."

"Oh."

"I told you the casual dating thing wasn't going to work."

Sid sighed. "I suppose I should be grateful for that."

I shrugged. "That's up to you."

He looked me over and shook his head. "I've got a t-shirt and some sweatpants in the other room. I'll put them in the bathroom, and you can go change."

"I'm okay."

"You're dribbling on my floor." A rueful smile flitted across his face, even though his tone said that he was a little annoyed.

"I'll wipe it up." I smiled back at him. "Thanks."

He went into the bedroom, then ushered me into the bathroom and left me alone. I changed quickly, laying out my t-shirt, sweater, and jeans over the edge of his bathtub, and my deck shoes alongside. I also washed my face.

"So, what happened?" Sid asked as I came into the living room. "I get the rain part, but what about the rest of it?"

"Well, Steve's been having trouble figuring us out and thought he had a shot at me. He's a nice guy. He just isn't you."

"I see." Sid smiled, looking somewhat relieved. "I guess now you're going to have to accept it when I tell you how attractive and sensual you really are. You can't just call it a quirk on my part or friendship."

He smiled his hot little smile, and I caught my breath, then flushed.

"Okay," I said, turning away. "Given Steve, I'll let you have attractive. But how sensual can I be when I'm always saying no?"

Sid laughed loudly. "You have no idea, my dear little ice maiden."

"Exactly my point."

Sid grabbed my hands. "No. You're not getting it. That's the joke. You are anything but an ice maiden. You are a very, very sensual, sexy woman. When the time comes, and I finally unlock that mental chastity belt of yours, pray forgive me for putting it this way, but you are going to make for one hot little lay."

I swallowed. "I'm glad you think so. But what difference does it make?"

"If it makes you feel better about yourself, maybe a lot."

I winced. He had, as he so often did, gotten me to my core.

"Which is why I'm here and not downstairs," I said. "You get me. You always have. He doesn't."

"I wasn't worried about that."

"Yeah, right."

Sid winced. "Okay. We're even. You get me like no one else."

I sighed and slid onto the couch. "I do think Steve had the right idea about the picnic. We've been going around and around and around on this case and have gotten nowhere. I've been reading my brains out on Merry Wives of Windsor. It's time to turn all that off and let our subconscious do its thing." I sat up. "Do you want me to make dinner?"

Sid laughed. "You can help. Once I figure out what we're going to have."

"Yeah. I did kind of barge in on you, didn't I? I can leave."

"Please don't. I'd rather spend the evening with you than just about anybody." He took one of my arms and pulled me up. "Now, come on, my darling locust, and let's see what I can feed you."

Sid's refrigerator and pantry were better stocked than he'd hinted. We ended up throwing together a chicken and vegetable stir-fry over brown rice, and Sid opened a nice imported Riesling to go with it. We'd had to make do with dried pepper flakes, however. We hadn't found any fresh chiles in Wisconsin.

After dinner, Sid put a tape full of John Denver tunes on the reel to reel. We snuggled on the couch, and he laughed as I sang along to Rocky Mountain High.

"Pretty bad, huh?" I said.

"No. You've got a nice voice and a decent ear. You just need to listen to yourself better and do better breath support."

I felt him nuzzling into my hair and I sighed happily.

"I'm glad I'm here," I said some minutes later. "It's been a really terrible week."

"I know. It's been pretty awful on my end, too."

"Hey, but I'm here now."

"Yeah." His eyes glowed, and he bent his head.

It was a glorious kiss. I melted into his arms. It didn't stop either. I let myself slide backwards onto the couch and he followed me down, his lips kissing my eyes, my nose, and back to my lips again and again. He stroked my hair, then moaned softly when I kissed the inside of his wrist. He dropped kiss after gentle kiss along my jawline to my ear, and then down the back of my neck and I moaned. I reached under his chin and lifted his head to look into his beautiful eyes. My heart nearly pounded itself out of my chest as we gazed at each other, then kissed some more.

The warmth and excitement spread through me. I loved this man like I had loved no one else, and all I wanted was to give myself to him, to be with him. I knew I was special. I knew I was unlike anyone else in his life. But that was the problem. I wasn't the only person in his life. I felt myself cooling and tried to focus on the excitement I'd felt.

I could be his only person. I knew it. The only reason he ran around was because I wouldn't give him what he needed. And I was ready at that point. I wanted to be ready. I needed to be ready. I kissed him harder.

He drew back.

"Getting a little carried away, are we?" he asked gently.

"I wish we were."

He chuckled sadly and stroked my face. "Lisapet, you're not ready. And I don't want you forcing yourself. It would ruin everything."

"I just wish I could be what you need."

"You are what I need." He sighed. "I promised you, when we come together, it will be in joy or it will not happen."

"I thought we had joy just now."

"Close, too damned close in some respects, but not entirely." He sat up. "And that's okay."

"Really?"

He made a face. "Yeah. You can't change who you are any more than I can change who I am. But we'll find a way. Somehow. I just don't know how yet."

"I don't either."

He pulled me up. "Then let's try not to worry about it."

Sid took me home rather later, when it was well after midnight, and it wasn't likely anyone would notice him doing it. I was kind of stuck since Steve had driven me there. The rain had slowed to a mist. I still had on Sid's t-shirt and sweats and my clothes were in a plastic bag. He let me off in the alley behind my apartment with a solid, sweet kiss. If the KGB saw us, all they saw was an illicit romance.

The rain continued well into the next day. It was as if some screenwriter was setting the scene for Eunice's memorial. The trees were almost bare and damp leaves littered streets and sidewalks.

I took off early to make my phone calls. Nick was happier, but still a little antsy. Mae was just sick and tired of dealing with five kids and a husband. I listened but had to cut Mae off to get back to Appleton in time for the memorial.

It was an emotional service. The stone walls of the gothic-style chapel still echoed loudly, even with the hushed voices. Dozens of students from all the different majors turned up, many of them young women, weeping openly. Steve Carmona sat near the front across the center aisle from me and gave me the occasional baleful stare. Ed/Sid sat in the back with Jason de Boeur, Rita Farley, Mark Ayers, Terry, and Sherry Van Wettering. The entire humanities staff was there, as were the wives of those who had them. Ernie, Cunningham, and Ted all looked particularly pale and shaky. I sat in the first row next to Fran and held her hand. Max was on her other side, and Dwight and his wife were on my other side.

The Madrigal Choir sang two lovely motets from a requiem mass, then a lively and slightly ribald madrigal that had all of us laughing and crying at the same time. Then they wound up with, of all things, The Philosopher's Song, from the Monty Python movie that had come out a couple of years before.

Max took the podium at that moment. Even with the slightly chilly air, his balding scalp glistened with perspiration.

"Some of you may think that a Monty Python tune might not be the most appropriate for a funeral," he said slowly. His hands twisted on the sides of the podium top. "But if anyone exemplified the ability to think you under a table, it was Eunice Blakely. Not to mention her ability to drink us all under the table without a sweat. She was vastly curious about everything, and while her passion was history, she loved exploring the sciences as well. Any new technology, she wanted it. My god, she had a personal computer back in 1977, when most of us didn't even know what one was. But to me, she was more than a friend. She was like my big sister, who hounded me and gave me grief, but let anyone give me trouble, and she'd be all over him." Max took a deep breath. "In many ways, she was like a big sister to all of us, one we loved, even as she made us crazy with her exacting standards and wild sense of humor."

I tried not to cry. I didn't want mascara all over my cheeks and have to risk messing up my contouring to get it off. But I was hardly the only one wiping my nose at Max's words. Then Fran took her place at the podium.

The tears streamed down her face. "I don't have much to say. Eunice was my mentor and champion, and now she's gone."

A soft wail rose through the chapel, and I realized that Eunice had been a mentor and champion for so many of the young women there.

"Eunice was also the best friend I've ever had," Fran continued. "She was closer to me than my own mother. Okay, maybe that's not saying much, but it made all the difference in the world to me. I loved her so dearly."

At that point, Fran broke down completely and Dwight Atwater helped her from the podium and returned her to the pew where we'd all been sitting. Max got up to let her in, then I put my arms around her as she cried.

The Madrigal Choir sang again, then the university president got up, read John Donne's Death be Not Proud, and gave a benediction. The choir sang two more motets, and then we all filed out of the chapel into the rain.

I was standing near Fran and Max when Jason and Sherry came up.

"Dr. Mayfield?" Jason asked tentatively, his umbrella bumping into mine. "Is there going to be Off Campus Office Hours today?"

I sighed and nodded. "Sure. Why not?" I turned to Fran and Max. "Would you two like to join us?"

"No," said Max quickly. "But, Fran, why don't you go? It might do you some good to get with the young people."

"Thanks." Fran blinked. "Both of you. But no." Her mouth took on a grim set. "I've got some things of my own to do. Janet, we need to have a meeting. Maybe later this week, after we've had some time to get ourselves together." Fran blinked and wept. "We now have to take up where Eunice left off in terms of protecting the women here."

"Of course. Let me know when you're ready." I dabbed at my eyes.

There was a small reception in the Faculty Dining Room, which had apparently been catered by some outside company. Not only was there enough food, it was good. There was wine, beer, and even shots of whiskey. I had no idea who was paying for it, but was grateful.

Cunningham was trying to look as if he were deeply grieved. I'm not sure if anybody bought it. The Madrigal Choir and some of the other music students gathered in one corner of the room and began singing Renaissance drinking songs. I saw Terry Michaels with a shot of whiskey in her hand and wondered why the catering staff wasn't being more careful about checking IDs. Steve Carmona seemed to be dedicated to getting drunk on someone else's dime. Given the way he kept looking sadly at me, I realized why and sighed.

As such parties do, things got louder as the afternoon wore on. Ted Curtis was the first to leave, with Cunningham following closely on his tail. Ryan Martin had found a chair in the corner and was already asleep, his wife glaring at him in fury in between chatting with Fred Wirth's wife. David Watts never showed up at all. I'd seen him in the crowd at the chapel with Ilona Swedburg by his side. I had finished my last plate of hors d'oeuvres and was debating getting some more when Ernie Lavalle sidled up next to me.

"Such a sad day," he said, as I stepped away from him. He stepped closer, bumping up next to me. "You must be feeling pretty bad right now."

"Back off, Ernie, or you'll be feeling worse."

"I could comfort you." He grabbed me with a surprisingly strong grip.

I tried to wriggle away, but he held on, his boozy breath hot on my neck.

"We both need comforting," he whined. "Come on!"

He tried to pull me away, but I twisted and caught his hand and bent it back. He wailed in pain.

"I said no." I bent some more, and he wailed again. People were staring.

I flushed and let go, then shoved Ernie toward the wall.

"Where did you learn to do that?" Dr. Ermengarde bellowed from across the room.

"Self-defense class." I gulped. "Doesn't everybody take one?"

"No, but we shall." Dr. Ermengarde raised her glass to me, and I nodded.

The room returned to their conversations, and I decided it was time to leave. Fran had already left, and Max was getting on his raincoat. Inside, I tried not to worry about my cover, about Ernie being significantly stronger than he looked and his attempt at grabbing me, about bursting into tears and wiping away my contouring. Ed/Sid winked at me from across the room.

I was late for Off Campus Office Hours. Marge Haver and Rick Waters were already there and had ordered pizzas, beer, and cola. Marge had a shapely brunette with her and introduced her as Stephanie O'Connor. I'd seen her at the chapel weeping freely.

"I was in Dr. Blakely's Elizabethan seminar," Stephanie said, offering me a watery smile. "I'm told we're going to be in your Shakespeare class now?"

"Yes. It should be interesting." I smiled, even though I knew I was woefully under-prepared.

"Okay." Stephanie frowned. "Are we really going to be reading Titus Andronicus?"

I patted her hand. "Don't worry. I've changed that. We're doing Merry Wives of Windsor. More tie-ins to Elizabeth I."

Stephanie brightened.

"Huzzah!" yelped Marge. "I was not looking forward to reading the miserable blood bath that is Titus Andronicus."

"It is pretty miserable," I said.

Ed/Sid and Jason arrived next. Jason was not entirely sober.

"Way to put Dr. Lavalle down, Dr. Mayfield!" he crowed. "He is such a slimeball, man."

I flushed, then caught a slightly angry cast to Ed's grin, as if he'd wanted a turn at Lavalle, too. He helped Jason to a chair and himself to a glass of beer.

Terry and Sherry showed up, with Kathy close behind. I thought I saw Tim Hannaford outside, but he'd apparently seen Ed and decided he'd better not show. Terry was a little tiddly and still managed to stuff several manilla envelopes into my purse without anyone noticing. I reached under the table and slid Kathy the Leticia Petrie novel I'd found. She slid me a note. The group got noisy and even maudlin. Soon the only sober people at the table were me, Kathy, and Ed. Terry had already left, taking Sherry with her, as Sherry had gotten sick. Jason passed out soon after, which was why Ed was hanging around. I took a chance and nodded slightly toward the door. He nodded, yes, he was still being tailed, and I saw a man sitting at the bar, casually glancing our way every now and then. Fortunately, the table was backed into the corner, so I don't think the man had seen Terry, Kathy, and me trading stuff around.

I suddenly sighed, the weight of the day finally getting unbearable.

"I'm going home, guys," I announced, getting up.

Jason snorted, and Marge gave me a very sloppy and beery hug. The man at the bar watched me leave, but as I drove home, there was no sign of a tail. The trip wires on my apartment were all sound, and no one was broadcasting anything. In fact, the only sound I heard as I stood in the foyer was sobbing from behind Fran's door. I knocked.

"Fran, you okay?"

"Please. I need to be by myself."

"I'll be upstairs if you need anything."

"Thanks."

The stairs creaked as I walked up them and hopefully drowned out the sound of my own crying.

October 29, 1984

I honestly don't know how I taught two sections of Basic Comp that next day, but I did. I got the mail sorted before classes and handed it to Ed and Tim with their homework. The police reports that Terry had slipped me noted the ampule in Eunice's house and it had not been sprung, nor had the coroner's screen for toxins shown any trace of nerve agent or even alcohol in her body. The prints in the house all belonged to Eunice, although the crime scene techs had picked up some glove smudges on the desk.

Kathy's note said that she and Tim had searched the house thoroughly, but had found nothing. Any floppy disks that had been there had been taken, and it looked like some files were missing, as well. It was probably safe to assume that Eunice's killer had taken them, although not certain. Steve posted on the bulletin board that he, Sid, and I should probably meet that night for a conference, and Steve suggested I get there around six. That was going to make things tight for weights and racquetball, and I decided that I was not in the mood, anyway.

In fact, with no one showing up for my regular office hours, I put a note on my office door and gathered up my purse and sweater. As I passed Max's office, I saw that he was in.

I probably shouldn't have used my pass key and walked in, given how skittish he was, but I needed some answers.

He looked up at me curiously. "Janet."

"We need to talk." I shut the door and made sure it was locked, then checked my bug finder. Nothing was transmitting.

Max got up and stood in front of his desk, which was again littered with papers.

"Relax, Max," I said, putting the bug finder back in my jeans' pocket. "Not only do I know what you're working on, I've got the clearance to look at it."

His eyebrows went up. "What division?"

"I'm fifty-three-Q."

"That's under FBI auspices."

"Yep. We got called in because of the formula theft."

"You weren't supposed to know about me."

"I didn't. Luckily for me, you bear down pretty hard when you write, and I picked it up off your desk blotter."

"Oh." Max looked deflated, but he went around to his desk chair and sat down. "You're good. I never suspected you."

"Thanks." I flopped into the chair in front of the desk. "The problem is, I need some answers, and I think you're the only one who has them."

"I don't know how it's being stolen." Max looked at me sadly. "I keep some of the files on the university system. I must because that's how I get them converted to machine language, and they're protected by a password that I change weekly. The print outs are meaningless to pretty much everyone, and even if someone compiles the program, it's incomplete unless you have the machine key on the other end. And, even then, there's a password to open the file."

"What did Eunice know?"

Max sighed and blinked. "Not much. I'd asked her to run the print outs to Chicago once or twice without telling her what they were, and even if she'd seen the formula, I don't think she would have been able to figure out what it was. It was all theoretical work, anyway. Eunice was good, but not that advanced, if you know what I mean."

"Did she invite you to her meeting that night?"

"No. I think she may have been trying to protect me. She did that a lot."

I shut my eyes. "Yeah. Do you have any idea what that meeting was about?"

Max thought. "She'd told me the day before that she thought somebody was spying on me. She had some evidence, but she didn't want to say who it was right away in case she was wrong. She said she needed a solid plan because it was pretty ticklish. I pointed out that it didn't matter who it was, it was ticklish because what I was working on was top secret. That's pretty much where it ended."

I looked at him. "So, how does a history professor end up working on a nerve gas formula?"

"It's an antidote," Max snarled. "I'm not doing any of that other stuff." Okay. He didn't say stuff. "I was a chemistry whiz kid. Had my PhD in chem by the time I was nineteen and The Company caught up with me. They sent me overseas to do my post-doc in West Germany. I got totally disenchanted with everything I was doing. At the same time, it was fun being around all those old buildings, and I got interested in history. So, I also took some undergraduate classes, and the next thing I knew, I was working on a second PhD." He looked up at me. "I got caught by the KGB. Got out with my life, but I'm now a known operative. Fortunately, that limited my usefulness, and I was able to finish my coursework here in the States, did my dissertation and got on here at Martin U. almost fifteen years ago." He shook his head. "Steve Carmona came on as an adjunct about ten years ago. I didn't know they'd set him up here to protect me. I thought I'd put that behind me." He snorted with disdain. "You know as well as I do that we don't retire from this business. About six years ago, The Company sucked me in to work on this antidote formula. I only agreed because no one, not even any handlers they assigned, was to know I was working on it. We still don't know how the KGB figured out that I was. They knew I was here. We weren't hiding it. Funny thing is, we're fairly sure the Soviets didn't get their hands on it until about a year ago."

"That's interesting. What about the two students that were killed? They were in your classes."

"Best I can figure, they were in the wrong place at the wrong time." Max closed his eyes. "They were good kids, damn it. And, as far as I knew, had no connection to anything but their own interests."

"And no clue who Eunice suspected."

Max shook his head. "None. Could be anyone at the university. I'm inclined to think it's probably faculty, given what Eunice said about it being ticklish."

"Like Joe Cunningham?"

Max snorted. "Not likely, but then again, no one would think that I'm writing chemical equations." He looked over at me. "I'm almost done. I'm hoping to make it to the end of the quarter for the students' sakes, but I've already called to have us extracted."

"Us?"

"Don't say anything about it, please. It's touchy. Anyway, I made up several phony bits, and sent them out with the good parts, just in case. Once I'm done, my life won't be worth two cents, so I'm taking the last part with me and getting out as soon as I can. It's just tricky. Who knew this business could be such a barrier to the people we care about?"

"Who knew, indeed?" I looked at the floor in front of me, then got up. "Okay. You know how to get a hold of me."

"I do."

"I did tell part of the team about you. They needed to know."

"I suppose."

"You'll be safer that way."

"Just find that thief and get him. He probably killed Eunice." Max looked angry.

"I'll do my best. If you think of anything, let me know."

As I left the office, a deep sadness filled me. The business was a barrier between me and my sister, between me and Nick, between Sid and Nick. Sid really wanted to take custody of his son, but couldn't, and worse yet, couldn't tell the poor kid why. Nick was left to wonder how much his father and I really loved him.

The autumn twilight had faded into dark by the time I pulled up to the Victorian mansion where Sid and Steve lived. There was no place to park in front, so I went down the street a little, parked there and walked back. As I came down the sidewalk, both Steve's and Sid's cars were in the driveway. Lights turned on behind the drawn blinds of the third-floor turret windows. I felt my bug finder buzz with a transmission. Then the turret blew up.

I stood gaping at the flames for I don't know how many minutes. Sirens wailed in the distance and grew closer. The other tenants hurried out of the building, one young couple helping an older woman, who I realized was the landlady. Neighbors gathered on the sidewalk. I kept hoping, but nowhere among the crowd did I see Sid or Steve.

The firefighters showed and went to work. I don't know how long it took to put out the fire, but it didn't seem to take that long. Still, they stayed around. As Sergeant Renecke pulled up, one of the firefighters called to the battalion chief.

"We've got a body!"

My heart in my throat, I ran over to the firefighter.

"What floor?" I shrieked.

"Second floor. Why?"

"Well, Dr. Mayfield." Sergeant Renecke came up. "What are you doing here?"

"I was going to dinner with Steve Carmona," I whimpered. "He's on the second floor. And one of my students, Ed Donaldson. He's on the third. And that's what blew up."

Renecke cursed. He went over to talk to the firefighters, and I slid away. I hid behind the hedge surrounding the back of the house, my eyes transfixed by the red lights flashing and the firefighters going back and forth. A coroner's van pulled up, with a county crime scene crew right behind it.

Suddenly, a hand clamped over my mouth and strong arms pulled me further behind the hedge. I started struggling until I realized the arms were so familiar, and his lips were kissing my hair.

"I'm sorry I had to do that," he whispered into my ear. "I didn't want you to scream."

"You're alive!" I broke down. "I was so scared. I saw your car and the lights go on. Then the bug finder went off."

"It went off?" Sid cursed. "Must have been radio detonated."

He suddenly kissed me hard on the mouth. I grabbed him and squeezed him as tightly as I could.

"I thought you were in there," he whispered. "I knew you were coming over to Steve's, and when I saw your car parked over there, and I didn't see you, I thought you were in there."

"I saw the lights in the window," I cried again. "That had to be you. And then they said there was a body."

Sid looked over to where the lights flickered through the hedge leaves.

"Whose?" he asked.

"I think Steve."

Sid cursed again. "Now what?"

"Maybe we shouldn't let people know you made it out." I looked at where my car was. "I don't think anybody's looking."

Sid picked up his daypack. "Let's go."

I went ahead and unlocked the passenger door, then looked around. The street was empty except for the crowd surrounding the fire engines and the mansion. I waved, and Sid sauntered over to the car.

"How did you get out of there?" I asked as I started the engine.

"My bug finder went off. The trip wires had been tampered with. So, I went in slowly, turned on the lights, saw the box on the table, and slammed the door and ran like hell down the stairs." He shuddered. "The blast hit as I got to the second-floor landing. I damn near fell down the rest of the way. But I went out the back and stayed in the hedges until I saw you."

It didn't take long to get to my apartment. I pulled around to the back alley, got out of the car and looked around for signs that someone was watching. No shadows, nothing. I waved at Sid, and we hurried up the back stairs.

"I'm calling the Dragon," I said. "She needs to know about this."

"Good," he said, gasping a little.

He followed me into the front room. The Dragon was the head of Quickline. I wasn't sure what support she'd be able to give us, largely because I didn't know how much she knew about the case. But someone had just tried to kill one of our people. She needed to know.

I got through right away on the living room phone and the Dragon agreed that we shouldn't tell anyone that Sid was alive.

"I'll see what I can find out from the local law enforcement," she told me. "Can you keep him hidden in the meantime?"

"Yeah. I'll be here until I hear from you."

I put the phone into its cradle and turned. Sid had collapsed onto my couch and was still breathing heavily.

"You're alive," I whispered, my eyes overflowing.

"Yeah. So are you."

A second later, I had flown into his arms, and we nearly bruised each other with our kisses. It was as if we wanted to swallow each other in the hopes of reassuring ourselves that we really were still there.

The intensity grew as we kissed. I loved the feel of his hands all over me, his rich, gentle kisses. I wanted to be with all of him, have him all to myself.

I could feel myself cooling but kept kissing him, anyway. It didn't help. He caught the coolness and pulled away with a curse.

"I'm sorry." The tears sprang to my eyes. "I'll try again."

"No." Sid growled and looked away. "Don't force it."

"But it's what you need."

He closed his eyes and got up. "Yes. No. Not this way, damn it all."

"I'm sorry!"

"It's who you are. You can't help it." He looked back at me. "But, damn it, Lisa, I'm getting tired of waiting."

"So, am I," I said.

"So it's not your religion." His eyes bore into me. "It's the fidelity thing, isn't it?"

I nodded and looked down at my hands. "It just feels like I'm not enough for you."

He came over and softly lifted my chin. "You are more than enough for me. How do I make you see that?"

I looked at the living room curtains, trying to find something to say.

"In a way, I do know that," I said, finally admitting it to myself, as well.

"Look, I can't promise I won't slip," he said softly.

"I know. That's the problem." I turned away, my tears getting the better of me again.

Sid cursed. "I am not going to make a promise to you unless I know damned well I can keep it." He swallowed and took a deep breath. "Believe it or not, I want to be faithful to you. I just don't think I can. I've been trying to. Really. But I keep giving in."

"So, it's not time yet." I shrugged and looked at my hands.

"What if it's never time?" Sid asked. His eyes were filled with fear. "What if I can't change?"

I got up and went over to him. "It's okay."

"No, it's not!" He pulled away. "There's nothing okay about this."

"Yes, it is! We have a good relationship. We have a terrific relationship. We're better than friends. There is so much here that I can manage. Yeah, the way things are is making me crazy. But putting up with it and being with you is still better than being without you."

"Oh, god, don't even hint at that." Sid sank onto the couch again. "That's my worst fear, you know. That you'll get fed up and move on."

I sat down next to him. "I'm not going to."

"You did last summer."

"Not really." I sighed. "I mean, there probably was a little of me being fried at you when I told George I'd marry him. You were kind of a pain in the butt that week. But I was coming to my right senses, and right now, there is no way I'm going anywhere."

Sid's arm slid around my shoulders, and he took my breath away, he held me so tight.

"How do I know you won't?"

"Because I love you, Sid."

He jumped up and away, cursing. "How...?" He saw me as I started weeping and winced. "Damn it! That's..." He cursed again as he began frantically pacing. "Lisa, why did you have to say that?"

"Because it's how I feel," I snapped.

"No! I mean, I get that." He looked at me. "I don't want to go tromping on your feelings. It's just that whenever I hear that, things get ugly." He paused. "I know when you say it that it's something different."

"I know. Kind of like how when you say I'm enough, it's true."

He looked at me and took a deep breath. "Lisa, I..." He cursed. "I just can't say it. You're everything to me, but I can't say it." He started pacing again. "To me, it's just a lie guys tell to get someone into bed. I don't do that to anyone, and I sure as hell can't do that to you."

"Good, because I don't want you to."

Sid paced toward the door and stopped. "Would it be so terrible if I slipped?"

"I don't know why, but it would," I said, trying not to sob. "Thinking about you with another woman, it just hurts. You'd think I'd be used to it, and in some ways, I am. It's part of who you are. But I hate the thought of you making love to someone else as much as you hate the thought of losing me."

"I see." Still gazing at the door, he shook his head. "I don't know what else to do." He turned to me. "Okay. As soon as we get home, we're getting married."

The anger rose in me. "What's that going to fix?"

"I don't know. You keep saying it changes things."

"Not if you're going into it like this!"

"Then what the hell else am I supposed to do? I can't take this much longer. And, yes, I will be faithful, somehow or other. Damn it, I will."

"That's not the point. I mean, yes, it is." I groaned as the words jammed in my mouth. I took a deep breath. "If we get married now, you'll only be doing it to appease me."

"Why is that a problem?"

"Because you're eventually going to resent it and resent me, and the friendship, the caring, the relationship will all go to hell."

"The one thing neither of us wants to lose." Sid gazed up at the ceiling, then let out another string of curses. "What do we do?"

I walked over to him. "Hang on?"

Sid softly pulled me into his arms. "That much I can do." He pressed his lips against my forehead.

I squeezed him. "Sid, you promised there will be joy when we come together. I believe in that promise."

"And I keep thinking I should never have made it."

"That's because you're trying to force yourself right now. Just like I keep going along with it when we get hot and heavy." I squeezed my eyes shut.

Sid let out a cross between a snort and a sigh. "Yeah, you have been doing that a lot lately." He pulled away just enough to look at me. "This is killing me. It's killing both of us. But strangely enough, for the first time in a long time, I'm beginning to feel some hope."

"Good. Sid, I want you to know that I'm in this for keeps."

"I know, but please don't make that a promise now." He put his forehead against mine. "There are just too many things that could go wrong yet."

"You're probably right."

Actually, I knew he was, which is why I let it go at that. We held each other a while longer, then finally, our exhaustion consumed us and we went to bed fully clothed, but still holding each other.

October 30, 1984

The phone rang just after six a.m. I could hear Sid moving about in the bathroom. Neither of us had slept that well. I picked up the phone.

It was the Dragon. She gave the caller code, and I gave the receiver. It was the usual routine for calls.

"I know it's early, but we've been pulling an all-nighter on this one," she said.

"Okay."

"Well, the explosion definitely took out your contact."

"Steve." I couldn't help choking a little. "He was a nice guy."

"I'm sure he was. They didn't find any remains in Big Red's apartment, which we knew. I've convinced the locals to release it that Ed Donaldson died in the explosion. He'll have to find a way to get home discreetly, but I think you guys can manage that."

"Sure."

The Dragon paused. "Our connection with The Company says that you found the developer."

"We did."

"If you want, I can send another team in to protect him."

"Oh."

"Don't you want to go home?"

I winced as I thought about it. "No. I don't. I want to find out who killed Eunice and Steve."

"If it was a KGB operative, you'll never be able to prove it, and there are good odds they'll be out of the country before you can try."

"I don't think it was. I mean, they're involved. But most of what's been happening, I think it's the amateur they have in their control. I don't know for sure yet, but I want to find out."

The Dragon chuckled. "That's my woman. I'm glad. Best of luck to you, then. Oh, one other thing that I hope will draw some of the attention away from you. We gave the locals permission to release it that Ed Donaldson was an undercover operative who was killed by a KGB assassin."

"He is not going to like that."

"Well, his cover was already blown with the KGB."

"Damn that Hannaford kid."

The Dragon sighed. "We should never have sent him in. He really doesn't have the temperament for teamwork."

"No kidding."

"Do you want a substitute?"

"I'm fine with the other two. It'll take too much time to set someone else up. And Hannaford isn't a complete liability."

"All right. Carry on then. Call me if you need anything."

"I will."

I hung up. Sid came into the bedroom.

"Was that...?"

I rolled onto my back. "The Dragon? Yes. You're going home."

"Oh."

"The locals have been asked to release it that Ed Donaldson died in the explosion and that he was an operative killed by a KGB assassin."

Sid cursed.

"I know. It stinks."

Sid shrugged. "Not much we can do about it, and I was practically impotent anyway with that tail on me."

The phone rang again. I picked it up.

"Hello?" I grunted.

"It's Max. Is this Janet?"

"Yes. What's up?"

"I need to be extracted and I need it now. After what happened last night, I can't afford to stick around."

"Your cover is still intact."

"They're stealing my formula, so no, it's not. And you know The Company. I'm only so much meat to them."

"What about your friend?"

"We'll have to figure something out."

I closed my eyes, then noticed Sid standing next to the bed. "Hold on a second." I covered the mouthpiece with my hand. "On your way out of town, do you mind doing an extraction?"

"Who?"

"Max. He's a little worried that he's next on the hit list."

"Not an entirely bad assumption, especially if the Soviets have enough of his formula to figure out the rest." Sid looked at me. "But how did he know to call you?"

"We had a little chat yesterday afternoon. Can you help?"

"Sure."

"Good." I uncovered the mouthpiece. "All right, Max. I can help." I closed my eyes. "We'll need to get a car first, but we should be able to get that by this evening. Will that be soon enough?"

"Yeah. We should probably do this under cover of darkness."

"Okay. There's that park by the river."

"Yeah, I know it."

"You're going to meet Ed Donaldson there at..." I looked at Sid. "Seven okay?"

Sid nodded.

"Seven," said Max. "But wait. The word's out that Donaldson's dead."

"Let's just say we want people to believe that. Meet him by the swings. How you two handle the rest of it, that's up to you."

"Good." Max hung up.

I rolled onto my back. "This is just too much trauma for this time of the day."

"I agree." Sid chuckled and sat down next to me on the bed. "You had a nightmare last night."

"A couple of them." I looked up at him. "I've got a feeling you did, too."

He looked away. "Oh?"

"When you were talking in your sleep, you sounded pretty anxious about a Robinson somebody."

Sid blew out his breath, then picked up my hand. "My dearest friend, as much as I would like to tell you all about that miserable incident, I don't think right now is the time." He kissed my fingers. "You've got a long day ahead of you, and so do I. Why don't you get a little more sleep?"

"That sounds nice. Would you like me to get you some underwear or a toothbrush or something?"

"Uh, I already had those in my daypack, which made it out of the house with me."

"Oh."

Given Sid's tendency to end up in someone else's bed at night, it made sense for him to keep a few personal items with him.

"At least they came in handy this morning," he said apologetically.

"They did." I reached up and touched his cheek. "Do you mind holding me a little longer?"

"Given that I don't know when I'll be able to again, I think that would be a good idea."

I awoke for good around eight. While I showered and got my makeup on, Sid made breakfast out of the few pieces of fruit I had, the last of the peanut butter, and some whole wheat bread I'd forgotten I'd bought. Luckily, I'd put the bread in my freezer, which may also have been why I forgot it was there.

I called Terry and told her what I needed, then asked her to meet me at my office after the Shakespeare seminar. While Sid and I ate, we talked over several scenarios for getting Max out of Appleton in a way that would keep the KGB from looking for him. Then I had to go to class. Sid kissed me soundly and sent me on my way, looking at me sadly as I closed the front door to the apartment.

I made it to Lawrence Hall a little early. Classes there were still on, but math/science classes had been canceled. Mrs. Spinetti stopped me as I got my mail from the inbox.

"Um, Janet, I just wanted to say that I'm sorry about Dr. Carmona. I'd heard you two were on the way to becoming, well, I guess you'd call it involved."

"Not really," I said, sniffing a little. "We were just friends, but he was a good one."

"Oh. Well, I'm sorry."

"Thanks."

I went upstairs and updated my notes for the Shakespeare seminar. I'd come up with a plan of action on Sunday night, when I'd forced myself to read Eunice's syllabus and notes, but I still felt woefully under-prepared. Oh, well. My mentor teacher had said that teaching was as much about improvisation as it was planning.

Admittedly, none of the students were thrilled when I announced the homework for the week. The Shakespeare seminar students would have to do a two-page essay, with quotes from the play, for their Julius Caesar take-home exam. The real exam was to have taken place the Thursday before but hadn't because of classes being canceled. I also had the Elizabethan students write up a two-page summation of what they'd covered in their class to that point and reminded them that I had Eunice's syllabus. Then we had a lively discussion on the overlaps between literature and history, and how each shed light on the other.

Kathy followed me to my office, where we found Tim Hannaford waiting for me, never mind that I didn't have office hours that day. He was a mess. I ushered both inside the office and turned on a radio I'd found on the shelf. The emotionless voice of a news reporter came out.

"Appleton PD has confirmed that the two dead men were Dr. Steve Carmona, a computer science teacher at

Martin University, and Ed Donaldson, a student at the same university."

Tim wailed.

"Sh!" I hissed at him and turned the dial to a Top-Forty station.

"But it's my fault," Tim said, weeping. "I blew his cover, and I killed him."

I glared at him. "Then learn from it."

Tim stepped back, a look of shock on his face.

There was a knock on the door. Kathy peeked out, then opened the door just wide enough to let Terry slip through.

"I have to pick it up this afternoon," Terry said. "But I've got the car."

"Can you get it by four?"

Terry nodded.

"Perfect. Leave it in the alley behind my place, keys in the glove compartment." I looked at the three of them. "Okay, gang, we've got an extraction to make happen."

Kathy's eyes opened wide with hope. "Ed?"

"No." I swallowed. "You'll figure it out soon enough. Tim, you know that park by the river?"

"Yeah."

"You'll need to meet the target near the swings at seven. Don't worry. You'll know him."

"Yes, ma'am."

"All right. Now get out of here."

Tim left the office quickly. I suppose I should have told him about Ed/Sid, but he'd find out that evening. Letting him stew in his guilt a little longer might just drive home the lesson that much better. I was just sorry that I wouldn't get to see Tim's face when he saw Sid. [It was priceless. - SEH]

I looked down at my desk, then at Terry and Kathy.

"Kathy, what did you find in that book I gave you?"

"Besides a really badly written romance?"

I couldn't help laughing, and Terry chuckled.

Kathy shrugged. "I don't think it's a code, or even a key map. If anything, it looks like textual analysis. I might be able to make more sense of it if I knew to what it was being compared to."

"Could there be a pass code or something in it?" I asked.

"Possibly. You think it could be somebody's computer password?" Kathy asked.

"Password!" I jumped up and turned on my computer. "I think you've got something." I looked at the two of them. "I've heard there's some sort of software that will help you find someone's computer password."

"Sure," said Terry. "But they take, like, days to work. What they do is enter every alpha-numeric combination of however many digits into the computer until the account opens."

"If you know the person whose account it is, it's usually faster to try guessing the password," Kathy said. "People usually use personal information, like their dog's name, or their kids' birthdates."

"But once you're in the account, you can see all their files, right?" I bit the nail on my thumb.

"Sure," said Terry. "You can open them, delete them, copy them onto a floppy drive. It would be just like being in your own account."

"Okay." I frowned. "All right. Eunice Blakely. She'd told someone that she had some evidence that our developer was being spied on. Maybe it's in her account. What would her password be?" I looked at Kathy. "Is it in that book, you think?"

"I don't know," Kathy said.

Terry snorted. "Why don't you break into the system administrator's account instead? That way, you'll get everybody's passwords."

"That's a good idea," I said, then looked at her. "Do you know who the system administrator is?"

"Probably Dr. Carmona."

"Crud." I sank back into my chair. "If I'd known this two days ago, I could have just asked him."

"Well, what do you know about him?" Kathy asked.

"Not much. He doesn't have a pet or kids that I know of." I fiddled with my keyboard. "I don't even know his birthdate."

"That's easy enough to look up." Terry gave me a shy grin. "So, I already got into the university system. I just can't get to the passwords because I'm sure Dr. Carmona has them under his account."

I sighed. In my mind, I could see Steve getting slowly more plastered as he looked balefully at me. I sat up.

"Let's try getting into Steve's account," I said.

"I've got an idea," said Terry. "Kathy, do you think you can get over to the computer center and find Dr. Carmona's floppy disks? He'd have backed up the passwords. He might have password protected the file, but he'd have it."

"I've got it." Kathy hurried out of the office.

I keyed through the directory to the university's system, found Steve's account and hit return.

"You can use your mouse," Terry pointed out.

"It doesn't always work, and I'm used to the keys, any-way. Okay." On the screen, the cursor blinked next to a request for a password. "Here goes."

I typed in "littlered." It was rejected. I tried again with "LittleRed." That didn't work, either. I sat back, thinking over all the conversations I'd had with Steve. Smiling, it hit. I typed in "BigRed."

The account opened. Terry giggled. I looked at the time on the computer screen.

"Shavings," I said, shutting the system down. "I've got to get lunch and get to class. See if you can get to Kathy. Let her know we got into the account, so she shouldn't take too many risks getting those floppies, okay?"

"Wait," said Terry.

"What?" I was a little irritated. I was hungry, and I only had about thirty minutes to get to the Commons, eat, and get back.

"Ed's not dead."

I sighed. "It's best if he is."

"No. You're not that broken up. If he really were dead, you'd be a mess. You can't tell me you wouldn't."

I thought back to the night before. Terry had a point.

"It doesn't matter. I should, technically, be more upset about Dr. Carmona. Ed was just one of my students. Let's leave it at that. Okay?"

Terry snorted, but left the office right before I did.

I managed to get through Basic Comp C without too much trouble. I knew I should have stayed and graded papers, but I didn't care. Instead, I hurried home as fast as I could. Sid was there. He'd somehow found enough ingredients in my kitchen to improvise a lasagna for me.

"Don't you want some?" I asked, lifting the corner of the foil-wrapped pan to sniff.

"I already ate." He smiled at me. "You keep that and a couple of other goodies I left in your freezer. That way, you won't have to go out to eat so much." He looked a little abashed. "I had time on my hands today, so I hope you don't mind."

"No." I blinked away more tears. "That's really sweet of you to do it."

The kitchen practically sparkled, so I figured he'd cleaned it.

"I also reorganized your cupboards in here," he said, sheepishly, as he put the lasagna in the fridge.

"Good lord, you were bored."

He shrugged. "It was very therapeutic. May just make a new hobby."

"Sure. Um, please stay away from the files, though?"

He laughed, and we held each other. When I'd first come to work for him, I'd redone the files so that they made more sense and put them in a database to keep track of them. It had taken Sid a while before he'd been able to find anything.

We didn't say or do much for the next hour and a half, just sat on the couch and held each other. There wasn't much to be said. Sid was going home. I was staying.

Finally, about twenty after six, the apartment was fully dark. Sid lifted his head.

"I should think about getting going," he said, his voice quiet and sad.

"Okay. The car is in the back alley. Keys are in the glove compartment. I checked before coming up."

"Good. Thanks." He shifted so that he could look me in the face. "Listen, I am fully confident that you will knock this case right out of the park, but will you do me one favor?"

"What?"

"Knock it out very carefully. Please?"

I laughed and held him. "I will." I put my hand on his face. "You be careful, too."

"I will."

We got up slowly and walked to the back of the apartment without turning on the lights. At the back door, we held each other tightly.

"Sid," I said. "I'll probably have to stay through the end of the term, assuming we wrap things up before then. And even if we don't, I'll definitely be home for Thanksgiving and probably Christmas."

He squeezed me. "I hope so."

I pulled away just enough to gaze into his eyes. "There is only one way that I am not coming back to you. And if that happens, then remembering will have to do."

"Yeah." He shuddered and squeezed me even tighter.

The line was from "You and Me Against the World." It was pretty much our song, mostly because that's how we felt a lot of the time, thanks to our business.

We kissed, long and slow. Neither of us really wanted to think about the possibility that we would not see the other again, but even at home, the potential was always there. The good thing was that we seldom took each other for granted.

Sid finally pulled away and opened the door. The wind whipped into the apartment in an icy blast. I found his daypack on the floor next to the door and handed it to him. He slung it over his shoulder and slid quietly down the stairs. I waited in the dark as he walked to the car. He opened the passenger side, got the keys, and quietly shut the door. As he opened the driver's side, he paused and looked up at me. I kissed my fingers, then he kissed his. I waited just long enough for him to get the car started and rolling down the alley.

I shivered slightly as I went back into the kitchen. Oddly enough, I wasn't hungry. It was probably the mixed stew of feelings roiling around my gut. There was an empty place in me where I was missing Sid already. I also felt excited that I was really going to find out what I could do on my own, but at the same time, I was utterly terrified because I was on my own and in charge of three others. I flipped on the lights and went to the front of the apartment hoping to distract myself by grading papers.

That's when I heard the creaking on the stairs. I went straight to the peephole. A minute later, Sergeant Renecke's balding head heaved into view. I waited for him to knock, gave it a minute, then opened the door.

"Can I help you, Sergeant?" I asked.

"I'd like to ask you a few more questions," he said.

"Sure. Come in. Can I get you some water?"

He followed me into the living room, and I shut the door behind him.

"I'm fine, thanks."

I pulled the desk chair over. "Why don't you take the couch?"

"Thanks." He eased his bulk down and got out his notebook. "How's it been going for you?"

"Pretty rocky," I said. "I've lost two friends in less than a week. What do you expect?"

"I can imagine. So, you're still calling Dr. Carmona a friend? I'd heard he'd spent the reception at Dr. Blakely's memorial getting drunk and looking all hang dog at you."

I flushed. "He had expressed an interest in being more than a friend. I had to say no. Bad relationship back home. I'm still a little raw." It was part of my original cover story. "I was hoping we could stay friends long enough for me to heal. Yesterday, he seemed to be willing to keep talking."

"So that's why you were there last night."

I shuddered. "Yeah. We were going to have dinner."

"Your student Ed Donaldson lived there, too."

"Yes."

Renecke looked at his notebook. "Rumor has it you were quite attracted to Mr. Donaldson."

I laughed in spite of myself. "Of course I was. Have you ever seen him? I mean, saw." I blinked back more tears. "He was gorgeous. You'd have to be dead not to be attracted to him."

"You ever do anything about it?"

"Of course not. He was a student. That would be utterly unethical."

"Doesn't stop some folks." Renecke shifted.

"It stopped me." I tried not to glare at him. He was only doing his job.

"You've heard about the spy thing, right?"

I nodded. "It totally surprised me."

"Really?" Renecke watched me.

"Who wouldn't be shocked to find out one of your students is James Bond?" I shook my head. "Okay, he looked the part, and I hear, slept around as if he was. But why would he even be here? This is an arts school. Unless they've hidden some missiles or something."

"Or something." Renecke grimaced and leaned back for a minute. He really wanted to share something, but couldn't. "The funny thing is, the Feds haven't told me to back off the case." He noticed me and cursed. "I wasn't planning on saying that. Open investigation."

"You look tired," I said, smiling softly.

He stretched his back for a second. "It's how the job goes. Did you see anything in Donaldson's papers that might tell us what he was working on?"

I thought about it. "No. It was basic stuff. The assignments are fairly structured. We did do a creative writing assignment, but that was about some high school kid trying to protect another. He got that paper back. The only thing of his that I have right now was Monday's assignment, which was an outline for his term paper. It was going to be on..." I bit my lip. I really hadn't remembered. "Oh, right. On how Johann Sebastian Bach developed the fugue."

"Oh." Renecke sighed. He flipped his notebook closed, then looked at me closely again. "You know, there is something going on around here. I don't know what it is, and I can't help but wonder if you do."

I shrugged my shoulders. "I don't know what to tell you. I've only been here since September."

Renecke got up. "That's right. Okay. Thanks for talking to me. If you think of anything, let me know."

I let him out and looked at my watch. It was just past seven. Sid and Max would have met up. Tim, hopefully, was well and truly shaken. I looked at my purse, then decided to heck with it. I went back to the university to work there.

But as I was going into Lawrence Hall, I met Fran in the department office.

"Oh, Janet, I was just leaving you a note," she said. "How are you?"

I shrugged. "Managing. How about you?"

"The same." She glanced back at Joe Cunningham's darkened office. "Say, have you got a few minutes? I'd like to talk about taking care of our women here."

"Sure."

"Let's go up to my office."

We walked up in silence to the third floor, where Fran's office was. Fran opened the door, then paused.

"You know what? I think I need to use the restroom. Why don't you go on in?"

I shut the door behind me and looked over the papers on her desk without touching them. There was one small scrap with an address on it. I didn't recognize the hand-writing, but there was something distinctive about it that made me think I should have. It was an address in Madison, but no name or other identification. Out of force of habit, I memorized it, then heard Fran coming back (the plumbing in the building being quite loud).

We started taking Cunningham's name in vain and didn't get much further than that. Fran started yawning, and I did, too, and then we both agreed it was probably time to go home. We left the building together and went to our separate cars. I still hadn't graded any papers.

October 31, 1984

I t was Halloween. Halloween on the campus of an arts school was... Okay, it was surreal. I mean, I like to think that I am reasonably culturally savvy, but these kids blew me away. The Dungeons and Dragons references were in the minority. Yes, we got a few Star Trek costumes. But I saw at least twelve costumes referencing the whole Dune universe - apparently the film was coming out later that year. The rest of them, well, they went way beyond the usual witches and ghouls.

There was a part of me that felt rather left out. I usually love dressing up for Halloween. But I realized that I'd had other things taking up space in my brain that week. I wore my Shetland wool sweater over a pair of jeans and my armored running shoes.

"Hey, Dr. Mayfield," Mark Ayers crowed as I walked into the first section of Basic Comp. At least, I was reasonably certain that it was him underneath the various growths that had sprouted all over his face. "Where's your costume?"

"Still trying to get the campus zeitgeist," I said, hoping I sounded more casual than I felt.

"Mark!" groaned Rita Farley. She, at least, had chosen not to dress up.

The rest of the class also shuffled uncomfortably.

I looked over the group. Even though two-thirds of them wore some elaborate costume, there was a sadness that overlaid everything.

"How many of you are a little messed up that one of your classmates is dead?" I asked.

No surprise, they weren't admitting it, but the way they shuffled and shifted told me what I'd guessed.

"I'll admit I'm behind on the grading," I said. "Why don't we talk about our feelings about what happened to Ed?"

There was more shuffling and shifting, but it wasn't long before the feelings and the fears started coming out. Most of them felt strange about what the police were saying about Ed.

"Like, a government agent?" Jason de Boeur said. "That's just, like, too weird."

"It doesn't mean he didn't like us," said Terry with a rather militant expression on her face. "And it doesn't mean he wasn't a really good person."

There wasn't much more for me to do than sit back and let things happen. Which they did. About mid-way through the class though, enough noise erupted in the halls that I went to check out what was going on.

When I came back into the classroom, I sank back against the desk.

"Okay, class. We've had yet another incident," I told them, playing into the shock I would have felt had I not known what was going on. "Apparently, sometime last night, Professor Max Beard's car landed in the Fox River.

I don't know much more than that, but if you want to stay around and talk about it, we can. Otherwise, class is dismissed."

There was a shocked silence, then the class fled. Terry stayed behind just long enough to agree to meet with me around five so that we could check out Steve Carmona's account. I went first to the department office to find out what I could. Classes were, indeed, canceled for the rest of the day, however, no faculty meeting had been scheduled.

"He refuses to come out of his office," Mrs. Spinetti said, with a nod toward Cunningham's door. "And he won't even talk to me. With luck, he's trying to figure out how he's going to live on his pension."

"Have they found out anything about Max?" I asked.

Mrs. Spinetti shook her head. "Not so far. They've been dragging the river all morning. Last I heard, they found his glasses and a shirt. His body probably got caught in an undertow and is halfway to the Illinois River by now." She put her hand on my shoulder. "Why don't you go home? Everyone else has left, except Joe and, I think, Fran. I'll be leaving in a few minutes, myself."

"I'm going to go up to my office first." I said, as listlessly as I felt.

It was time to do some searches, but my heart wasn't in it. I got out my leather gloves, then locked my purse in my desk and started up the stairs to the third floor, anyway. The lights were on in Fran's office. She'd been so broken up about Eunice, I couldn't help but wonder how Max's disappearance was affecting her. I stuffed the gloves in my back pocket and knocked on her door.

"Please leave," Fran called.

"It's Janet," I said.

"Oh, Janet. Come on in. It's open."

She sat at her desk, glumly staring at nothing.

"Are you okay?" I asked, shutting the door behind me.

"I..." Fran shrugged. "I don't know. I really don't." She looked at me. "Eunice trusted you. Do you know why?"

"Not really." I kept my face puzzled and tried to hide my fear as I sat down on the couch. "I liked her a lot, probably even loved her."

Fran smiled. "You know what she told me after the Faculty Luncheon at the beginning of the quarter? That we had another ally. That's why I thought the meeting was about getting rid of Joe Cunningham. But earlier today, when I heard about Max's car, I remembered a couple of things." She took a deep breath. "About a year and a half ago, one night after Joe had been acting particularly badly, Eunice and I got fed up. We sat in her office and drank ourselves silly. We staggered downstairs to go home, and Eunice stole the department pass key. Mrs. Spinetti keeps it in the top drawer of her desk in case somebody loses their office key. The next thing I knew, I had a copy of it. How Eunice had gotten it, I don't know. I do know she had a copy. Then, about a week before she died, she told me that we were finally going to need our pass keys. I asked her if this meant we were going to get Joe, and she said, no, it was more serious than that. I let it go. It wasn't that unusual for Eunice to get cryptic."

"Okay. But why are you telling me this?"

"Eunice trusted you, and I need help. Max said to let it go, but I can't."

"Because he's gone now?"

"Because he's up to his neck in it." Fran chuckled. "I don't know how. He wouldn't tell me, and I'm fairly certain Eunice didn't know, either." She looked at me. "Max and I are lovers."

I raised my eyebrows. "I never guessed." Then something occurred to me. "You're speaking about him in the present tense."

"He's not dead," Fran's blinking grew even worse. "Don't ask me how I know and please keep that under your hat. I need to find Eunice's killer. It's connected to something Max was doing. It must be. That's why she didn't ask him to the meeting. She wanted to protect him, I'm sure."

"Do you think Max could have killed her?"

"Absolutely not. He was completely shocked to hear." Fran's eyes flitted my way. "I went over there after the police let us go that night. I didn't know what else to do. I also asked Steve the next day if Max had been signed into his account that night, and Steve said that Max had signed out around ten thirty. I wanted to be sure that Max wasn't a suspect."

I made a mental note to check the sign in logs for that night when I got back into Steve's account.

"So, who do you think is?" I asked.

"Well, that's what I need the help for," Fran said. "Practically everyone else in this department could be. I've got a passkey. We need to search some offices. Maybe we can find some evidence or something."

"Um," I tried to think of something to say. "Shouldn't we leave this to the police?"

"We can't. Whatever Max was working on, he needed to keep it a secret."

"You can't be planning on taking out Eunice's killer by yourself." I gulped.

"Oh, no. But depending on what evidence we find, we'll figure what to do with it then." Fran got up. "Come on. I want to get as much done today as I can."

"Now?" I swallowed. I wanted to talk her out of it, but I knew I couldn't. I needed to do the searches, anyway, and maybe working with her, I could keep her out of trouble.

"It's for Eunice," Fran said.

I sighed. "All right. Let's go."

We started on the third floor. Fran only wanted to go through the desks, but I checked a few of the bookshelves. David Watts' office was clean. Ernie Lavalle had a complete collection of Playboy Magazines on his shelves, which I'd already seen and ignored. Somehow, I thought his interest in the articles was limited. His desk was clean, even of syringes. Carson Osgood's desk was also clean, but he had a dirty little secret on his shelf. He'd pasted an incredible collection of pornographic pictures in between the pages of his academic journals.

Fran was disgusted. "I always thought he found those more interesting than they warranted."

We moved on. Perry Addington's, then downstairs, Dwight Atwater's and Ted Curtis' offices were all clean. Ryan Martin had a couple bottles of Jack Daniels in his desk, but nothing incriminating. Fran didn't think it would be worth searching Eunice's or Max's offices, so we went on to the first floor. Cunningham was still sulking in his office, so we were extra quiet as we went through Robert Farnsworth's office (clean), the Zaners' office (also clean) and Fred Wirth's (clean, but more pornography).

"What is it with men and porn?" Fran grumbled as we went back up to my office.

"I have no idea," I said. "Beyond the whole objectification thing."

Fran snorted. "So now, what do we do?"

I looked at my watch. "Actually, I'm meeting with a student in a couple. Terry Michaels. She was close to Ed, so I'm letting her cry on my shoulder. How about we set up a plan tonight when I get home?"

"That's a good idea." Fran headed for her office. "I'll go get my purse and you'll lock up?"

"Sure."

I kept watch until I saw her coming down the stairs. She passed Terry, who was coming up the stairs. I waved at Terry to keep watching what Fran did. Terry paused and looked back, then hurried over to me.

"She's gone."

"Good. Let's keep our ears open, okay?"

We got into Steve's account quickly. Terry spotted the password file. We saved it to a floppy disk on my computer, then opened it up. It was a spreadsheet that hadn't been sorted, but Terry found Max's account near the bottom. I wrote the password down, then found Eunice's.

Outside, college students began to make party noises, and it sounded like someone had set up a loudspeaker system on the lawn.

"It's going to be a really big party," Terry said. "They've even got a pit dug for a bonfire."

"Good." I signed out of Steve's account and into Max's.

It was empty. Every single file was gone, and I didn't doubt that Max had been the one to empty it. I signed out and signed into Eunice's account. Most of the files there related to her course work. There were also a couple journal articles. I pulled out the box of floppy disks that

I'd found in her desk. The labels corresponded to the file names on her computer account.

"That's funny," said Terry, who was looking over my shoulder.

"What?"

Terry pointed to the screen. "The last file was created on October first. She's been creating files at least once a week up until that time. She must have erased a bunch of files. I wonder why."

"Evidence," I said. "She told Max that someone was spying on him and that she had some evidence. But why would she erase the files? She'd need them to back herself up."

"Because she made backups." Terry's face fell. "Oh, no! The floppies that were missing from her house."

"Wait a minute." I looked at the box of floppy disks on my desk. "She left these out and they were untouched. I wonder if this is a second box of backups. I have a friend who always talks about making backups of backups. So, if Eunice erased the files from the university system, she wouldn't have made just one backup."

"You're right." Terry glowed. "Why didn't I think of that? But where would the second backup be?"

"She wouldn't tell Max who she thought was doing the spying. If she was that skittish, then she probably hid them. But where?"

"Kathy was pretty sure it wasn't in her house."

I shook my head. "It wasn't in her office, either." I thought about all the offices I'd searched and realized that I hadn't searched Fran's since Eunice was killed. "I wonder if it's in Fran's. Eunice was already getting ready to ask her for help." I opened my desk drawer. "Stuff your pack in here and I'll lock it."

Terry did, and we left my office for Fran's. Fortunately, Fran had left her lights on again. I found the manila envelope stuck between a couple of People Magazines that Fran had on her shelf. There was a note on the front asking Fran not to open it until after their meeting.

I took the envelope and pushed Terry back to my office. Outside, music started playing, and the students cheered loudly.

"I hope those kids will be in shape for class tomorrow," I grumbled as I opened the envelope.

"Tomorrow's a day off," Terry said. "Remember?"

I thought, then realized it was. "It's a faculty in-service day or something."

"They call it that." Terry giggled. "One of the sophomores in my other classes said it's because so many of the students are hung over, no one comes to class, anyway."

"You're right. I had heard that." I turned back to the contents of the envelope.

There were several sheets of paper, including two dot matrix printouts and a floppy disk. The printouts had chemical formulae on them. One was marked "Max."

I didn't get a chance to read more. We could hear someone in the hall coming toward the office. I shoved everything back into the envelope, slid it into my desk drawer, and relocked the desk.

I was just in time. The door rattled, then splintered. Two men wearing black clothes and masks burst into the office. I screamed loudly, which made one of them laugh.

"No one is going to hear you."

He and the other man pulled their guns. Terry was rooted in place and utterly terrified.

"Now, come along nicely," the first man said.

I eased my way around the desk.

"Please don't hurt us," I whimpered.

"If you are good, we don't." He grabbed my arm and shoved me forward.

I stomped on his foot. He let go, howling. I charged the second man. Terry finally woke up and ran out the door. The second man didn't back down and finally got me pinned and shoved out the door. I kept struggling until I saw Terry. A third man held her with a gun to her head.

November 1 – 2, 1984

S unlight filtered through the bars on the window as I awoke the next morning. I blinked my eyes. Terry stood at the door, listening. We'd been fed decently the night before, and we hadn't been searched. They'd taken the blindfolds and hand cuffs off us right before they'd shoved us into the small room we were in.

We'd had to find the one twin bed in the dark, though. When we'd flipped the light switch, no lights had come on.

It was very puzzling, although Terry and I hadn't said much to each other. She had been very frightened, and I was glad. It made us look less like operatives.

"They bought it," Terry whispered.

"Bought what?"

Terry put her finger to her lips, listened a minute more, then came over and sat next to be on the bed.

"They're talking in Russian now," she said softly. "But one of them just made a phone call. It was a ransom demand. The person on the other end is to turn over Max Beard or they'll kill us. The weird thing is, they think we're civilians."

"Oh, thank God!" I made the sign of the cross. "We've got some time then."

I looked out the window, but it overlooked a street. Most of the houses were the same yellow brick I'd been seeing everywhere, so I thought we were still in Wisconsin. We were also on a second floor with nothing between us and the pavement.

"How do you know?" Terry's eyes were wide with fear.

"They'll need us alive to exchange for Dr. Beard. And nobody likes killing civilians."

"They don't?"

I snorted. "It's not fine feeling. Killing civilians calls attention to yourself. That's what brought us in, remember? The two students?"

"But why take us if they think we're civilians?" Terry swallowed.

I shrugged. "Wait. There was the party outside, and we were the only ones in the building. They probably saw that the lights were on in my office. They needed hostages and figured we would be the easiest to get. How many on the other side?" I nodded at the door.

"Two. There was a third, but she left."

I checked my watch. It was a quarter after seven. I pulled my bug finder from my pocket. Nothing was broadcasting. Then I did something that had Terry gaping. I opened up the sole of my running shoes.

"You can always hide something." I looked at her. "You don't faint at the sight of blood or anything like that, do you?"

"No," she said, her voice shaking a little.

I pulled the small stiletto out of the chamber in the sole of my shoe, then got a small screwdriver out of the other sole and flipped both shoes shut.

"Here." I handed her the stiletto. The smell of bacon wafted in through the door. "I think they're going to feed us now. You ready?"

"Sure." She trembled, but set her chin in defiance.

I backed up against the wall next to the door. It swung open, covering me, and the university janitor came in with a plate of eggs and bacon. I shut the door behind him, and he turned toward me. Terry jumped on him, and he howled as he got the stiletto in his kidneys. Spotting the handgun on his belt, I grabbed it just as his partner came running in. I put a shot into his shoulder, then got his gun, as well.

I looked out the door. There was a big, furnished front room on the other side. I nodded and Terry followed me out of the little room we'd been in. I nodded again, and she shut the door and locked it. We probably didn't have much time, but I took a quick look around, anyway.

The phone was on an end table next to a brown sofa. Paper grocery sacks littered a dining room table just a bit further on. I picked up a binder and thumbed through the dot matrix paper inside. Not unlike the sheets I'd found in Eunice's envelope, these sheets were filled with chemical formulae. I went over to the dining room table and noticed several emptied plastic produce bags laying there. I handed a couple to Terry.

"Keep these on your hands and do a quick search. I'll call in the code nine."

Code nine was the request for an arrest. After using two of the plastic bags to make the call, I put the binder and the guns I'd taken into one of the paper bags and grabbed a bag of potato chips for each of us.

"Let's go. We've got to figure out where we are and how to get some money." I opened the front door to the apartment slowly.

We slid out and down to the sidewalk, moving quickly but as casually as we could. A few blocks away, I found a gas station and went over to the phone booth. There was a phone book there, mostly decimated, but the cover was sufficiently intact.

"We're in Madison," I told Terry.

She looked around and pointed. "That must be the state house over there."

The white dome and pinnacle towered over the other buildings. I gazed at it, my thoughts elsewhere. The address that I had found on Fran's desk. It was in Madison. Suddenly, what had been so distinctive about it came to life. It had been written in pencil, and the point had made deep grooves in the paper. The way Max's desk blotter had been grooved.

I blew out my breath and saw it fog in front of me. Terry shivered a little. The day was clear, but frosty.

"I think I know how we can get some money," I told her.

"I have some in my pocket. About twenty dollars."

"Well, let's see what we can do with it," I said, heading in the direction of the statehouse.

As I expected, the traffic was starting to grow, and I saw a couple taxis drive past. Looking back down the street, one approached with its light on. I waved it down and asked the driver how much it would cost to get to the address I'd seen on Fran's desk.

"About fifteen bucks."

"That's fine." I opened the back door and waved Terry in. "Let's go."

It took about twenty minutes to get there. Terry handed the driver her twenty, and we got out of the cab in front of a medical building. The office I wanted was in the back on the second floor. Terry and I walked into the waiting room of an obstetrician's office. Two women, one very pregnant, looked up curiously at us.

"Hi," I told the receptionist. "We're trying to find a friend of ours."

"Name, please?" She was sweet looking, but with a jaw set like steel.

The phone buzzed next to her. Glaring briefly at us, she picked it up.

"Yes, sir," she said into it, then hung up. She jerked a thumb over her shoulder. "Go down to the last door on the left."

"Thanks."

Terry was shocked to see Max Beard on the other side of the door. I was less so. The room had no windows and only a couple floor lamps lighting it up. The far wall was filled with a bank of video monitors, including one showing the reception desk. Max sat in an office chair next to the monitors, but faced us.

"Why are you here?" Max asked, again more curious than anything.

"We were taken hostage last night," I said. "By two KGB operatives. Terry, here, heard them making a ransom demand. Us for you."

"As if that would work," said Max.

"They thought we were civilians." I sighed. "Look, we need to get back to Appleton as soon as possible, and I'm sure your friends in The Company will be happy to know that they don't need to do any prisoner swaps. But..." I paused. "Fran Mercer is looking for Eunice's killer. She said you told her to drop it, but that's not stopping her."

Max sighed. "I didn't think it would." He looked wistfully at me. "How is she?"

"Managing. She told me about the two of you."

"She did?" Max suddenly looked positively animated. "Does she know your cover?"

"I don't think so."

"Did she tell you not to tell anyone else?"

"No." I looked at him, completely puzzled.

"Hallelujah!" Max paced about the room. "It's terrific." He turned to me. "She wanted to keep our relationship a secret, not me. She was afraid of giving Joe Cunningham another excuse to deny her tenure. If she told you about it and didn't swear you to secrecy, then she doesn't care about tenure anymore. She's coming to me. I was so worried about that."

I put the paper bag I still had on the floor. "She told me she'd talked to you but wouldn't say how or what you said."

"I called her at home that night. I told her that they were going to find my car in the river, but that I was all right." Max sank into the desk chair happily. "I couldn't explain much, but I told her that I had been doing work for the U.S. government. I had to escape because of what had happened to Ed Donaldson and Steve Carmona." He grinned at me. "She doesn't know Ed made it out okay. Anyway, I told her I had to go into hiding, and that I wanted her to join me. She didn't believe me, at first, but then I told her about the address I'd left on her desk that morning. I told her to send me a letter there when she was ready, and I'd set it up for her to come to me. She was worried about her students and finishing the quarter, so I said I'd wait. Which I am. I was just afraid she wouldn't want to after all. But if she doesn't care about tenure there, then she's coming. She's got to be."

I had to smile. "Okay. I'm glad for you." My stomach gurgled. I looked down at the paper bag and thought of something else. I pulled out the binder. "Max, does anything in this binder look familiar?"

He opened it and swore. "It's the formula. But it's not compiled into machine language. How the hell did that happen?"

Terry gulped. "Dr. Beard, did you have any of those files on the university system?"

"Yes. That's how they get compiled into the machine language for the printouts. But I change my password every week, and it's a strong random alpha-numeric one."

I rolled my eyes. "Which doesn't mean a thing if someone has gotten to the system administrator's file with the passwords." I looked at Terry. "You think somebody got one of those password programs?"

"What do you mean?" asked Max.

Terry sighed. "There are programs out there that will run every possible combination of alpha-numeric characters in a set number of digits, which can basically try every possible password out there."

Max swore. "But who?"

"That we don't know," I said. I thought about the dot matrix print outs from Eunice's envelope. "Eunice probably did."

"You don't think...?" Max turned pale.

"No," I said. "She was protecting you from what I've seen. I'm guessing it's someone else on the campus, which is one of the reasons we need to get back to Appleton as fast as we can. And we need some cash to do it with."

Max nodded. "That will be no problem."

It took about an hour, but by nine-thirty, Terry and I were in the back seat of a car heading up the interstate to Appleton. Max had seen to it that we'd gotten some breakfast, and we left with a couple hundred dollars in cash between us.

"I'm sorry," Terry suddenly sobbed.

"For what?" I asked.

"It's just that you were so scared last night, and that really scared me."

"So?" I sighed. "They thought we were civilians. They wouldn't have thought that if we hadn't been acting scared."

"But I really was."

"So was I." I put my arm around her shoulders. "But letting myself be scared has saved my butt more than once in this business. The key thing is, you didn't let being scared cloud your thinking or make you afraid to act. I was impressed with the way you handled that stiletto. You'll make a good operative yet."

Terry sniffed. "I'm not sure I want to anymore."

"We all feel that way sometimes." I gave her a quick squeeze.

When we got back to Martin U., a hush had fallen over the campus. The bare trees waved their branches in the breeze, and the lawn and walkways were empty of human life. The speakers from the night before had been removed, but there was a huge black hole in the center of the main lawn. Beer cans and bottles lay scattered here and there. I had the driver let Terry and me off near the computer center.

Now that we knew what we were looking for, it was a matter of looking at everyone's accounts to see if we could find who had the formula files. Terry took one computer in the deserted center. I took one next to her. I logged into Eunice's account first and was surprised to find the formula files there. Terry said she'd found some in Carson Osgood's account. I got into Cunningham's account and didn't find any formula files but laughed out loud when I found a bunch of files with manuscripts by Leticia Petrie.

"What?" asked Terry.

"Oh, I think I've finally got Joe Cunningham by the short hairs," I said. "Sadly, however, he doesn't have the formula files."

"Ted Curtis doesn't, either."

I logged into Ernie's account. "Lavalle does."

"So does Dwight Atwater."

"Shavings." I glared at the screen. "It looks like somebody uploaded the files into the accounts of several other people and deleted their copies."

"Yeah." Terry looked at me. "All the files with the formula were created today, about eight-thirty or so."

"Right after we busted out of our prison." I made a face, thinking. "All right, Terry. Why don't you head back to your dorm? I'll call you if I need anything."

She sighed. "Okay. Are you going to be okay?"

I couldn't help grinning. "I'm going to be fine. I haven't had this much backup before, even with him." I reached over and patted her arm. "You did a great job today. Thanks."

Terry smiled, but still looked a little worried. Nonetheless, she left the computer center.

Once alone, I made my way back to Lawrence Hall and my office. I sighed when I saw Terry's daypack in my desk, but that couldn't be helped. The good news was that the envelope with Eunice's evidence was undisturbed.

I pulled out the several sheets. There was a note buried in the mess.

"Fran," it read. "I hope like hell we've already had our meeting, but just in case, I've blacked out my suspect's name. It's too dangerous right now. Once we have our plan in place, then all will be well. In the meantime, stay the hell away from Ilona Watts. As far away as you can."

There was another sheet with dot matrix and a series of times and notes about how the subject had met with various people, including Ilona Swedburg. Okay, Ilona Watts. There was a photocopy of a news story about a KGB assassin who had been taken into custody about six years before. The picture gracing the article was of Ilona. But the most damning of all was a letter from a small university in Massachusetts, or rather a photocopy of the original letter.

"Dear Dr. Blakely," it read. "Thank you for your enquiry into..." The name was blacked out. "We can confirm that he was a PhD candidate at our institution, finishing in 1975. However, shortly after his dissertation was passed, we discovered that he had falsified certain data that he had used to prove his thesis and rescinded his degree. We hope this answers your question. Sincerely..."

I looked at the sheet with the times and notes. One of the dates was September twenty-second, the evening after the canoeing party. It noted that Ilona Watts had shown up at the bar and the subject had disappeared shortly after. So Eunice had been watching, too, that night.

At that point, I had a rather good idea of who our amateur under KGB control was. I only had one more question and the person who could answer it was in Los Angeles. It was just after three o'clock Wisconsin time, which meant one o'clock L.A. time. I probably shouldn't have, but I used the phone on my desk to make the call. I used one of our long-distance card codes to do it, though, which would make it harder to track.

He picked up after three rings.

"It's me," I told him.

"Hey. You doing okay?"

"Oh, fine. You?"

"Good enough. Not much going on around here, although I did touch base with a couple editors for more assignments. Looks like I'll be pretty busy through the end of the month."

"Great."

"Nick's coming in for the weekend tomorrow."

"Oh, good. Tell him I love him, will you?"

"Sure."

"I do have a couple questions for you. Um. When Tim blew your cover, was there anyone else around besides what's-his-name, Timorivich?"

"Yeah. That sociology professor. Come to think of it, I saw him a few times before the tailing team showed."

"That does not surprise me. I think we've got some evidence, but this helps. I saw Max this morning."

He chuckled. "Good. How's he doing?"

"He was a little worried about his girlfriend."

"Ah. Dr. Mercer."

"He told you about that?"

"Oh, yeah. We had an extended conversation about being in love." He sighed. "He and Terry Michaels both called me on it."

"On what?"

"On my feelings for you." He paused. "If it makes you feel any better, I'd like to put it that way, but it still feels like a line to me."

"That's okay. I mean that."

"I know you do." He paused again. "I miss you already."

"I miss you, too." I swallowed. "I may have this wrapped up, but I'll probably have to stay through the end of the quarter. My students, you know, not to mention my cover."

He laughed. "I love it. Students first, then your cover."

"What can I say? I'll call on Sundays. Will that work?"

"I'll make it work."

"Thank you."

"Thank you, honey."

"I'll see you by Thanksgiving."

"I'm looking forward to it."

"Me, too."

I hung up. I spent another hour or so mulling over ways to handle the situation, but then, eventually, picked up the phone and dialed Fran at home. She'd been worried when I hadn't called her the night before. I told her I'd fallen asleep in my office, and she bought it.

I must give Fran a lot of credit. Once she saw all the evidence that Eunice had gathered, she came up with an almost sensible plan for how to deal with it.

"Shouldn't we call Sergeant Renecke?" I asked her the next morning as we waited in her apartment. We'd both called in sick that day and our classes had been canceled.

"I already did." Fran snorted. "He didn't entirely take me seriously. He just told me to not do anything dangerous."

"Which is exactly what I think we're about to do," I said.

Fran shrugged. "I think we can handle it. You took down Ernie at Eunice's funeral with no problem."

I rolled my eyes. "Self-defense class. This is different."

"Don't be such a worrywart. We'll be fine."

"I sure hope so."

The knock on Fran's door came a little late, but when Fran opened it, Ted was there. I surreptitiously turned on the cassette recorder hidden under the coffee table.

"Come on in, Ted," she said. "I've got tea ready. Would you like a cup?"

"Uh, sure." Ted wandered into the living room.

Thanks to the many years Fran had been at Martin U., her apartment was much more nicely decorated than mine. There were some good prints on the walls. She had a lovely mix of antiques and modern furniture in her living room. Ted settled on the dark blue velvet couch, while I landed in the overstuffed chair on one end and Fran sat in the matching chair on the opposite end of the couch. Fran poured the tea from a pot that she'd set on the end of the coffee table in front of the couch and handed Ted the cup.

"Here's the problem, Ted," Fran said. "As you know, Eunice invited Janet and me and a couple of other folks to a meeting the night she died."

"Yeah." Ted squirmed a little, but didn't give anything away.

"We didn't know what the meeting was about," Fran continued. "Until we found an envelope in my office yesterday. Turns out there was a pile of evidence that implicated you in stealing some sort of chemical formula from Max Beard."

Ted turned pale, but laughed nonetheless. "Me? What would I know about any sort of formula?"

"That is the question, Ted," I said. "However, you had told me about some fudged data in your past and part of the evidence is a letter from your alma mater that says your degree was rescinded because you had falsified data."

"It wasn't." Ted put the cup down. "I fixed it. I told you."

"Then why would Eunice be tracking your every contact with Ilona Watts?" Fran asked. "The funny thing is, Ilona apparently works for the KGB. You do know what that is, don't you, Ted?"

"Everyone knows what the KGB is," Ted snorted. "Ilona has nothing to do with them."

"Then explain this," I said, handing him the photocopy of the news story about Ilona. "I'm sorry, Ted, but we have to believe that Eunice had figured out that you were stealing Max's formula, whatever that was, and that was why you killed her."

"I didn't kill her!" Ted bounced up, then sank onto the couch. "I didn't."

I shook my head. "Then why were you there that night?"

"Who said I was there?" Ted gasped.

"Oh, come on, Ted," Fran snapped. "Who else could it have been?"

"Anybody! Not me!" Ted looked frantic.

"Right." I rolled my eyes. "Eunice was tracking your every contact with Ilona Watts. Why would she if she didn't suspect you were up to no good?"

"And the letter we have from your alma mater says they rescinded your doctorate," Fran continued without mercy. "They didn't say anything about you fixing your data."

"I didn't want to kill her." He started sobbing. "They made me. They made me do everything. They came after me when my dissertation was rescinded. Told me that they could make it all right if I would do the odd chore or two for them. They sent me here to spy on Max. I didn't think it was that big a deal. I mean, it was Max, for God's sakes. The ultimate space cadet. I have no idea what he was working on. I just knew they were in his system files, and they were important."

"But what about his students?" I asked.

"The students? I had to kill them. I really didn't want to do it, but they said I had to."

"Why Eunice?" Fran glared at him.

His shoulders collapsed. "She caught me setting up an ampule of nerve agent in her house. I'd never killed anybody directly before. But I had to. She knew about me and was going to tell everyone else. If my handlers found out, I'd be dead. I had to do it."

I sighed. "What about Steve Carmona and Ed Donaldson?"

"Them, too." Ted sniffed. "I mean, I didn't mean to kill Steve. And I did call in the alarm on the fire. I didn't want to hurt anybody else." He got up suddenly. "I still don't, but you're forcing me to."

He pulled a pistol from the back of his pants. Okay, I had one strapped to my shin, but wasn't sure how I was going to get it pulled and ready with Fran there. Not to mention before Ted could shoot us both.

"Ted, we believe you," I said in as calm a voice as I could manage. "It obviously wasn't your fault."

I approached him. He backed up toward the hallway to the back of the apartment.

"No!" he screamed. "Don't make me use this!"

"We don't want you to," I said, again trying to force my voice to sound soothing. "We want you to come out of this alive. Really. We do."

"I have to kill you," Ted sobbed. "They'll kill me."

"We'll find a way to keep you safe," Fran said.

Ted continued backing up into the hallway, right into Sergeant Renecke's arms. I concentrated on keeping my face blank until Renecke bumped into Ted. The gun went off and both Fran and I screamed. But the bullet went into the ceiling and before we knew it, Renecke had Ted in handcuffs.

I turned on Fran. "Renecke's been here the whole time?"

"I couldn't have you giving him away to Ted." Fran shrugged.

I snorted and got the tape from the recorder and handed it to Renecke.

"Thanks," the cop said. "This should help a lot."

I glared at Fran as Renecke pulled Ted from the apartment. A minute later, we heard two gunshots. Fran and I ran to the window. Renecke was bent over Ted, who had fallen back-first onto the sidewalk. Another minute later, I saw Ilona Swedburg Watts walking away down the street with a musical instrument bag over her shoulder.

November 3 – 24, 1984

F ran and I spent the rest of that weekend together, grading papers and drinking heavily. Well, Fran drank heavily. I graded papers. Sunday afternoon, we went to Steve Carmona's memorial service, then we spent that night in my office while I entered grades into the system.

"Janet," Fran said as I finished. "I'm not going to be here next quarter. Do you think you can manage?"

"I think so." I smiled. "You know Ted had found out about Max because he'd broken into the systems administration account and stolen Max's passwords, right?"

"Yes."

"Um. It's entirely possible that I may have done the same thing." I winced.

"Really?" Fran's eyes widened.

"I have a couple of students who are good at that sort of thing." I shrugged. "The important thing is, I now know Joe Cunningham's greatest secret."

"I was so hoping he was behind this."

"So was I." I grinned. "But we can still get him. You ever hear of a romance novel writer named Leticia Petrie?"

"No." Fran grinned. "Tell me more."

The rest of the quarter passed quietly. Yes, Cunningham had scrambled, but he'd found enough adjuncts to cover both Max's and Ted's classes. The rumor was he was sweating bullets, and who could blame him? He'd lost three staff members in the space of a month, and while he didn't know it yet, he was about to lose two more.

As for me, somehow, I stayed on top of all the grading. Cunningham tried to give me trouble here and there, but once I mentioned Leticia Petrie, suddenly, he was content to leave me be.

Tim Hannaford quietly flunked out shortly after Ted was arrested, which did not surprise me. Kathy hung on but told me that she was getting her transfer from Las Vegas to San Francisco. Terry told me near the end of the quarter that she was going back to systems and was happy to be there.

David Watts remained blissfully unaware of his wife's other career, but there wasn't much I could do about that. I later heard that Ilona had stayed there, leaving only for short assignments.

The last week of the quarter, I made sure that I had all my finals finished before that Wednesday. The term papers had all been graded the weekend before. I spent Thursday grading finals and got those entered into the system. Joe Cunningham had yet to find out that I had a connected computer in my office.

I took my faculty keys off my key ring and picked up the envelope containing the letter I'd typed the night before. Slinging my purse over my shoulder, I smiled at the print of Thomas Hardy on the wall next to the door.

"Dr. Pendergast," I said out loud. "I'm sorry I moved Mr. Hardy, but I kind of like him there. So, I'm leaving him. I hope you don't mind."

Laughing at myself, I left the office, locked it, and went downstairs to the department office. Dwight Atwater was standing at Mrs. Spinetti's desk and having an intense conversation with her.

"Oh," I said. "I didn't mean to interrupt. Is Cunningham around?"

Dwight looked up and grinned. "You didn't hear? He turned in his resignation last night. The trustees made me department chair pro tem."

"As if Joe had a choice," Mrs. Spinetti said smugly.

Dwight came over to me. "Janet, I know this was a really bad quarter, but it's not normally like this around here." He stopped as he saw me hold out the envelope. "Not you, too."

I shrugged. "I got an exceptionally good offer from the school where I really want to be. I like it here, and I know this past quarter was a once in a lifetime. But it's missing one major compensation, and he's in L.A."

"Ah." Dwight took the envelope sadly. "Well, best of luck to you."

"In the letter, I blamed everything on Joe," I said, handing Mrs. Spinetti my keys. "Oh, do I call you Dr. Atwater now?"

"Dwight's fine." He laughed weakly. "All right, Mrs. Spinetti, please add a request for an English adjunct, and that's who all?"

"One for communications, two history, one sociology, and now one English."

Dwight swore, and I left, taking just enough time to visit the provost's office and get signed out there as well.

Early the next day, Fran came up to my apartment.

"Hey, what's up?" I asked her, ushering her inside to my living room.

"I need a ride to Madison tomorrow," she said.

"Oh?"

"Yes. Uh. The movers will be here in the morning. I do need to get some packing done." She smiled. "But I mostly need a ride down to Madison."

"What about your car?"

"I'm leaving it."

"Okay. And I can help pack, I guess."

"Oh, that would be wonderful."

While Fran had a fair amount to pack, we got it done by eight that evening. We went to the Cider Keg to have a final meal and Bloody Mary there and had a lovely time. The only problem was, I still had some packing to do myself.

It took longer than I expected, but I didn't care. What Fran didn't know was that the movers who were coming to move her stuff were also coming to move mine. It was kind of scary how much stuff I'd picked up in the few months I'd been there.

I kept the argyle sweater with me. Fran also didn't see the two suitcases and carry on I put in my car before I knocked on her door that Friday morning. She dropped her keys on a small table in the building foyer and I dropped mine when she wasn't looking.

"Well, we're off," she said as I pulled onto the interstate.

"I suppose you are," I said.

She laughed. "Not just me. You're leaving, too."

"Um. Yeah."

She looked at me. I shrugged.

"You remember that broken heart I told you about?" I said.

"Ah. What about tenure?"

"I found a school near him in L.A. that liked my CV. I start in January. What about you?"

Fran shrugged. "I don't know. That's going to be the interesting part." She looked out the window at the green pasture lands and red barns going past. "We're going into the witness protection plan."

"We?"

"Max and me. He couldn't arrange it sooner and I didn't want to leave my students high and dry." She looked at me. "But I think you know about that already."

"Know about what?"

Fran sighed. "You're not just an English professor."

I laughed. "I don't know where you got that idea. But I'm glad you and Max are getting together." I glanced her way. "You two deserve it."

Fran snorted.

We made it to Madison in record time. Okay, I have a bit of a lead foot, which is why. Fran directed me to the obstetrics office. I went in with her to help her with her suitcases. Max was in the waiting room and the two ran into each other's arms and simply held each other for several minutes. My eyes filled with tears, but I blinked them back.

We had an early lunch together, still I could tell they really wanted to be alone, so I told them that I needed to be moving on. Fran hugged me tightly on the sidewalk.

"Thank you for everything, Janet," she said. "I hope we come across each other again."

"I'd like that," I said.

There was a part of me that felt sad because I seriously doubted we would. I headed back to the interstate and drove south. Almost three hours later, I was in the Chicago area. The car got abandoned in Morton Grove. It was no small trick to haul the two suitcases, carry on and my purse onto the bus to O'Hare airport, but I did it. I bought a ticket for the first flight I could find to LAX. I barely had time to wash my face in the airport bathroom and make a phone call before boarding. As soon as I got into my seat on the plane, I stashed my glasses.

Sid and Nick were at the gate when the plane arrived. Sid was clean-shaven and wearing his contact lenses. He held me tightly, and we kissed. Then I hugged Nick. He looked and even acted so much like Sid, but was so different at the same time. Eleven years old, he was nearsighted like his father, but wore glasses. He could be just as gentle as Sid, although he had an exuberance that was utterly unlike his father.

"And we've got kittens," Nick told me as we waited for my suitcases.

"Kittens?" I asked. I looked at Sid, who rolled his eyes.

"Long John Silver," Nick said. "I named her before I knew she was a she. I made friends with her a couple weekends ago. She's this gray cat, and she only has one eye. And Dad said she kept coming back and sitting in his lap."

"What female can resist?" Sid's eyes twinkled.

"Anyway, she was pregnant. She had the kittens last week. There's four of them. Isn't that the coolest thing ever?"

I looked at Sid, who shrugged. He had one of my hands in his and hadn't let go since I'd gotten off the plane.

"What did you do with your hair?" Nick asked. "I liked it all curly and brown."

"I just cut it, Nick," I said. "I'll get my natural color and style back as soon as I can."

Back at the house, I ooh'd and ah'd over the kittens, who were with their mother in a box in the rumpus room. Long John Silver was, as advertised, a one-eyed gray cat with a mangled ear.

Nick helped me bring my suitcases into my little suite of rooms at the back. There was a workroom in the front, which led to my actual bedroom. I looked around. Sid had clearly been in both rooms. Everything was perfectly organized and in place.

Later that night, Sid and I sat together in the living room of his house, the house where I also lived. He shifted as he dug something out of his shirt pocket.

"I've got something for you," he said.

He placed the gold ring and battered nickel chain in my hand. The ring came from San Francisco High School, class of '68, and featured a blue faceted stone.

"This is it, huh?" I asked softly as I examined the ring. "You didn't get to wear it much."

"I'd gotten my job at that restaurant by then and had to take it off when I went to work so they wouldn't know how old I really was." He picked up the chain and looked at the ring as it dangled. "Why don't you wear it? It kept another virgin out of trouble."

"Sure." I let him drape the chain around my neck, then sniffed a little. "This means so much."

"I'm not going anywhere, Lisa." He picked up the ring, then let it fall onto my chest. "I want you to know that."

"I know. I'm not going anywhere, either." I thought of something and got up. "I'll be right back."

I was only gone a minute. I slid under his arm again and put something into his free hand.

"What's this?" He asked, looking at the white gold ring with the light blue faceted stone from South Lake Tahoe High, class of '76.

"My class ring, obviously," I said. "But why don't you call it reassurance?"

"Thank you." He chuckled and slid it into the front pocket of his dress slacks. "I think I will."

"Good."

"You did a hell of a job in Wisconsin." He gave me a warm squeeze.

"Thanks. I couldn't have done it without you."

"You could have and did."

"Yeah, I guess I did," I said, after thinking about it for a moment.

He sighed. "I really missed you, though. I am so glad to have you back."

"You knew I would be."

"Yeah. But there's that part of me that's afraid. You worry that you can't be what I need. Well, I worry that I can't be what you need."

"You are what I need, Sid."

"And you are what I need." He sighed. "And you were right. What we do have, our friendship and caring and all that. That's the most important part. That's what makes all this mess worthwhile. I really am happier with you, even with the mess, than I am without you. I don't think I understood that until now, but it's certainly true."

"I'm glad. I missed you, too." I snuggled in closer to him. "But at the same time, I'm glad I had a chance to do something on my own. Makes it feel like we really are equal partners."

"You needed to know what you could do apart from me."

"Yeah." I smiled and looked up at him. "I'm still better with you."

"We are a hell of a team, aren't we?" Sid chuckled. "Good."

"Very good," I whispered.

Thank You for Reading

I do hope you enjoyed the book.

If you can do me one small favor, please. Can you go to one of the social media/retail profiles below and leave a short review? It doesn't need to be a lot, just honest.

a amazon.com/author/annelouisebannon

BB bookbub.com/profile/anne-louise-bannon

g goodreads.com/author/show/513383.Anne_Louise _Bannon

Coming Soon

Book Seven in the Operation Quickline series, *My Sweet Lisa*

Finally, it's real love... Now what?

Lisa Wycherly's surprise birthday party ends in a terrifying disaster when she's kidnapped off the street. Her partner, Sid Hackbirn, is so devastated that he loses his interest in sleeping around - the one thing keeping the two of them apart. The kidnapping gets messy enough when it comes to light that the kidnappers got the wrong target. There's also a defecting KGB agent playing games with the CIA, who are involved with the Colombian kidnappers.

Then Lisa's recovery sets in motion a whole other set of challenges as she and Sid deal with her trauma and try to get the KGB agent under control, only to find that Sid's randy past will continue to haunt them. The only thing worse? Figuring out how to be a couple.

Other books by Anne Louise Bannon

I'm so glad you liked this book! Check out my other novels, available in print or ebook at your favorite retailer:

Old Los Angeles Series:

Death of the Zanjero

Death of the City Marshal

Death of the Chinese Field Hands

Death of an Heiress

Operation Quickline Series:

That Old Cloak and Dagger Routine

Stopleak

Deceptive Appearances

Fugue in a Minor Key

Sad Lisa

These Hallowed Halls

My Sweet Lisa

A Little Family Business

Just Because You're Paranoid

Freddie and Kathy Series:

Fascinating Rhythm

Bring Into Bondage

The Last Witnesses

Blood Red

Daria Barnes:

Rage Issues

Mrs. Sperling:

A Nose for a Niedeman

Brenda Finnegan:

Tyger, Tyger

Romantic Fiction:

White House Rhapsody, Book One and Two

Fantasy and Science Fiction:

A Ring for a Second Chance

But World Enough and Time

And I would be honored if you left a review for this and any of my books on the below sites. It really helps.

amazon.com/author/annelouisebannon

bookbub.com/profile/anne-louise-bannon

goodreads.com/author/show/513383.Anne_Louise _Bannon

Connect with Anne Louise Bannon

Thank you for sticking it out this long! Please join my newsletter. It's the best way to stay up-to-date on my upcoming projects, blog posts and even the occasional game and giveaway.

You can sign up for the Robin Goodfellow Newsletter here: http://eepurl.com/zH0Ab or by visiting my website, annelouisebannon.com

And don't forget to connect with me on your favorite social media platforms:

BB bookbub.com/profile/anne-louise-bannon

f facebook.com/RobinGoodfellowEnt

a amazon.com/author/annelouisebannon

g goodreads.com/author/show/513383.Anne_Louise _Bannon

in linkedin.com/in/annelouisebannon.com

 twitter.com/albannon

About Anne Louise Bannon

Anne Louise Bannon is an author and journalist who wrote her first novel at age 15. Her journalistic work has appeared in Ladies' Home Journal, the Los Angeles Times, Wines and Vines, and in newspapers across the country. She was a TV critic for over 10 years, founded the YourFamilyViewer blog, and created the OddBallGrape.com wine education blog with her husband, Michael Holland. She is the co-author of Howdunit: Book of Poisons, with Serita Stevens, as well as author of the Freddie and Kathy mystery series, set in the 1920s, the Old Los Angeles series, set in 1870, and the Operation Quickline series, plus several stand alones. She and her husband live in Southern California with an assortment of critters.

www.ingramcontent.com/pod-product-compliance
Lightning Source LLC
Chambersburg PA
CBHW071231190726
48292CB00007B/2223